Val McDermid

Val McDermid grew up in a Scottish mining community then read English at Oxford. She was a journalist for sixteen years, spending the last three years as Northern Bureau Chief of a national Sunday tabloid. She is now a full-time writer and lives outside Manchester. *Blue Genes* is her fifth crime novel to feature Kate Brannigan.

Val McDermid is also the author of *The Mermaids Singing*, the 1995 winner of the Crime Writers' Association's Gold Dagger Award for Best Crime Novel of the Year. *The Wire in the Blood*, featuring Tony Hill, the criminal profiler from *The Mermaids Singing*, is now available in hardcover.

VAL McDERMID

BLUE GENES

HarperCollins*Publishers*

HarperCollins*Publishers*
77–85 Fulham Palace Road,
Hammersmith, London W6 8JB

This paperback edition 1997
3 5 7 9 8 6 4 2

First published in Great Britain by
HarperCollins*Publishers* 1996

ISBN 0 00 649831 0

Set in Meridien and Bodoni

Printed and bound in Great Britain by
Caledonian International Book Manufacturing Ltd, Glasgow

ACKNOWLEDGEMENTS

What is outlined in this novel is entirely within the realms of possible science. Somebody somewhere is almost certainly carrying out these procedures, probably for very large sums of money.

I'm grateful to Dr Gill Lockwood for most of my medical and scientific information, and to David Hartshorn of Cellmark Diagnostics for background on DNA testing. For other matters, I'm indebted to Lee D'Courcy, Diana Cooper, Yvonne Twiby, Jai Penna, Paula Tyler, Brigid Baillie and the press office of the Human Fertility and Embryology Authority.

For Fairy, Lesley and all the other lesbian mothers who prove that moulds are there to be broken.
And for Robyn and Andrew and Jack

1

The day Richard's death announcement appeared in the *Manchester Evening Chronicle*, I knew I couldn't postpone clearing up the mess any longer. But there was something I had to do first. I stood in the doorway of the living room of the man who'd been my lover for three years, Polaroid in hand, surveying the chaos. Slowly, I swept the camera lens round the room, carefully recording every detail of the shambles, section by section. This was one time I wasn't prepared to rely on memory. Richard might be gone, but that didn't mean I was going to take any unnecessary risks. Private eyes who do that have as much chance of collecting their pensions as a Robert Maxwell employee.

Once I had a complete chronicle of exactly how things had been left in the room that was a mirror image of my own bungalow next door, I started my mammoth task. First, I sorted things into piles: books, magazines, CDs, tapes, promo videos, the detritus of a rock journalist's life. Then I arranged them. Books, alphabetically, on the shelf unit. CDs ditto. The tapes I stacked in the storage unit Richard had bought for the purpose one Sunday when I'd managed to drag him round Ikea, the 1990s equivalent of buying an engagement ring. I'd even put the cabinet together for him, but he'd never got into the habit of using it, preferring the haphazard stacks and heaps strewn all over the floor. I buried the surge of emotion that came with the memory and carried on doggedly. The magazines I shoved out of sight in the conservatory that runs along the back of both our houses, linking them together more firmly than we'd ever been prepared to do in any formal sense with our lives.

I leaned against the wall and looked around the room. When people say, 'It's a dirty job, but somebody's got to do it,' how come we never really believe we'll be the ones left clutching the sticky end? I sighed and forced myself on. I emptied ashtrays of the roaches left from Richard's joints, gathered together pens and pencils and stuffed them into the sawn-off Sapporo beer can he'd used for the purpose for as long as I'd known him. I picked up the assorted notepads, sheets of scrap paper and envelopes where he'd scribbled down vital phone numbers and quotes, careful not to render them any more disordered than they were already, and took them through to the room he used as his office when it wasn't occupied by his nine-year-old son Davy on one of his regular visits. I dumped them on the desk on top of a remarkably similar-looking pile already there.

Back in the living room, I was amazed by the effect. It almost looked like a room I could sit comfortably in. Cleared of the usual junk, it was possible to see the pattern on the elderly Moroccan rug that covered most of the floor and the sofas could for once accommodate the five people they were designed for. I realized for the first time that the coffee table had a central panel of glass. I'd been trying for ages to get him to put the room into something approaching a civilized state, but he'd always resisted me. Even though I'd finally got my own way, I can't say it made me happy. But then, I couldn't get out of my mind the reason behind what I was doing here, and what lay ahead. The announcement of Richard's death was only the beginning of a chain of events that would be a hell of a lot more testing than tidying a room.

I thought about brushing the rug, but I figured that was probably gilding the lily, the kind of activity that people found a little bizarre after the death of a lover. And bizarre was not the impression I wanted to give. I went back through to my house and changed from the sweat pants and T-shirt I'd worn to do the cleaning into something more appropriate for a grieving relict. A charcoal wool wraparound skirt from the French Connection sale and a black lamb's-wool turtleneck I'd chosen for the one and only reason that it made me look like death. There are times in a private eye's working life when looking like she's about to keel over is an image preferable to that of Wonder Woman on whizz.

I was about to close the conservatory door behind me as I returned to Richard's house when his doorbell belted out an inappropriate blast of the guitar riff from Eric Clapton's 'Layla'. 'Shit,' I muttered. No matter how careful you are, there's always something you forget. I couldn't remember what the other choices were on Richard's 'Twenty Great Rock Riffs' doorbell, but I was sure there must be something more fitting than Clapton's wailing guitar. Maybe something from the Smiths, I thought vaguely as I tried to compose my face into a suitable expression for a woman who's just lost her partner. Just how was I supposed to look, I found a second to wonder. What's the well-bereft woman wearing on her face this season? You can't even go for the mascara tracks down the cheeks in these days of lash tints.

I took a deep breath, hoped for the best and opened the door. The crime correspondent of the *Manchester Evening Chronicle* stood on the step, her black hair even more like an explosion in a wig factory than usual. 'Kate,' my best friend Alexis said, stepping forward and pulling me into a hug. 'I can't believe it,' she added, a catch in her voice. She moved back to look at me, tears in her eyes. So much for the hard-bitten newshound. 'Why didn't you call us? When I saw it in the paper . . . Kate, what the hell happened?'

I looked past her. All quiet in the street outside. I put my arm round her shoulders and firmly drew her inside, closing the door behind her. 'Nothing. Richard's fine,' I said, leading the way down the hall.

'Do what?' Alexis demanded, stopping and frowning at me. 'If he's fine, how come I just read he's dead in tonight's paper? And if he's fine, how come you're doing the "Baby's in Black" number when you know that's the one colour that makes you look like the Bride of Frankenstein?'

'If you'd let me get a word in edgeways, I'll explain,' I said, going through to the living room. 'Take my word for it, Richard is absolutely OK.'

Alexis stopped dead on the threshold, taking in the pristine tidiness of the room. 'Oh no, he's not,' she said, suspicion running through her heavy Scouse accent like the stripe in the toothpaste. 'He's not fine if he's left his living room looking like this. At the very least, he's having a nervous breakdown. What the hell's going on here, KB?'

'I can't believe you read the death notices,' I said, throwing myself down on the nearest sofa.

'I don't normally,' Alexis admitted, subsiding on the sofa opposite me. 'I was down Moss Side nick waiting for a statement from the duty inspector about a little bit of aggravation involving an Uzi and a dead Rottweiler, and they were taking so long about it I'd read everything else in the paper except the ads for the dinner dances. And it's just as well I did. What's going on? If he's not dead, who's he upset enough to get heavy-metal hassle like this?' She stabbed the paper she carried with a nicotine-stained index finger.

'It was me who put the announcement in,' I said.

'That's one way of telling him it's over,' Alexis interrupted before I could continue. 'I thought you two had got things sorted?'

'We have,' I said through clenched teeth. Ironing out the problems in my relationship with Richard would have taken the entire staff of an industrial laundry a month. It had taken us rather longer.

'So what's going on?' Alexis demanded belligerently. 'What's so important that you have to give everybody a heart attack thinking me laddo's popped his clogs?'

'Can't you resist the journalistic exaggeration for once?' I sighed. 'You know and I know that nobody under sixty routinely reads the deaths column. I had to use a real name and address, and I figured with Richard out of town till the end of the week, nobody's going to be any the wiser if I used his,' I explained. 'And he won't be, unless you tell him.'

'That depends on whether you tell me what this is all in aid of,' Alexis said cunningly, her outrage at having wasted her sympathy a distant memory now she had the scent of a possible story in her nostrils. 'I mean, I think he's going to notice something's going on,' she added, sweeping an eloquent arm through the air. 'I don't think he knows that carpet has a pattern.'

'I took Polaroids before I started,' I told her. 'When I'm finished, I'll put it back the way it was before. He won't notice a thing.'

'He will when I show him the cutting,' Alexis countered. 'Spill, KB. What're you playing at? What's with the grieving widow number?' She leaned back and lit a cigarette. So much for my clean ashtrays.

'Can't tell you,' I said sweetly. 'Client confidentiality.'

'Bollocks,' Alexis scoffed. 'It's me you're talking to, KB, not the bizzies. Come on, give. Or else the first thing Richard sees when he comes home is . . .'

I closed my eyes and muttered an old gypsy curse under my breath. It's not that I speak Romany; it's just that I've refused to buy lucky white heather once too often. Believe me, I know exactly what those old gypsies say. I weighed up my options. I could always call her bluff and hope she wouldn't tell Richard, on the basis that the two of them maintain this pretence of despising each other's area of professional expertise and extend that into the personal arena at every possible opportunity. On the other hand, the prospect of explaining to Richard that I was responsible for the report of his death didn't appeal either. I gave in. 'It's got to be off the record, then,' I said ungraciously.

'Why?' Alexis demanded.

'Because with a bit of luck it will be sub judice in a day or two. And if you blow it before then, the bad guys will be out of town on the next train and we'll never nail them.'

'Anybody ever tell you you've got melodramatic tendencies, KB?' Alexis asked with a grin.

'A bit rich, coming from a woman who started today's story with, "Undercover police swooped on a top drug dealer's love nest in a dawn raid this morning," when we both know that all that happened was a couple of guys from the Drugs Squad turned over some two-bit dealer's girlfriend's bedsit,' I commented.

'Yeah, well, you gotta give it a bit of topspin or the boy racers on the newsdesk kill it. But that's not what we're talking about. I want to know why Richard's supposed to be dead.'

'It's a long and complicated story,' I started in a last attempt to lose her interest.

Alexis grinned and blew a long stream of smoke down her nostrils. Puff the Magic Dragon would have signed up for a training course on the spot. 'Great,' she enthused. 'My favourite kind.'

'The client's a firm of monumental masons,' I said. 'They're the biggest provider of stone memorials in South Manchester. They came to us because they've been getting a string of complaints from people saying they've paid for gravestones that haven't turned up.'

'Somebody's been nicking *gravestones*?'

'Worse than that,' I said, meaning it. Far as I was concerned, I was dealing with total scumbags on this one. 'My clients are the incidental victims of a really nasty scam. From what I've managed to find out so far, there are at least two people involved, a man and a woman. They turn up on the doorsteps of the recently bereaved and claim to be representing my client's firm. They produce these business cards which have the name of my clients, complete with address and phone number, all absolutely kosher. The only thing wrong with them is that the names on the cards are completely unknown to my client. They're not using the names of his staff. But this pair are smart. They always come in the evening, out of business hours, so anyone who's a bit suspicious can't ring my client's office and check up on them. And they come single-handed. Nothing heavy. Where it's a woman who's died, it's the woman who shows up. Where it's a man, it's the bloke.'

'So what's the pitch?' Alexis asked.

'They do the tea-and-sympathy routine, then they explain that they're adopting the new practice of visiting people in their homes because it's a more personal approach to choosing an appropriate memorial. Then they go into a special-offer routine, just like they were selling double glazing or something. You know the sort of thing – unique opportunity, special shipment of Italian marble or Aberdeen granite, you could be one of the people we use for testimonial purposes, limited period offer.'

'Yeah, yeah, yeah,' Alexis groaned. 'And if they don't sign up tonight, they've lost the opportunity, am I right, or am I right?'

'You're right. So these poor sods whose lives are already in bits because they've just lost their partner or husband or wife, or mother or father, or son or daughter get done up like a kipper just so some smart bastard can go out and buy another designer suit or a mobile bloody phone,' I said angrily. I know all the rules about never letting yourself get emotionally involved with the jobs, but there are times when staying cool and disinterested would be the mark of inhumanity rather than good sense. This was one of them.

Alexis lit another cigarette, shaking her head. 'Pure gob-shites,' she said in disgust. 'Twenty-four-carat shysters. So they take the cash and disappear into the night, leaving your clients to pick up the pieces when the headstone remains a ghostly presence?'

'Something like that. They really are a pair of unscrupulous bastards. I've been interviewing some of the people who have been had over, and a couple of them have told me the woman has actually driven them to holes in the wall to get money for a cash deposit.' I shook my head, remembering the faces of the victims again. They showed a procession of emotions, each more painful to watch than the last. There was grief revisited in the setting of the scene for me, then anger as they recalled how they'd been stung, then a mixture of shame and resentment that they'd fallen for it. 'And there's no point in me telling them that in their shoes even a streetwise old cynic like me would probably have fallen for it. Because I probably would have done, that's the worst of it,' I added bitterly.

'Grief gets you like that,' Alexis agreed. 'The last thing you're expecting is to be taken for a ride. Look at how many families end up not speaking to each other for years because someone has done something outrageous in the immediate aftermath of death, when everyone's staggering round feeling like their brain's in the food processor along with their emotions. After my Uncle Jos's second wife Theresa wore my gran's fur coat to the old dear's funeral, she might as well have been dead too. My dad wouldn't even let my mum send them a Christmas card for about ten years. Until Uncle Jos got cancer himself, poor sod.'

'Yeah, well, us knowing these people haven't been particularly gullible doesn't make it any easier for them. The only thing that might help them would be for me to nail the bastards responsible.'

'What about the bizzies? Haven't they reported it to them?'

I shrugged. 'Only one or two of them. Most of them left it at phoning my client. It's pride, isn't it? People don't want everybody thinking they can't cope just because they've lost somebody. Especially if they're getting on a bit. So all Officer Dibble has to go on is a few isolated incidents.' I didn't need to tell a crime correspondent that it wasn't something that was going to assume a high priority for a police force struggling to deal with an epidemic of crack and guns that seemed to claim fresh victims every week in spite of an alleged truce between the gangs.

Alexis gave a cynical smile. 'Not exactly the kind of glamorous case the CID's glory boys are dying to take on, either. The only way they'd have started to take proper notice would have been if some journo like me had stumbled across the story and given it some headlines. Then they'd have had to get their finger out.'

'Too late for that now,' I said firmly.

'Toerags,' Alexis said. 'So you've put Richard's death notice in to try and flush them out?'

'Seemed like the only way to get a fix on them,' I said. 'It's clear from what the victims have said that they operate by using the deaths column. Richard's out of town on the road with some band, so I thought I'd get it done and dusted while he's not around to object to having his name taken in vain. If everything goes according to plan, someone should be here within the next half-hour.'

'Nice thinking,' Alexis said approvingly. 'Hope it works. So why didn't you use Bill's name and address? He's still in Australia, isn't he?'

I shook my head. 'I would have done, except he was flying in this afternoon.' Bill Mortensen, the senior partner of Mortensen and Brannigan, Private Investigators and Security

Consultants, had been in Australia for the last three weeks, his second trip Down Under in the past six months, an occurrence that was starting to feel a lot like double trouble to me. 'He'll be using his house as a jet-lag recovery zone. So that left Richard. Sorry you had a wasted journey of condolence. And I'm sorry if it upset you,' I added.

'You're all right. I don't think I really believed he was dead, you know? I figured it must be some sick puppy's idea of a joke, on account of I couldn't work out how come you hadn't told me he'd kicked it. If you see what I mean. Anyway, it wasn't a wasted journey. I was coming round anyway. There's something I wanted to tell you.'

For some reason, Alexis had suddenly stopped meeting my eye. She was looking vaguely round the room, as if Richard's walls were the source of all inspiration. Then she dragged her eyes away from the no longer brilliant white emulsion and started rootling round in a handbag so vast it makes mine look like an evening purse. 'So tell me,' I said impatiently after a silence long enough for Alexis to unearth a fresh packet of cigarettes, unwrap them and light one.

'It's Chris,' she exhaled ominously. More silence. Chris, Alexis's partner, is an architect in a community practice. It feels like they've been together longer than Mickey and Minnie. The pair of them had just finished building their dream home beyond the borders of civilization as we know it, part of a self-build scheme. And now Alexis was using the tone of voice that BBC announcers adopt when a member of the Royal family has died or separated from a spouse.

'What about Chris?' I asked nervously.

Alexis ran a hand through her hair then looked up at me from under her eyebrows. 'She's pregnant.'

Before I could say anything, the doorbell blasted out the riff from 'Layla' again.

2

I looked at her and she looked at me. What I saw was genuine happiness accompanied by a faint flicker of apprehension. What Alexis saw, I suspect, was every piece of dental work I've ever had done. Before I could get my vocal cords unjammed, Alexis was on her feet and heading for the conservatory. 'That'll be your scam merchant. I'd better leg it,' she said. 'I'll let myself out through your house. Give me a bell later,' she added to her slipstream.

Feeling stunned enough to resemble someone whose entire family has been wiped out by a freak accident, I walked to the front door in a bewildered daze. The guy on the other side of it looked like a high-class undertaker's apprentice. Dark suit, white shirt that gleamed in the streetlights like an advert for soap powder, plain dark tie. Even his hair was a gleaming black that matched his shoeshine. The only incongruity was that instead of a graveyard pallor, his skin had the kind of light tan most of us can't afford in April. 'Mrs Barclay?' he asked, his voice deep and dignified.

'That's right,' I said, trying for tremulous.

A hand snaked into his top pocket and came out with a business card. 'Will Allen, Mrs Barclay. I'm very sorry for your loss,' he said, not yet offering the card.

'Are you a friend of Richard's? Someone he works – *worked* – with?'

'I'm afraid not, Mrs Barclay. I didn't have the good fortune to know your late husband. No, I'm with Greenhalgh and Edwards.' He handed the card over with a small flourish. 'I wonder if I might have a quiet word with you?'

I looked at the card. I recognized it right away as one of

18

the ones that come out of machines at the motorway-service areas. The ones on the M6 at Hilton Park are the best; they've got really smart textured card. Drop three quid in the slot, choose a logo, type in the text and you get sixty instant business cards. No questions asked. One of the great mysteries of the universe is how villains catch on to the potential of new technology way ahead of the straight community. While most punters were still eyeing the business card machines warily on their way to the toilets, the bad guys were queuing up to arm themselves with bullshit IDs. This particular piece of fiction told me Will Allen was Senior Bereavement Consultant with Greenhalgh and Edwards, Monumental Masons, The Garth, Cheadle Hulme. 'You'd better come in,' I said tonelessly and stepped back to let him pass me. As I closed the door, I noticed Alexis emerging from my house with a cheery wave in my direction.

Allen was moving tentatively towards the living room, the one open door off the hallway. I'd drawn the line at cleaning the whole house. 'Come on through,' I said, ushering him in and pointing him at the sofa Alexis had just vacated. He sat down, carefully hitching up his trousers at the knees. In the light, the charcoal grey suit looked more like Jasper Conran than Marks and Spencer; ripping off widows was clearly a profitable business.

'Thanks for agreeing to see me, Mrs Barclay,' Allen said, concern dripping from his warm voice. He was clean cut and clean shaven, with a disturbing resemblance to John Cusack at his most disarming. 'Was your husband's death very sudden?' he asked, his eyebrows wrinkling in concern.

'Car accident,' I said, gulping back a sob. Hard work, acting. Almost convinces you Kevin Costner earns every dollar of the millions he gets for a movie.

'Tragic,' he intoned. 'To lose him in his prime. Tragic.' Much more of this and I wasn't going to be acting. I was going to be weeping for real. And not from sorrow.

I made a point of looking at his business card again. 'I don't understand, Mr Allen. What is it you're here about?'

'My company is in the business of providing high quality memorials for loved ones who pass away. The quality element is especially important for someone like yourself, losing a loved one so young. You'll want to be certain that whatever you choose to remember him by will more than stand the test of time.' His solemn smile was close to passing the sincerity test. If I really was a grief-stricken widow, I'd have been half in love with him by now.

'But the undertaker said he'd get that all sorted out for me,' I said, going for the sensible-but-confused line.

'Traditionally, we have relied on funeral directors to refer people on to us, but we've found that this doesn't really lead to a satisfactory conclusion,' Allen said confidentially. 'When you're making the arrangements for a funeral, there are so many different matters to consider. It's hard under those circumstances to give a memorial the undivided attention it deserves.'

I nodded. 'I know what you mean,' I said wearily. 'It all starts to blur into one after a while.'

'And that's exactly why we decided that a radical rethink was needed. A memorial is something that lasts, and it's important for those of us left behind that it symbolizes the love and respect we have for the person we have lost. We at Greenhalgh and Edwards feel that the crucial issue here is that you make the decision about how to commemorate your dear husband in the peace of your own home, uncluttered by thoughts of the various elements that will make up the funeral.'

'I see,' I said. 'It sounds sensible, I suppose.'

'We think so. Tell me, Mrs Barclay, have you opted for interment or cremation?'

'Not cremation,' I said very firmly. 'A proper burial, that's what Richard would have wanted.' But only after he was actually dead, I added mentally.

He snapped open the locks on the slim black briefcase he'd placed next to him on the sofa. 'An excellent choice, if I may say so, Mrs Barclay. It's important to have a place where you can mourn properly, a focus for the communication I'm sure you'll feel between yourself and Mr Barclay for a long time to come. Now, because we're still in the trial period of this new way of communicating with our customers, we are able to offer our high quality memorials at a significant discount of twenty per cent less than the prices quoted on our behalf by funeral directors. So that means you get much better value for your money; a memorial that previously might have seemed out of your price range suddenly becomes affordable. Because, of course, we all want the very best for our loved ones,' he added, his voice oozing sympathy.

I bit back the overwhelming desire to rip his testicles off and have them nickel-plated as a memorial to his crass opportunism and nodded weakly. 'I suppose,' I said.

'I wonder if I might take this opportunity to show you our range?' The briefcase was as open as the expression on his face. How could I refuse?

'I don't know . . .'

'There's absolutely no obligation, though obviously it would be in your best interests to go down the road that offers you the best value for money.' He was on his feet and across the room to sit next to me in one fluid movement, a display file from his briefcase in his hand as if by magic. Sleight of hand like his, he could have been the new David Copperfield if he'd gone straight.

He flipped the book open in front of me. I stared at a modest granite slab, letters stuck on it like Letraset rather than incised in the stone. 'This is the most basic model we offer,' he said. 'But even that is finest Scottish granite, quarried by traditional methods and hand-finished by our own craftsmen.' He quoted a price that made my daily rate seem like buttons. He placed the file on my lap.

'Is that with or without the discount?' I asked.

'We always quote prices without discount, Mrs Barclay. So you're looking at a price that is twenty per cent less than that. And if you want to go ahead and you're prepared to pay a cash deposit plus cheque for the full amount tonight, I am authorized to offer you a further five per cent discount, making a total of one quarter less than the quoted price.' His hand had moved to cover mine, gently patting it.

That was when the front door crashed open. 'Careful with that bag, it's got the hot and sour soup in it,' I heard a familiar voice shout. I closed my eyes momentarily. Now I knew how Mary Magdalene felt on Easter Sunday.

'Kate? You in here?' Richard's voice beat him into the room by a couple of seconds. He arrived in the doorway clutching a fragrant plastic carrier bag, a smoking spliff in his other hand. He looked around his living room incredulously. 'What the hell's going on? What have you done to the place?'

He stepped into the room, followed by a pair of burly neo-punks, each with a familiar Chinese takeaway carrier bag. It was the only remotely normal thing about them. Each wore heavy black work boots laced halfway up their calves, ragged black leggings and heavy tartan knee-length kilts. Above the waist, they had black granddad shirts with strategic rips held together by kilt pins and Celtic brooches. Across their chests, each had a diagonal tartan sash of the kind worn on television on Hogmanay by the dancers on those terrible ethnic fantasias the Scottish TV companies broadcast to warm the cockles of their exiles' hearts and make the rest of us throw up into our champagne. The one on Richard's left had bright red hair left long and floppy on top. The sides of his head were stubbled. The other had a permed, rainbow striped Mohican. Each was big enough to merit his own postcode. They looked like Rob Roy dressed by Vivienne Westwood. Will Allen goggled at the three of them, aghast.

Richard dropped the bag of Chinese food and his jaw as the transformation to the room really sank in. 'Jesus, Brannigan, I turn my back for five minutes and you trash the place. And who the hell are you?' he demanded, glowering at Allen.

Allen reassembled his face into something approaching a smile. 'I'm Will Allen. From Greenhalgh and Edwards, the monumental masons. About Mr Barclay's memorial?'

Richard frowned. 'Mr Barclay's memorial? You mean, as in gravestone?'

Allen nodded. 'That's not the term we prefer to use, but yes, as in gravestone.'

'Mr Richard Barclay, would that be?'

'That's right.'

Richard shook his head in disbelief. He stuck his hand into the inside pocket of his leather jacket and pulled out a press card with his photograph on it. He thrust it towards Allen. 'Do I look dead to you?'

Allen was on his feet, his folder pulled out of my grasp. He threw it into the briefcase, grabbed it and shouldered past Richard and the two Celtic warriors. 'Ah shit,' I swore, jumping to my feet and pushing through the doorway in Allen's wake.

'Come back here, Brannigan, you've got some explaining to do,' I heard Richard yell as I reached the door. Allen was sprinting down the path towards the car-parking area. I didn't have my car keys on me; the last thing I'd anticipated was a chase. But Allen was my only lead and he was getting away. I had to do something. I ran down the path after him, glad that the only respectable pair of black shoes in my wardrobe had been flat pumps. As he approached a silver Mazda saloon, the lights flashed and I heard the doors unlock. Allen jumped into the car. The engine started first time. Another one of the joys of modern technology that makes life simpler for the bad guys. He reversed in a scream of tyres and engine, threw the car into a three-point turn and swept out of the cul-de-sac where I live. Anyone seeing him burn rubber as he swung on to the main drag would only mark him down as one of the local car thieves being a little indiscreet.

Dispirited, I sighed and walked back to the house. I'd got the number of his car, but I had a funny feeling that wasn't going to take me a whole lot further forward. These people were too professional for that. At least I had the whole thing on tape, I reminded myself. I stopped in my tracks. Oh no, I didn't. In the confusion of Alexis's visit and the fallout from her shock announcement, I'd forgotten to switch on the radio mikes I'd planted in Richard's living room. The whole operation was a bust.

Not only that, but I was going to have to deal with an irate and very much alive Richard, who was by now standing on his doorstep, arms folded, face scowling. Swallowing a sigh, I walked towards him. If I'd been wearing heels, I'd have been dragging them. 'I know you think being on the road with a neo-punk band is a fate worse than death, but it doesn't actually call for a tombstone,' Richard said sarcastically as I approached.

'It was work,' I said wearily.

'Am I supposed to be *grateful* for that? There's a man in my living room – at least, I *thought* it was my living room, but looking at it, I'm not so sure any more. Maybe I walked into the wrong house by mistake? Anyway, there's some smooth bastard in *my* living room, sitting on *my* settee discussing *my* gravestone with *my* so-called girlfriend –'

'Partner,' I interjected. 'Twenty-nine, remember? Not a girl any more.'

He ignored me and steamrollered on. 'Presumably because I'm supposedly dead. And I'm supposed to be calm and laid back about it because it was *work*?' he yelled.

'Are you going to let me in, or shall I sell tickets?' I asked calmly, gesturing over my shoulder with my thumb at the rest of the close. I didn't have to look to know that half a dozen windows would be occupied by now. TV drama's been so dire lately that the locals have taken up competitive Neighbourhood Watching.

'Let you in? Why? Are we expecting the undertaker next? Coffin due to be delivered, is it?' Richard demanded, thrusting his head forward so we were practically nose to nose. I could smell the sweetness of the marijuana on his breath, see the specks of gold in his hazel eyes. Good technique for dealing with anger, focusing on small details of your environment.

I pushed him in the chest. Not hard, just enough to make him back off. 'I'll explain inside,' I said, lips tight against my teeth.

'Well, big fat hairy deal,' Richard muttered, turning on his heel and pushing past the two neo-punks who were leaning against the wall behind him, desperately trying to pretend they were far too cool to be interested in the war raging around them.

I followed him back into the living room and returned to my seat. Richard sat opposite me, the coffee table between us. He started emptying the contents of the three carrier bags on to the table. 'You'll find bowls and chopsticks in the kitchen,' he said to his giant Gaelic gargoyles. 'First on the right down the hall. That's if she hasn't emptied it as well.' The redhead left in search of eating implements. 'This had better be good, Brannigan,' Richard added threateningly.

'It *smells* good,' I said brightly. 'Yang Sing, is it?'

'Never mind the bloody Chinese!' I waited for the jolt while the world stopped turning. Never mind the bloody Chinese? From the man who thinks it's not food if it doesn't have soy sauce in it? 'What was that creep doing here?' Richard persisted.

'Pitching me into a gravestone,' I said as the redhead returned and dumped bowls, chopsticks and serving spoons in front of us. I grabbed a carton of hot and sour soup and a spoon.

'I realized *that*. But why here? And why *my* gravestone?' Richard almost howled.

The punk with the Mohican exchanged apprehensive looks with his mate. The redhead nodded. 'Look,' the Mohican said. 'This mebbe isnae a good time for this, Richard, know what ah mean, but?' The Glasgow accent was so strong you could have built a bridge with it and known it would outlast the civilization that spawned it. Once I'd deciphered his sentiment, I couldn't help agreeing with him.

'We could come back another time, by the way,' the redhead chipped in, accent matching. Like aural bookends.

'Never mind coming back, you're here now,' Richard said. 'Get stuck in. She loves an audience, don't you, Brannigan?' He piled his bowl with fried noodles and beansprouts, added some chunks of aromatic stuffed duck and balanced a couple of prawn wontons on top, then leaned back in his seat to munch. 'So why am I dead?'

He always does it to me. As soon as there's the remotest chance of me getting my fair share of a Chinese takeaway, Richard asks the kind of questions that require long and complicated answers. He knows perfectly well that my mother has rendered me incapable of speaking with my mouth full. Some injunctions you can rebel against; others are in the grain. Between mouthfuls of hot and sour soup so powerful it steam-cleaned my sinuses, I filled him in on the scam.

Then, Richard being too busy with his chopsticks to

comment, I went on the offensive. 'And it would all have gone off perfectly if you hadn't come blundering through the door and blowing my cover sky-high. Two days early, I might point out. You're supposed to be in Milton Keynes with some band that sounds like it was chosen at random from the Neanderthal's dictionary of grunts. What was it? Blurt? Grope? Fart?'

'Prole,' Richard mumbled through the Singapore vermicelli. He swallowed. 'But we're not talking about me coming back early to my own house. We're talking about this mess,' he said, waving his chopsticks in the air.

'It's cleaner and tidier than it's ever been,' I said firmly.

'Bad news, but,' the Mohican muttered. 'Hey, missus, have you thought about getting your chakras balanced? Your energy flow's well blocked in your third.'

'Shut up, Lice. Not everybody's into being enlightened and that,' the redhead said, giving him a dig in the side that would have left most people with three cracked ribs. Lice only grunted.

'You still haven't said why you came home early,' I pointed out.

'It was two things really. Though looking at what I've come home to, I don't know why I bothered about one of them,' Richard said, as if that were some kind of explanation.

'Do I have to guess? Animal, vegetable or mineral?'

'I'd got all the material I needed for the pieces I've got lined up on Prole, and then I bumped into the lads here. Boys, meet Kate Brannigan, who, in spite of appearances to the contrary, is a private investigator. Kate, meet Dan Druff, front man with Glasgow's top nouveau punk band, Dan Druff and the Scabby Heided Bairns.' The redhead nodded gravely and sketched a salute with his chopsticks. 'And Lice, the band's drummer.' Lice looked up from his bowl and nodded. I found a moment to wonder if their guitar players were called Al O'Pecia and Nits.

'Delighted to make your acquaintance,' I said. 'Richard, pleased though I am to be sharing my evening with Dan and Lice, why exactly have you brought them home?' My subtlety, good manners and discretion had passed their sell-by date. Besides, Dan and Lice didn't look like the kind who'd notice anyone being offensive until the half-bricks started swinging.

'My good deed for the year,' he said nonchalantly. 'They need a private eye, and I've never seen you turn down a case.'

'A paying case,' I muttered.

'We'll pay you,' Dan said.

'Something,' Lice added ominously.

'For your trouble,' Dan added, even more ominously.

'Why do you need a private eye?' I asked. It wouldn't be the first time Richard's dropped me in it, and this time I was determined that if I agreed, it was going to be an informed decision.

'Somebody's trying to see us off,' Dan said bluntly.

'You mean . . . ?' I asked.

'How plain do you need it?' Lice demanded. 'They're trying to wipe us off the map. Finish us. Render us history. Consign us to our next karmic state.'

There didn't seem to be two ways of taking Lice's words. I was hooked, no question.

3

This was definitely a lot more interesting than rehashing the cockup of my gravestone inquiries. There would be plenty of time for me to beat myself up about that later. Dealing with the seriously menaced, even if they were barely comprehensible Glaswegian musicians, has always seemed a better way of passing the time than contemplating my failures. 'You've had death threats?' I asked.

Lice looked at Dan, shaking his head pityingly. Dan looked at Richard, his eyebrows steepling in a demand for help. 'Not as such,' Richard explained. 'When Lice talks about being wiped out, he means metaphorically.'

'That's right,' Lice confirmed. 'Poetic licence and that.' My interest was dropping faster than a gun barrel faced with Clint Eastwood.

'Somebody's out to get us *professionally* is what we're trying to say,' Dan butted in. 'We're getting stuffed tighter than a red pudding.'

'What's a red pudding?' Richard demanded. I was glad about that; we private eyes never like to display our ignorance.

'For fuck's sake,' Lice groaned.

'What do you expect from a country where the fish and chip shops only sell fish and chips?' Dan said. 'It's like a sausage only it's red and it's got oatmeal in it and you deep-fry it, OK? In batter,' he added for the benefit of us Sassenachs.

I wasn't about to ask any more. I still hadn't recovered from the shock of asking for a pizza in a Scottish chip shop. I'd watched in horrified amazement as the fryer expertly folded it in half and dumped it in the deep fat. No, I didn't eat it. I fed it to the seagulls and watched them plummet into the waves afterwards, their ability to defeat gravity wiped out in one meal. 'So this metaphorical, poetically licensed professional stitch-up consists of what, exactly?'

'Essentially, the boys are being sabotaged,' Richard said.

'Every time we're doing a gig around the town, some bastard covers all our posters up,' Dan said. 'Somebody's been phoning the promoters and telling them not to sell any more tickets for our gigs because they're already sold out. And then we get to a gig and there's hardly any genuine fans there.'

'But there's always a busload of Nazis on super lager that tear the place to bits and close the gig down,' Lice kicked in bitterly. 'Now we've been barred from half the decent venues in the north and we're getting tarred with the same brush as they fascist bastards that are wrecking our gigs. The punters are starting to mutter that if these guys follow us around from place to place, it must be because there's something in our music that appeals to brainless racists.'

'And actually, the boys' lyrics are quite the opposite of that.' Richard with the truly crucial information as usual. 'Even the most PC of your friends would be hard pressed to take offence.'

'The only PC friend I've got is the one next door with the Pentium processor,' I snapped. To my surprise, Dan and Lice guffawed.

'Nice one,' Dan said. 'Anyway, last night put the tin lid on it. We were doing this gig in Bedford, and while we were inside watching the usual wrecking crew smashing the place up, some total toerag torched our Transit.'

'Have you talked to the police about this?' I said. Silly me. The boys scowled and shook their heads. Richard cast his eyes heavenward and sighed deeply. I tried again. 'This sounds like a campaign of systematic harassment to me. They've got the resources to pursue something like that properly. And they're free,' I added.

'I thought you said she knew her arse from a hole in the ground?' Lice demanded of Richard. '"Have you talked to the police about this,"' he mimicked cruelly. The last time I felt that mimsy I was nine years old and forced to wear my cousin's cast-off party frock in lemon nylon with blue roses, complete with crackling petticoat, to my best friend's birthday party. 'For fuck's sake, look at us. If we walked into the local nick, they'd arrest us. If we told them we were being harassed, they'd piss themselves laughing. I don't think that's the answer, missus.'

Dan picked up the last salt and pepper rib and stood up. 'Come on, Lice,' he said. 'I don't want to embarrass the woman. Richard, I know you meant well, but hey, your missus obviously isnae up to it. You know what they're like, women today. They cannae bring themselves to admit there are things that are way beyond them.'

That did it. Through clenched teeth, I said, 'I am nobody's missus and I am more than capable of sorting out any of the assorted scumbags that have doubtless got their own very good reasons for having it in for Dan Druff and the Scabby Heided Bairns. You want this sorting, I'll sort it. No messing.'

When I saw the smile of complicity that flashed between Richard and Dan, I nearly decked the pair of them with the flying sweep kick I'd been perfecting down the Thai boxing gym. But there's no point in petulance once you've been well and truly had over. 'I think that little routine makes us quits,' I told Richard. He grinned. 'I'm going to need a lot more details.'

Dan sat down again. 'It all started with the flyposting,' he said, stretching his long legs out in front of him. I had the feeling it was going to be a long story.

It was just after midnight when Dan and Lice left Richard and me staring across the coffee table at each other. It had taken a while to get the whole story, what with Lice's digressions into the relationship between rock music and politics, with particular reference to right-wing racists and the oppression of the Scots. The one clear thread in their story that seemed impossible to deny was that someone was definitely out to get them. Any single incident in the Scabby Heided Bairns's catalogue of disaster could have been explained away, but not the accumulation of cockups that had characterized the last few weeks in the band's career.

They'd moved down to Manchester, supposedly the alternative music capital of the UK, from their native Glasgow in a bid to climb on to the next rung of the ladder that would lead them to becoming the Bay City Rollers of the nineties. Now, the boys were days away from throwing in the towel and heading north again. Bewildered that they could have made so serious an enemy so quickly, they wanted me to find out who was behind the campaign. Then, I suspected, it would be a matter of summoning their friends and having the Tartan Army march on some poor unsuspecting Manchester villain. I wasn't entirely sure whose side I was on here.

'You are going to sort it out for them?' Richard asked.

I shrugged. 'If they've got the money, I've got the time.'

'This isn't just about money. You owe me, Brannigan, and these lads are kicking. They deserve a break.'

'So give them a good write-up in all those magazines you contribute to,' I told him.

'They need more than that. They need word of mouth, a following. Without that, they're not exactly an attractive proposition to a record company.'

'It would take more fans than Elvis to make Dan Druff and his team attractive to me,' I muttered. 'And besides, I don't owe you. It was you and your merry men who screwed up my job earlier tonight, if you remember.'

Richard looked astonished, his big tortoiseshell glasses slipping down his nose faster than Eddie the Eagle on a ski jump. 'And what about this place?' he wailed, waving his arm at the neat and tidy room.

'Out of the goodness of my heart, I'm not going to demand the ten quid an hour that good industrial cleaners get,' I said sweetly, getting up and tossing the empty tinfoil containers into plastic bags.

'What about killing me off?' he demanded, his voice rising like a Bee Gee. 'How do you think I felt, coming home to find my partner sitting discussing my gravestone with a complete stranger? And while we're on the subject, I hope you weren't going to settle for some cheap crap,' he added indignantly.

I finished what I was doing and moved across to the sofa.

'Richard, behave,' I said, slipping my legs over his, straddling him.

'It's not very nice, being dead,' he muttered as my mouth descended on his.

Eventually, I moved my lips along his jaw, tongue flickering against the angle of the bone. 'Maybe not,' I said softly, tickling his ear. 'But isn't resurrection fun?'

Richard barely stirred when I left his bed next morning just after seven. I scribbled, 'Gone 2 work, C U 2night?' on a Post-It note and stuck it on the forearm that was flung out across the pillow. I used to write messages straight on to his arm with a felt-tip pen until he complained it ruined his street cred to have 'Buy milk' stencilled indelibly across his wrist. Nothing if not sensitive to people's needs, I switched to Post-Its.

Back in my own home, I stood under the shower, taking my first opportunity to consider Alexis's ballistic missile. I knew that having a baby had climbed to the top of her and Chris's partnership agenda now that they had put the finishing touches to their house on the edge of the Pennines, but somehow I hadn't realized parenthood was quite so imminent a project. I'd had this mental picture of it being something that would rumble on for ages before anything actually happened, given that it's such a complicated business for lesbian couples to arrange.

First they've got to decide whether they want an anonymous donor, in which case their baby could end up having the same father as half the children of lesbians in the Greater Manchester area, with all the potential horrors that lines up for the future.

But if they decide to go for a donor they know, they've got to be careful that everyone agrees in advance what his relationship to the child is going to be. Then they've got to wait while he has two AIDS tests with a gap of at least six months in between. Finally, they've got to juggle things so that sperm and womb are in the same place at the optimum moment. According to Alexis, it's not like a straight couple where the woman can take her temperature every five

32

minutes till the time is right then seize her bloke by the appropriate body part and demand sex. So I'd been banking on a breathing space to get used to the idea of Chris and Alexis as parents.

I've never been smitten with the maternal urge, which means I always feel a bit bemused when my friends get sandbagged by their hormones and turn from perfectly normal women into monomaniacs desperate to pass their genes on to a waiting world. Maybe it's because my biological clock has still got a way to go before anything in my universe starts turning pumpkin-shaped. Or maybe, as Richard suggests when he's in sentimental father mode, it's because I'm a coldhearted bastard with all the emotional warmth of Robocop. Either way, I didn't want a child and I never knew if I was saying the right thing to those who did.

Selfishly, my first thought was for the difference it was going to make to my life. Alexis is my best friend. We go shopping for clothes together. We play seriously competitive and acrimonious Scrabble games together. When Chris and Richard aren't there to complain about the results, we concoct exotic and bizarre snacks (oatcakes with French mayonnaise and strawberry jam; green banana, coconut and chicken curry . . .) and wash them down with copious amounts of good vodka. We pick each other's brains and exploit each other's contacts. Most of all, we're there for each other when it counts.

As the hot water cascaded over me, I felt like I was already in mourning for the friendship. Nothing was ever going to be the same again. Alexis would have responsibilities. When Chris's commitments as a partner in a firm of community architects took her out of town, Alexis would be shackled without time off for good behaviour. Instead of hanging out with me after work, she'd be rushing home for bathtime and nursery tea. Her conversation would shrink to the latest exploits of the incredible child. And it would be incredible, no two ways about it. They always are. There would be endless photographs to pore over. Instead of calling me to say, 'Get down here, girl, I've just found a fabulous silk shirt in your size in Kendal's sale,' Alexis would be putting the child on the phone to say, 'Wo, gay,' and claiming it as 'Hello, Kate'. Worst of all, I had this horrible suspicion I was going to become Auntie Kate. Even Richard's son Davy has never tried to do that to me.

I rinsed the last of the shampoo out of my auburn hair and stepped out of the shower. At least I didn't have to live under the same roof as it, I thought as I towelled my head. Besides, I told myself, nothing healthy stays the same. Friendships change and grow, they shift their emphases and sometimes they even die. 'Everything must change,' I said out loud. Then I noticed a grey hair. So much for healthy change.

I brushed my hair into the neat bob I've opted for recently. Time to get my brain into gear. I knew where I needed to go next on Dan and Lice's problem, but that was a source that might take a little time and a lot of deviousness to tap. More straightforward was a visit to the dark side of the moon.

Gizmo is one of my silver linings. The cloud was a Telecom engineer that I'd had a brief fling with. He'd caught me at one of those weak moments when you kid yourself into believing a nice smile and cute bum are a reasonable basis for a meaningful relationship. After all, if it's a good enough principle for most of the male population . . . His lectures on telephone technology had been mildly interesting the first time round. After a month of them, there wasn't a court in the land that would have convicted me of anything other than self-defence if I'd succumbed to the temptation of burying a meat cleaver in his skull. But he had introduced me to Gizmo, which gave me something good to remember him by.

If Judy Garland was born in a trunk, Gizmo was born in an anorak. In spite of having the soul of a nerd, he had too much attitude for the passivity of train spotting. So he became a computer whizz. That was back in the steam age of computers, when the most powerful of machines took so long to scroll to the end of a ten-page document that you could go off and drip a pot of filter coffee without missing a thing. When 99.99% of the population still thought bulletin boards were things you found on office walls, Gizmo was on line to people all over the world. The teenagers who invented phone phreaking and hacking into the Pentagon were close personal friends of his. He'd never met them, you understand, just spent his nights typing his end of conversations with them and like-minded nutters all over the planet.

When the FBI started arresting hackers and phreakers on the grounds that America has never known what to do with nonconformists, and the British police started to take an interest, Gizmo decided it was time to stop playing Butch Cassidy and the Sundance Kid and come out into the sunlit uplands. So he started working for Telecom. And he manages to keep his face straight when he tells people that he's a computer systems manager there. Which is another way of saying he actually gets paid to keep abreast of all the information technology that allows him to remain king of the darkside hackers. Gizmo's like Bruce Wayne in reverse. When darkness falls on Gotham City, instead of donning mask and cape and taking on the bad guys, Gizmo goes on line and becomes one of the growing army who see cyberspace as the ultimate subversive, anarchic community. And Telecom still haven't noticed that their northern systems manager is a renegade. It's no wonder none of Gizmo's friends have Telecom shares.

If I had to pick one thing that demonstrates the key difference between the UK and the USA, it would be their attitudes to information. Americans get everything unless there's a damn good reason why not. Brits get nothing unless a High Court judge and an Act of Parliament have said there's a damn good reason why we should. And private eyes are just like ordinary citizens in that respect. We don't have any privileges. What we have are sources. They fall into two groups: the ones who are motivated by money and the ones who are driven by principle. Gizmo's belief that information is born free but everywhere is in chains has saved my clients a small fortune. Police records, driver and vehicle licensing information, credit ratings: they're all there at his fingertips and, for a small donation to Gizmo's Hardware Upgrade Fund, at mine. The only information he won't pass on to me is anything relating to BT phone bills or numbers. That would be a breach of confidence. Or something equally arbitrary. We all have to draw the line somewhere.

I draw it at passing Gizmo's info on to clients. I use him either when I've hit a dead end or I know he can get something a lot faster than I can by official routes, which means the client saves money. I know I can be trusted not to abuse that information. I can't say the same about the people who hire me, so I don't tell them. I've had people waving wads of dosh under my nose for an ex-directory phone number or the address that goes with a car licence plate. Call me a control freak, but I won't do that kind of work. I know there are agencies who do, but that doesn't keep me awake at night. The only conscience I can afford to worry about is my own.

Gizmo had recently moved from a bedsit in the busiest red-light street in Whalley Range to a two-bedroomed flat above a shop in Levenshulme, a stretch of bandit country grouped around Stockport Road. The shop sells reconditioned vacuum cleaners. If you've ever wondered where Hoovers go when they die, this is the place. I've never seen a customer enter or leave the place, though there's so much grime on the windows they could be running live sex shows in there and nobody would be any the wiser. And Gizmo reckons he's moved up in the world.

I was going against the traffic flow on the busy arterial road, so it didn't take me long to drive the short distance to Levenshulme and find a parking space on a side street of red-brick terraces. I pressed the bell and waited, contemplating a front door so coated with inner-city pollution that it was no longer possible to tell what colour it had originally been. The only clean part of the door was the glass on the spyhole. After about thirty seconds, I pressed the bell again. This time, there was a thunder of clattering feet, a brief pause and then the door opened a cautious couple of inches. 'Kate,' Gizmo said, showing no inclination to invite me in. His skin looked grey in the harsh morning light, his eyes red-rimmed like a laboratory white rat.

'All right, Giz?'

'No, since you ask.' He rubbed a hand along his stubbled jaw and scratched behind one ear with the knuckle of his index finger.

'What's the problem? Trouble with the Dibble?'

His lips twisted in the kind of smile dogs give before they remove your liver without benefit of anaesthetic. 'No way. I'm always well ahead of the woodentops. No, this is serious. I've got the bullet.'

'From Telecom?'

'Who else?'

I was taken aback. The only thing I could think of was that someone had got wise to Gizmo's extra-curricular activities. 'They catch you with your hand in somebody's digital traffic?'

'Get real,' he said indignantly. 'Staff cuts. The section head doesn't like the fact that I know more than anybody else in the section, including him. So it's good night Vienna, Gizmo.'

'You'll get another job,' I said. I would have found it easier to convince myself if I hadn't been looking at him as I spoke. As well as the red-rimmed eyes and the stubble, a prospective employer had to contend with a haircut that looked like Edward Scissorhands on a bad hair day, and a dress sense that would embarrass a jumble sale.

'I'm too old.'

'How old?'

'Thirty-two,' he mumbled with a suspicious scowl, as if he thought I was going to laugh. I didn't have enough years on him for that.

'You're winding me up,' I said.

'The guys who do the hiring are in their forties and scared shitless that they're going to get the tin handshake any day now, and they know nothing about computer systems except that someone told them it's a young man's game. If you're over twenty-five, twenty-seven if you've got a PhD, they won't even look at your CV. Believe me, Kate, I'm too old.'

'What a bummer,' I said, meaning it.

'Yeah, well. Shit happens. But it's nicer when it happens to somebody else. So what did you come round for? Last orders before I have to put my rates up?'

I handed him the piece of paper where I'd noted Will Allen's licence plate. 'The name and address that goes with the car.'

He didn't even look at it. He just said, 'Some time this afternoon,' then started to close the door.

'Hey, Giz?' He paused. 'I'm really sorry,' I said. He nodded and shut the door.

I walked back towards the street where I'd parked the zippy Rover 216 that Mortensen and Brannigan had bought for me a couple of months before. Until then, I'd been driving a top-of-the-range sports coupé that we'd taken in part payment for a long and complicated car-finance fraud case, but I'd known in my heart of hearts it was far too conspicuous a set of wheels for the kind of work I do. Given how much I enjoy driving, it had been a wrench to part with it, but I'd learned to love the Rover. Especially after my mate Handbrake had done something double wicked to the engine which made it nippier than any of its German siblings from BMW.

As I rounded the corner, I couldn't believe what I saw. There was a spray of glittering glass chunks like hundreds of tiny mosaic tiles all over the pavement by the driver's door of the Rover. The car was twenty yards from the main road, it was half past eight in the morning and I'd been gone less than ten minutes, but someone had had it away on their toes with my stereo.

4

It took me an hour and a half round at Handbrake's back-street garage to get a new window and stereo cassette. I knew the window had come from a scrapyard, but it would have been bad manners to ask about the origins of the cassette. I wouldn't have been entirely surprised if my own deck had arrived in the bike pannier of one of the young lads who supply Handbrake with spare parts as an alternative to drug-running round Moss Side, but it clearly wasn't my lucky day and I had to settle for a less sophisticated machine. While that might increase the shelf life of my new driver's-door window, it wouldn't improve the quality of my life in Manchester's orbital motorway traffic jams, so I wasn't in the best of moods when I finally staggered through the door of the office just after ten.

I knew at once that something was badly wrong. Shelley, our office manager, made no comment about my lateness. In all the years I've been working with her, she'd never before missed the opportunity to whip me into line like one of her two teenage kids. I'd once found her son Donovan, a six-foot three-inch basketball player, engineering student and occasional rapper with a local band, having to give up a week-end to paint my office because he hadn't come home till four in the morning. After that, I'd always had a good excuse for being late into work. But this morning, she scarcely glanced up from her screen when I walked in. 'Bill's in,' was all she said.

Worrying. 'Already? I thought he only flew in yesterday afternoon?'

Shelley's lips pursed. 'That's right,' she said stiffly. 'He said to tell you he needs a word,' she added, gesturing with her head towards the closed door of my partner's office. Even more worrying. Shelley is Bill's biggest fan. Normally when he returns from one of his foreign security consultancy trips, we all sit around in the outside office and schmooze the morning away over coffee, catching up. Bill's a friendly soul; I'd never known him to hide behind a closed door unless he needed absolute peace and quiet to work out some thorny computer problem.

I tapped on the door but didn't wait for an answer before I opened it and walked in on the sort of scene that would have been more appropriate in the new Dancehouse a few doors down Oxford Road. Bill Mortensen, a bearded blond giant of a man, was standing behind his desk, leaning over a dark woman whose body was curved back under his in an arc that would have had my spine screaming for mercy. One of Bill's bunch-of-bananas hands supported the small of her back, the other her shoulders. Unlike the ballet, however, their lips were welded together. I cleared my throat.

Bill jumped, his mouth leaving the woman's with a nauseating smack as he straightened and half turned, releasing his grip on the woman. Just as well her arms were wrapped round his neck or she'd have been on the fast track to quadriplegia. 'Kate,' Bill gasped. His face did a double act, the mouth smiling, the eyes panicking.

'Welcome back, Bill. I wasn't expecting to see you this morning,' I said calmly, closing the door behind me and making for my usual perch on the table that runs along one wall.

Bill stuttered something about wanting to see me while the woman disentangled herself from him. She was a good six inches taller than my five feet and three inches. Strike one. Her hair was as dark as Bill's was blond, cut in the sort of spiky urchin cut I'd recently abandoned when even I'd noticed it was getting a bit passé. On her, it looked terrific. Strike two. Her skin was burnished bronze, an impossible dream for those of us with the skin that matches auburn hair. Strike three. I didn't have the faintest idea who Bill's latest companion was, but I hated her already. She grinned and moved towards me, hand stuck out in front of her with all the enthusiasm of an extrovert teenager who hasn't been put down yet. 'Kate, it's great to meet you,' she announced in an Australian accent that made Crocodile Dundee sound like a BBC newsreader. 'Bill's told me so much about you, I feel like I know you already.' I tentatively put out a hand which she gripped fervently and pumped up and down. 'I just know we're going to be mates,' she added, clapping her other hand on my shoulder.

I looked past her at Bill, my eyebrows raised. He moved towards us and the woman released my hand to slip hers into his. 'Kate,' he finally said. 'This is Sheila.' His eyes warned me not to laugh.

'Don't tell me, let me guess,' I said. 'You met in Australia.'

Sheila roared with laughter. I could feel her excessive response thrusting me into the role of repressed Englishwoman. 'God, Kate, he was right about your sense of humour,' she said. I forced my lips into what I seemed to remember was a smile. 'Hey, Bill, you better tell her the news.'

Bill stood chewing his beard for a moment, then said, 'Sheila and I are getting married.'

To say I was gobsmacked would be like saying Tom Hanks can act a bit. It's not that Bill doesn't like women. He does. Lots of them. He also likes variety. As a serial monogamist, he makes Casanova and Don Juan look like absolute beginners. But he'd always been choosy about who he hung out with. While he preferred his girlfriends good-looking, brains and ambition had always been just as high on his agenda. So while Sheila might appear more of a bimbo than anyone I'd ever seen Bill with, I wasn't about to make a snap judgement on the basis of what I'd seen so far. 'Congratulations,' I managed without tripping over too many of the syllables.

'Thanks, Kate,' Sheila said warmly. 'It's big of you to be generous about losing your partner.'

I looked at Bill. He looked like he'd swallowed an ice cube. 'I thought that in these situations one said something like, "Not so much losing a partner as gaining a secretary,"' I said ominously. 'I have this feeling that there's something you haven't got round to telling me yet, William.'

'Sheila, Kate and I need to have boring business talks. Why don't you get Shelley to point you in the direction of all the best clothes shops? You can come back at lunch time and we'll all go to the Brasserie?' Bill said desperately, one eye on the toe I was tapping on the floor.

'No problems, Billy boy,' Sheila said, planting a kiss smack on his lips. On her way past me, she sketched a wave. 'Can't wait to get to know you better, Kate.'

When the door closed behind her, there was a long silence. ' "Why don't you get Shelley to point you in the direction of the clothes shops?" ' I mimicked as cruelly as I could manage.

'She owns three dress shops in Sydney,' Bill said mildly. I might have known. That explained the tailored black dress she'd almost been wearing.

'This is not a good way to start the day, Bill,' I said. 'What does she mean, I'll be losing a partner? Is she the pathologically jealous type who doesn't want her man working alongside another woman? Is Shelley getting the bum's rush from Waltzing Matilda too?'

Bill threw himself into his chair and sighed. 'Sheila knows I was dreading this conversation, and she said what she did to force me into having it,' he explained. 'Kate, this is it. Sheila's the one I want.'

'Let's face it, Bill, you've run enough consumer tests to make an informed decision,' I said bitterly. I wanted to be happy for him. I would have been happy for him if it hadn't been for the stab of fear that Sheila's words had triggered in me.

He looked me in the eye and smiled. 'True. Which means that now I've found her, I don't want to let her go. Marriage seems like the sensible option.' He looked away. 'And that means either Sheila moves over here or I move to Australia.'

Silence. I knew what was coming but I didn't see why I should let him off the hook. I leaned back against the wall and folded my arms across my chest. Bill the Bear was turning from teddy to grizzly before my eyes, and I didn't like the transformation. Finally, a few sighs later, Bill said, 'Me moving is the logical step. My work's more portable than hers. The jobs I've already been doing in Australia have given me some good contacts, while she has none in the rag trade over here. Besides, the weather's nicer. And the wine.' He tried a pleading, little-boy-lost smile on me.

It didn't play. 'So what happens to Mortensen and Brannigan?' I demanded, my voice surprising even me with its harshness.

Bill picked up the curly Sherlock Holmes pipe he occasionally smokes when he's stuck on a problem, and started fiddling with it. 'I'm sorry, Kate, but I'm going to have to sell my share of the partnership. The problem I've got is that I need to realize the capital I've got tied up in the business so I can start again in Sydney.'

'I don't believe I'm hearing this,' I said. 'You think you can just *sell* us to the highest bidder? Your parents own half the farmland in Cheshire. Can't you get them to stake you?'

Bill scowled. 'Of course I bloody can't,' he growled. 'You didn't go cap in hand to your father when you wanted to become a partner. You funded it yourself. Besides, life's not exactly a bed of roses in cattle farming right now. I doubt they've got the cash to throw around.'

'Fine,' I said angrily. 'So who have you sold out to?'

Bill looked shocked. 'I haven't sold to anyone,' he protested. 'How could you think I'd go behind your back like that?'

I shrugged. 'Everything else seems to have been cut and dried without consulting me. Why should that be any different?'

'Didn't you bother reading the partnership agreement when we drew it up? Paragraph sixteen. If either of us wants to sell our share of the business, we have to offer first refusal to the other partner. And if the remaining partner doesn't want to buy, they have the power of veto over the sale to any third party on any reasonable ground.'

'"The final decision as to the reasonableness or otherwise of that ground to be taken by the partners in consultation with any employees of the firm,"' I quoted from memory. I'd written most of the agreement; it wasn't surprising I knew by heart what the key parts of it said. 'It's academic, Bill. You know I can't afford to buy you out. And you also know damn

43

well that I'm far too fond of you to stand in the way of what you want. So pick your buyer.'

I jumped to my feet and wrenched the door open. 'I'm out of here,' I said, hoping the disgust and anger I felt was as vivid to him as it was to me. Sometimes, the only things that make you feel good are the same ones that worked when you were five. Yes, I slammed the door.

I sat staring into the froth of a cappuccino in the Cigar Store café. The waitress was having an animated conversation with a couple of her friends drinking espressos in the corner, but apart from them, I had the place to myself. It wasn't hard to tune out their gossip and focus on the implications of what Bill had said. I couldn't believe what he planned to do to me. It undercut everything I thought I knew about Bill. It made me feel that my judgement wasn't worth a bag of used cat litter. The man had been my friend before he became my business partner. I'd started my career process-serving for him as a way of eking out my student grant because the hours and the cash were better than bar work. I'd toiled with him or for him ever since I'd jacked in my law degree after the second year, when I realized I could never spend my working days in the company of wolves and settled for the blond bear instead.

There was no way I could afford to buy him out. The deal we'd done when I'd become a partner had been simple enough. Bill had had the business valued, and I'd worked out I could afford to buy thirty-five per cent. I'd borrowed the money on a short-term loan from the bank and paid it back over four years. I'd managed that by paying the bank every penny I earned over and above my previous salary, including my annual profit shares. I'd only finished paying the loan off three months previously, thanks in part to a windfall that couldn't be explained either to another living soul or to the taxman without risking the knowledge getting back to the organized criminals who had inadvertently made me the gift. It had been a struggle to meet the payments on the loan, and I had no intention of standing under the kind of trees that deliver such dangerous windfalls ever again.

I had to face it. There was no way I could raise the cash to buy out Bill's sixty-five per cent at the prices of four years ago, never mind what the agency would now be worth, given the new clients we'd both brought in since then. I was going to be the victim of anyone who decided a two-thirds share in a profitable detective agency was a good investment.

A second cup clattered on to the table in front of me. Startled, I looked up and found myself staring into Shelley's amber eyes. 'I thought I'd find you here,' she said, tossing her mac over a chair and sitting down opposite me. Her face looked like one of those carved African ceremonial masks, all polished planes and immobility, especially now she'd abandoned the beads she used to wear plaited in her hair and moved on to neat cornrows. I couldn't tell from looking at her if she'd come to sympathize or to tell me off for my tantrum and plead Bill's case.

'And we thought Lincoln freed the slaves,' I said bitterly. 'How do you feel about being bought and sold?'

'It's not as bad for me as it is for you,' Shelley said. 'I don't like the new boss, I just walk out the door and get me another job. But you're tied to whoever Bill sells his share to, am I right?'

'As usual. Back on the chain gang, Shell, that's what I am. Like Chrissie Hynde says, circumstance beyond our control.'

Shelley's eyebrows flickered. 'Doesn't have to be that way, does it?'

'I'm not with you.'

'This behaviour from Bill is not what we're used to.'

'Of course it's bloody not,' I interrupted petulantly. 'It's this Sheila, isn't it? Like the man said, when you've got them by the balls, their hearts and minds will follow. And there's no doubting which part of Bill's anatomy Sheila's got a grip on.'

'Doesn't matter who's behind it, the end result is the same,' Shelley pointed out. 'Bottom line is, Bill is not behaving like your friend, and in my book that absolves you from behaving like his friend.'

'And?'

'You own thirty-five per cent of the business, don't you?'

I nodded. 'Free and clear.'

'So you put your share on the market. Either as an independent entity, or as part of the whole package.'

I frowned. 'But that would devalue the business quite a lot. It's a different kettle of fish buying into an established agency where one of the partners is staying on to maintain the existing clients and another thing altogether to go for something that's nothing more really than a name and a bunch of office equipment.'

'My point exactly,' Shelley said.

'But I'd lose a lot of the money I've put in,' I said.

'But Bill would stand to lose a hell of a lot more,' Shelley said. 'And he needs the cash a lot more than you do right now. What it would do is buy you a bit of time and a lot of say-so on the deal. It gives you a bargaining chip.'

Slowly, I nodded. 'Shelley, you are one mean mother,' I said, admiration in my voice. 'And I thought Bill was your blue-eyed boy.'

Shelley's lips tightened. I noticed that between her nose and mouth, a couple of creases were graduating to lines. 'Listen, Kate, when I was growing up, I saw a lot of women doing the "my kids, right or wrong" routine with teachers, with cops. And I see their kids now, running drugs, living behind bars. I've seen the funerals when another one gets shot in some stupid gang war. I don't like the end result of blind loyalty. Bill has been my friend and my boss a long time, but he's behaving like an arsehole to us both, and that's how he deserves to be treated.'

I admired her cold determination to get the best result for both of us. I just didn't know if I could carry it through as ruthlessly as Shelley would doubtless demand. 'You're right,' I said. 'I'll tell him I want to sell too.'

Shelley smiled. 'I bet you feel better already,' she said shrewdly. She wasn't wrong. 'So, haven't you got any work to do?'

I told her about the previous evening's adventures, and, predictably enough, she had a good laugh at my expense. 'So now I need to see Dennis,' I finished up. 'Richard might know all there is to know about the music side of the rock business, but when it comes to the criminal side, he thinks seedy is

something you listen to on your stereo. Whereas Dennis might not know his Ice T from his Enya, but he could figure out where to make a bent earner in the "Hallelujah Chorus".'
The only problem was, as I didn't have to remind Shelley, my friend and sometime mentor Dennis wasn't quite as accessible as normal, Her Majesty the Queen being unreasonably fussy about keeping her guests to herself.

When I met Dennis, like so many people in their late thirties, he'd just gone through a major career change. After a stretch in prison, he'd given up his previous job as a professional and highly successful burglar to the rich and famous and taken up the more demanding but less dangerous occupation of 'a bit of ducking and diving' on the fringes of the law. Which included, on occasion, a bit of consultancy work for Mortensen and Brannigan. Thanks to Dennis, I'd learned how to pick locks, defeat alarm systems and ransack filing cabinets without leaving a trace.

Unfortunately, a little enterprise of Dennis's aimed at separating criminals from their cash flow had turned sour when he'd inadvertently arranged one of his handovers in the middle of a Drugs Squad surveillance. Instead of grabbing a couple of major-league traffickers and one of those cocaine hauls that get mentioned in the news, the cops ended up with a small-time villain and the kind of nothing case that barely makes three paragraphs in the local paper. Inevitably, Dennis paid the price of their pique, seeing his scam blown sufficiently out of proportion in court to land him with an eighteen-month sentence. Some might say he got off lightly, given his CV and what else I happened to know he'd been up to lately, but speaking as someone who would go quietly mad serving an eighteen-day sentence, I wouldn't be one of them.

'When can you get in to see him?' Shelley asked.

Good question. I didn't have a Visiting Order nor any immediate prospect of getting one. Once upon a time, I'd have rung up and pretended to be a legal executive from his firm of solicitors and asked for an appointment the next day. But security had grown tighter recently. Too many prisoners had been going walkabout from jails that weren't supposed to be open prisons. Now, when you booked a brief's appointment at Strangeways, they took the details then rang back the firm you allegedly represented to confirm the name of the person attending and to give them a code consisting of two letters and four numbers. Without the code, you couldn't get in. 'I thought about asking Ruth to let me pose as one of her legal execs,' I said.

Shelley snorted. 'After the last time? I don't think so!'

The last time I'd pretended to be one of Ruth Hunter's junior employees it had strained our friendship so severely it had to wear a truss for months afterwards. Shelley was right. Ruth wasn't going to play.

'I don't mean to teach you to suck eggs,' Shelley said without a trace of humility or apology. 'And I know this goes against the grain. But had you thought about doing it the straight way?'

5

I pivoted on the ball of my right foot, bending the knee as I straightened my left leg, using the momentum to drive me forward and round in a quarter-circle. The well-muscled leg whistled past me, just grazing the hip that moments before had been right in its path. I grunted with effort as I sidestepped and jabbed a short kick at the knee of my assailant.

I was too slow. Next thing I knew, my right leg was swept from under me and I was lying on my back, lungs screaming for anything to replace the air that had been slammed out of them. Christie O'Brien stood above me, grinning. 'You're slowing down,' she observed with the casual cruelty of adolescence. Of course I was slow compared to her; she was, after all, a former British under-fourteen championship finalist. But Christie – Christine until she discovered fashion and lads – was above all her father's daughter. She'd learned at an early age that nothing succeeds like kicking them when they're down.

One of the other things I'd learned thanks to Dennis was Thai kick boxing, a sport he insisted every woman should know. The theory goes, a woman as small as I am is never going to beat a guy in a fair fight, so the key to personal safety is to land one good kick either in the shins or the gonads. Then it's 'legs, don't let me down' time. Kick boxing teaches you how to land the kick and keeps you fit enough to leg it afterwards.

When he'd been sent down, Dennis had asked me to keep an eye on Christie. She'd inherited her mother's gleaming blonde hair and wide blue eyes, but her brains had come from a father who knew only too well the damage a teenage girl can wreak when the only adult around to keep an eye on things has a generous spirit and fewer brain cells than the average goldfish. Because she'd always been accustomed to seeing me around the gym, Christie had either failed to notice or decided not to resent the fact that I'd been spending a lot more time with her recently.

She filled me in on the latest school dramas of who was hanging out with whom and why as we showered next to each other – our club's strictly breeze block. You want cubicles, go somewhere else and pay four times as much to join. By the time we were towelling ourselves dry, I'd managed to swing the conversation round to Dennis. 'You told your dad about this Jason, then,' I asked her casually. She'd mentioned the lad's name once too often.

'You've got to be joking,' she said. 'Tell him about somebody he can't check out for himself and have the heavy mob kicking Jason's door in for a reference? No way. When he comes out'll be well soon enough.'

'When you seeing him next?' I asked.

'Mum's got a VO for Thursday afternoon. I'm supposed to be going with her, but I've got cross-country trials and I don't want to miss them,' she grumbled as she pulled a sweatshirt over her head. 'Dad wouldn't mind. He'll be the one giving me a go-along if I miss getting on the team. But Mum gets really depressed going to Strangeways on her own, so I feel like I've got to go with her.'

'I could go instead of you,' I suggested.

Christie's face lit up. 'Would you? You don't mind? I'm warning you, it's a three-hankie job coming home.'

'I don't mind,' I said. 'I'd like to see your dad. I miss him.'

Christie sighed and stared at her trainers. 'Me too.' She looked up at me, her eyes candid. 'I'm really angry with him, you know? After he came out last time, he promised me he'd never do anything that would get him banged up again.'

I leaned over and gave her a hug. 'He knows he's let you down. It's hard, recognizing that your dad's not perfect, but he's just like the rest of us. He needs you to forgive him, Christie.'

'Yeah, well,' she said. 'I'll tell Mum you'll pick her up dinner time Thursday, then.' She got to her feet and stuffed her sweaty sports clothes into one of the counterfeit Head holdalls Dennis had been turning out the previous spring. 'See ya, Kate,' she said on her way out the door.

Knowing I was doing her a favour made me feel less like the exploitation queen of South Manchester. But not a lot less. So much for doing it the straight way.

When I emerged from the gym, I decided to swing round by Gizmo's to see if he'd got anywhere with my earlier request. If the old axiom, 'If I was going there, I wouldn't start from here,' didn't exist, they'd have to invent it for the journey from Sale to Levenshulme in mid-morning traffic. I knew before I started it was going to be hell on wheels, but for once, I didn't care. Me, reluctant to face Bill?

I crawled along in second while Cyndi Lauper reminded me that girls just wanna have fun. I growled at the cassette deck and swapped Cyndi for Tanita Tikaram's more gloomy take on the world. I knew exactly what she meant when she accused someone of making the whole world cry. I sat in the queue of traffic at the lights where Wilbraham Road meets Oxford Road in the heart of undergraduate city, watching them going about their student lives, backpacked and badly barbered. I couldn't believe it when the fashion world created a whole industry round grunge as if it was something that had just happened. The rest of us knew it wasn't anything new: students have been wearing layers against the cold, and workmen's heavy-duty checked shirts for cheapness, ever since I was a student a dozen years ago. Shaking my head, I glanced at the wall alongside the car. Plastered along it were posters for bands appearing at the local clubs. Some of the venues I recognized from razzing with Richard; others I knew nothing about. I hadn't realized quite how many live music venues there were in the city these days. I looked more closely at the posters, noticing one that had peeled away on the top right corner. Underneath, I could see, in large red letters, 'UFF'. It looked like Dan and Lice hadn't been making it up as they went along.

The impatient horn of the suit in the company car behind

me dragged my attention away from the posters and back to the road. After the lights, the traffic eased up, and I actually managed to get into fourth gear before I reached Gizmo's. This time, I reckoned it would be cheaper to take my chances with the traffic wardens than the locals, so I left the car illegally parked on the main drag. Judging by the other drivers doing the same thing, the wardens were about as fond of hanging out in Levenshulme as I was. I hit the hole in the wall for some cash for Gizmo, then I crossed the road and rang his bell.

Gizmo frowned when he saw me. 'Didn't you get the e-mail?' he asked.

'I've not been back to the office,' I said, holding a tightly rolled wad of notes towards him. 'Do I take it you've had some joy?'

'Yeah. You better come in,' he said reluctantly, delicately removing the cash from my hand and slipping it into the watch pocket of a pair of grey flannels that looked as if they'd first drawn breath around the time of the Great War. 'Somebody dressed as smart as you on the pavement around here looks well suspicious to the local plod. I mean, you're obviously not a native, are you?' he added as I followed him up the narrow stairs, the soles of my shoes sticking to the elderly cord carpet. It was the first time he'd let me past his front door, and frankly, I wasn't surprised.

I followed Gizmo into the front room of the flat. It was a dislocating experience. Instead of the dingy grime and chipped paint of the stairway, I was in a spotlessly clean room. New woodblock flooring, matt grey walls, no curtains, double-glazed windows. A leather sofa. Two desks with computer monitors, one a Mac, one a PC. A long table with an assortment of old computers – an Atari, a Spectrum, an Amiga, an Amstrad PCW and an ancient Pet. A couple of modems, a flat-bed scanner, a hand-held scanner, a couple of printers and a shelf stacked with software boxes. There was no fabric anywhere in the room. Even the chair in front of the PC monitor was upholstered in leather. Gizmo might look like Pigpen, but the environment he'd created for his beloved computers was as near to the perfect dust-free room as he could get.

'Nice one,' I said.

He thrust his hands into the pockets of a woollen waistcoat most bag ladies would be ashamed to own and said, 'Got to look after them, haven't you? I've had that Pet since 1980, and it still runs like a dream.'

'Strange dreams you have, Giz,' I commented as he hit some keys on his PC and located the information I'd asked for. Within seconds, a sheet of paper was spitting out of one of the laser printers. I picked up the paper and read, 'Sell Phones, 1 Beaumaris Road, Higher Crumpsall, Manchester.' There was a phone number too. I raised an eyebrow. 'That it?'

'All I could get,' he said.

'No names?'

'No names. They're not listed at Companies House. They sound like they're into mobies. I suppose if you wanted to go to the trouble and *expense*' – stressing the last word heavily – 'I could do a trawl through the mobile phone service providers and see if this lot are among their customers. But –'

'Thanks, but no thanks,' I said. Breaking the law too many times on any given job is tempting fate. 'Once is sufficient,' I added. 'Anything more would be vulgar.'

'I'll be seeing you then,' Gizmo said pointedly, staring past my shoulder at the door. I took the hint. Find what you're good at and stick to it, that's what I say.

Beaumaris Road was a red-brick back street running parallel to the main drag of Cheetham Hill Road. Unsurprisingly, number one was on the corner. Sell Phones occupied what had obviously once been a corner shop, though it had been tarted up since it had last sold pints of milk at all hours and grossly inflated prices. I parked further down the street and pulled on a floppy green velvet cap and a pair of granny specs with clear glass to complete the transformation from desolate widow to total stranger. They didn't really go with my Levis and beige blazer, but fashion's so eclectic these days that you can mix anything if you don't mind looking like a borderline care-in-the-community case or a social worker.

I walked back to the corner, noting the heavy grilles over the window of Sell Phones. I paused and looked through to an interior that was all grey carpet, white walls and display cabinets of mobile phones. A good-looking black guy was leaning languidly against a display cabinet, head cocked, listening to a woman who was clearly telling the kind of lengthy tale that involves a lot of body language and lines like, 'So she goes, "You didn't!" and I go, "I did. No messing." And she looks at me gone out and she goes, "You never!" ' She was a couple of inches taller than me, but slimmer through the shoulders and hips. Her hair was a glossy black bob, her eyes dark, her skin pale, her cheekbones Slavic, scarlet lips reminding me irresistibly of Cruella De Vil. She looked like a Pole crossed with a racehorse. She was too engrossed in her tale to notice me, and the black guy was too busy looking exquisite in a suit that screamed, *'Ciao, bambino.'*

I peered more closely through the glass and there, at the back of the shop, sitting behind a desk, head lowered as he took notes of the phone call he was engrossed in, was Will Allen in all his glory. I might not know his real name, but at least now I knew where he worked. I carried on round the corner and there, in the back alley behind the shop, was the Mazda I'd last seen parked outside my house the night before. At last something was working out today.

Now for the boring bit. I figured Will Allen wouldn't be going anywhere for the next hour or two, but that didn't mean I could wander off and amble back later in the hope he'd still be around. I reckoned it was probably safe to nip round the corner to the McDonald's on Cheetham Hill Road and stock up with some doughnuts and coffee to make me feel like an authentic private eye as I staked out Sell Phones, but that was as far away as I wanted to get.

I moved my Rover on to the street that ran at right angles to Beaumaris Road and the alley so that I had a good view of the end of Allen's car bonnet, though it meant losing sight of the front of the shop. I slid into the passenger seat to make it look like I was waiting for someone and took off the cap. I kept the glasses in place, though. I slouched in my seat and brooded on Bill's perfidy. I sipped my coffee very slowly, just enough to keep me alert, not enough to make me want to pee. By the time I saw some action, the coffee was cold and so was I.

The nose of the silver Mazda slipped out of the alleyway and turned left towards Cheetham Hill Road. Just on five, with traffic tight as haemoglobin in the bloodstream. Born lucky, that's me. I scrambled across the gear stick and started the engine, easing out into the road behind the car. As we waited to turn left at the busy main road, I had the chance to see who was in the car. Allen was driving, but there was also someone in the passenger seat. She conveniently reached over into the back seat for something, and I identified the woman who had been in Sell Phones talking to the Emporio Armani mannequin. I wondered if she was the other half of the scam, the woman who went out to chat up the widowers. They don't call me a detective for nothing.

The Mazda slid into a gap in the traffic heading into Manchester. I didn't. By the time I squeezed out into a space that wasn't really there, the Mazda was three cars ahead and I was the target of a car-horn voluntary. I gave the kind of cheery wave that makes me crazy when arseholes do it to me and smartly switched lanes in the hope that I'd be less visible to my target. The traffic was so slow down Cheetham Hill that I was able to stay in touch, as well as check out the furniture stores for bargains. But then, just as we hit the straight, he peeled off left down North Street. I was in the right-hand lane and I couldn't get across, but I figured he must be heading down Red Bank to cut through the back doubles down to Ancoats and on to South Manchester. If I didn't catch him before Red Bank swept under the railway viaduct, he'd be anywhere in a maze of back streets and gone forever.

I swung the nose of the Rover over to the left, which pissed off the driver of the Porsche I'd just cut up. At least now the day wasn't a complete waste. I squeezed round the corner of Derby Street and hammered it for the junction that would sweep me down Red Bank. I cornered on a prayer that nothing was coming up the hill and screamed down the steep incline.

There was no silver Mazda in sight. I sat fuming at the junction for a moment, then slowly swung the car round and back up the hill. There was always the chance that they'd stopped off at one of the dozens of small-time wholesalers and middlemen whose tatty warehouses and storefronts occupy the streets of Strangeways. Maybe they were buying some jewellery or a fur coat with their ill-gotten gains. I gave it ten minutes, cruising every street and alley between Red Bank and Cheetham Hill Road. Then I accepted they were gone. I'd lost them.

I'd had enough for one day. Come to that, I'd had enough for the whole week. So I switched off my mobile, wearily slotted myself back into the thick of the traffic and drove home. Plan A was to run a hot bath lavishly laced with essential oils, Cowboy Junkies on the stereo, the pile of computer magazines I'd been ignoring for the last month and the biggest Stoly and grapefruit juice in the world on the side. Plan B involved Richard, if he was around.

I walked through my front door and down the hall, shedding layers like some sixties starlet, then started running the bath. I wrapped myself in my bathrobe which had been hanging strategically over a radiator, and headed for the freezer. I'd just gripped the neck of the vodka bottle when the doorbell rang. I considered ignoring it, but curiosity won. Story of my life. So I dumped the bottle and headed for the door.

They say it's not over till the fat lady sings. Alexis is far from fat, and from her expression I guessed singing wasn't on the agenda. Seeing the stricken look on her face, I kissed Plan A goodbye and prepared for the worst.

6

'Chris?' I asked, stepping back to let Alexis in.

She looked dumbly back at me, frowning, as if trying to call to mind why I should be concerned about her partner.

'Has something happened to Chris?' I tried. 'The baby?'

Alexis shook her head. 'Chris is all right,' she said impatiently, as if I'd asked the kind of stupid question TV reporters pose to disaster victims. She pushed past me and walked like an automaton into the living room, where she subsided onto a sofa with the slack-limbed collapse of a marionette.

I left her staring blankly at the floor and turned off the bath taps. By the time I came back with two stiff drinks, she was smoking with the desperate concentration of an addict on the edge of cold turkey. 'What's happened, Alexis?' I said softly, sitting down beside her.

'She's dead,' she said. I wasn't entirely surprised that somebody she knew was. I couldn't imagine anything else that would destroy the composure of a hard-bitten crime reporter like this.

'Who is?'

Alexis pulled a scrunched up copy of the *Yorkshire Post* out of her handbag. I knew it was one of the out-of-town papers that the *Chronicle* subscribed to. 'I was going through the regionals, looking to see if anybody had any decent crime feature ideas,' Alexis said bleakly as she spread the *YP* out on the table. DOCTOR DIES IN RAID, I read in the top right-hand section of the front page. Under the headline was a photograph of a dark-haired woman with strong features and a wide, smiling mouth. I read the first paragraph.

Consultant gynaecologist Sarah Blackstone was fatally stabbed last night when she disturbed an intruder in her Headingley home.

'You knew her?' I asked.

'That's the doctor who worked with us on Christine's pregnancy.'

It was a strange way of expressing it, but I let it pass. Alexis clearly wasn't in command of herself, never mind the English language. 'I'm so sorry, Alexis,' I said inadequately.

'Never mind being sorry. I want you working,' she said abruptly. She crushed out her cigarette, lit another and swallowed half her vodka and Diet Coke. 'Kate, there's something going on here. That's definitely the woman we dealt with. But she wasn't a consultant in Leeds called Sarah Blackstone. She had consulting rooms here in Manchester and her name was Helen Maitland.'

There are days when I'm overwhelmed with the conviction that somebody's stolen my perfectly nice life and left me with this pile of shit to deal with. Right then, I was inches away from calling the cops and demanding they track down the robber. After the day I'd had, I just wasn't in the mood for chapter one of an Agatha Christie mystery. 'Are you sure?' I asked. 'I mean, newspaper photographs . . .'

Alexis snorted. 'Look at her. She's not got a face that blends into the background, has she? Of course it's Helen Maitland.'

I shrugged. 'So she uses an assumed name when she's treating lesbians. Maybe she just doesn't want the notoriety of being the dykes' baby doctor.'

'It's more than that, KB,' Alexis insisted, swallowing smoke as if her life depended on it. 'She's got a prescription pad and she writes prescriptions in the name of Helen Maitland. We've not had any trouble getting them filled, and it's not like it was a one-off, believe me. There's been plenty. Which also makes me worried, because if the bizzies figure out that Sarah Blackstone and Helen Maitland are the same person, and they try and track down her patients, all they've got to do is start asking around the local chemists. And there we are, right in the middle of the frame.'

All of which was true, but I couldn't see why Alexis was getting so wound up. I knew the rules on human fertility treatment were pretty strict, but as far as I was aware, it wasn't a crime yet to give lesbians artificial insemination, though if the Tories started to get really hysterical about losing the next election, I could see it might have its attractions as a possible vote winner. 'Alexis,' I said gently. 'Why exactly is that a problem?'

She looked blankly at me. 'Because they'll take the baby off us,' she said in a tone of voice I recognized as the one I used to explain to Richard why you can't wash your jeans in the dishwasher.

'I think you might be overreacting,' I said cautiously, aware that I wasn't wearing protective clothing. 'This is a straight-forward case, Alexis,' I continued, skimming the story. 'Bur-glar gets disturbed, struggle, burglar panics, pulls a blade and lashes out. Tragic waste of talented test-tube baby doctor.' I looked up. 'The cops aren't going to be interviewing her Leeds patients, never mind trying to trace people she treated in a different city under a different name.'

'Maybe so, but maybe there's more to it than meets the eye,' Alexis said stubbornly. 'I've been doing the crime beat long enough to know that the Old Bill only tell you what they want you to know. It wouldn't be the first time there's been a whole other investigation going on beneath the sur-face.' She finished her drink and her cigarette, for some reason avoiding my eye.

I had a strong feeling that I didn't know what the real story was here. I wasn't entirely sure that I wanted to know what it was that could disconcert my normally stable best buddy as much as this, but I knew I couldn't dodge the issue. 'What's really going on here, Alexis?' I asked.

She ran both hands through her wild tangle of black hair and looked up at me, her face worried and frightened, her eyes as hollow as a politician's promises. 'Any chance of another drink?'

I fetched her another Stoly and Diet Coke, this one more than a little weaker than the last. If she was going to swallow them like water, I didn't want her passing out before she'd explained why she was in such a state about the death of a woman with whom she'd had nothing more than a professional relationship. I slid the drink across the table to her, and when she reached out for it, I covered her hand with mine. 'Tell me,' I said.

Alexis tightened her lips and shook her head. 'We haven't told another living soul,' she said, reaching for another cigarette. I hoped she wasn't smoking like this around Chris or the baby was going to need nicotine patches to get through its first twenty-four hours.

'You said a minute ago you wanted me working on this. If I don't know what's going on, there's not a lot I can do,' I reminded her.

Alexis lifted her eyes and gazed into mine. 'This has got to stay between us,' she said, her voice a plea I'd never heard from her before. 'I mean it, KB. Nobody gets to hear this one. Not Della, not Ruth, not even Richard. Nobody.'

'That serious, eh?' I said, trying to lighten the oppressiveness of the atmosphere.

'Yeah, that serious,' Alexis said, not noticeably lightened.

'You know you can trust me.'

'That's why I'm here,' she admitted after a pause. The hand that wasn't hanging on to the cigarette swept through her hair again. 'I didn't realize how hard it was going to be to tell you.'

I leaned back against the sofa, trying to look as relaxed and unshockable as I could. 'Alexis, I'm bombproof. Whatever it is, I've heard it before. Or something very like it.'

Her mouth twisted in a strange, inward smile. 'Not like this, KB, I promise you. This is one hundred per cent one-off.' Alexis sat up straight, squaring her shoulders. I saw she'd made the decision to reveal what was eating her. 'This baby that Chris is carrying – it's ours.' She looked expectantly at me.

I didn't want to believe what I was afraid she was trying to tell me. So I smiled and said, 'Hey, that's a really healthy attitude, acting like you've really got a stake in it.'

'I'm not talking attitude, KB. I'm talking reality.' She sighed. 'I'm talking making a baby from two women.'

The trouble with modern life is that there isn't any etiquette any more. Things change so much and so fast that even if Emily Post were still around, she wouldn't be able to devise a set of protocols that stay abreast of tortured human relationships. If Alexis had dropped her bombshell in my mother's day, I could have said, 'That's nice, dear. Now, do you like your milk in first?' In my Granny Brannigan's day, I could have crossed myself vigorously and sent for the priest. But in the face of the encroaching millennium, all I could do was gape and say, 'What?'

'I'm not making this up, you know,' Alexis said defensively. 'It's possible. It's not even very difficult. It's just very illegal.'

'I'm having a bit of trouble with this,' I stammered. 'How do you mean, it's possible? Are we talking cloning here, or what?'

'Nothing so high tech. Look, all you need to make a baby are a womb, an egg and something to fertilize it with.'

'Which traditionally has been sperm,' I remarked drily.

'Which traditionally has been sperm,' Alexis agreed. 'But all you actually need is a collision of chromosomes. You get one from each side of the exchange. Women have two X chromosomes and men have an X and a Y. With me so far?'

'I might not have A level biology, but I do know the basics,' I said.

'Right. So you'll know that if it's the man's Y chromosome that links up with the woman's X chromosome, you get a little baby boy. And if it's his X chromosome that does the business, you get a girl. So everybody knew that you could make babies out of two X chromosomes. Only they didn't shout too much about it, did they? Because if they did more than mention it in passing, like, it wouldn't take a lot of working out to understand that if all you need for baby girls is a pair of X chromosomes from two different sources, you wouldn't need men.'

'You're telling me that after twenty-five years of feminist theory, scientists have only just noticed that?' I couldn't keep the irony out of my voice.

'No, they've always known it. But certain kinds of experiments are against the law. That includes almost anything involving human embryos. Unless, of course, it's aimed at letting men who produce crap sperm make babies. So although loads of people knew that theoretically it was possible to make babies from two women, nobody could officially do any research on it, so the technology that would make it possible science instead of fantasy just wasn't happening.' The journalist was in control now, and Alexis paused for effect. She couldn't help herself.

'So what happened to change that?' I asked, responding to my cue.

'There was a load of research done which showed that men didn't react well to having their wives inseminated with donor sperm. Surprise, surprise, they didn't feel connected to the kids and more often than not, families were breaking up because the men didn't feel like they were proper families. Given that more men are having problems with their sperm production than ever before, the pressure was really on for doctors to find a way of helping inadequate sperm to make babies. A couple of years ago, they came up with a really thin needle that could be inserted right into the very nucleus of an egg so that they could deliver a single sperm right to the place where it would count.'

I nodded, light dawning. 'And somebody somewhere figured that if they could do it with a sperm, they could do it with another egg.'

'Give the girl a coconut,' Alexis said, incapable of being solemn and scared for long.

'And this doctor, whatever her real name is, has been doing this in *Manchester*?' I asked. I know they say that what Manchester does today, London does tomorrow, but this seemed to be taking things a bit far.

'Yeah.'

'Totally illegally?'

'Yeah.'

'With lesbian couples?'

'Yeah.'

'Who are therefore technically also breaking the law?'

'I suppose so.'

We looked at each other across the table. I didn't know

62

about Alexis, but I couldn't help banner headlines flashing across my mind. The thought of what the tabloids would do with a story like this was enough in itself to bring me out fighting for the women who had gone underground to make their dreams come true, let alone my feelings for Alexis and Chris. 'And the baby Chris is carrying belongs to both of you?' I asked.

'That's right. We both had to have a course of drugs to maximize our fertility, then Helen harvested our eggs and took them off to the lab to join them up and grow them on till she was sure they were OK. She did four altogether.'

If I looked as aghast as I felt, Alexis's face didn't reflect it. 'Chris is having *quads*?' I gasped.

'Don't be soft. 'Course she's not. There's a lousy success rate. You have to transplant at least three embryos to be in with a shout, and then it's only a seventy per cent chance that one of them's going to do the business. Helen transplanted three, and one of them survived. Believe me, in this game, that's a result.'

'So what happened to the other one?' I asked. I had a horrible feeling I wasn't going to like the answer.

'It's in the freezer at home. In a flask of liquid nitrogen.'

I'd been right. I felt slightly queasy at the thought and reminded myself never to go looking for a snack in Alexis's kitchen. I cleared my throat. 'How do you know it works? How do you know the babies are . . . OK?'

Alexis frowned. 'There was no way of proving it objectively. We had to take Helen's word for it. She introduced us to the first couple she had a success with. Their little girl's about eighteen months now. She's a really bright kid. And yes, I know they could have been bullshitting us, that it could have been a racket to rip us off, but I believed those two women. You had to be there, KB.'

I thought I could probably make it through the night without the experience. 'I see now why you thought they'd take the baby off you,' was all I said.

'You've got to help us,' Alexis said.

'What exactly did you have in mind?' I asked.

'Helen Maitland's files,' Alexis said. 'We've got to get rid of them before the police find them.'

'Why would the police be looking for them in the first place?' I asked. 'Like I said, it's a straightforward burglary gone wrong.'

'OK, OK, I know you think I'm being paranoid. But this is our child's future that's at stake here. I'm entitled to go a bit over the top. But there's two reasons why I'm worried. One, suppose it didn't happen like the *YP* says? Suppose the person who killed Helen Maitland wasn't a burglar. Suppose it was some woman whose treatment hadn't worked and she'd gone off her box? Or suppose it was somebody who'd found out what was going on and was blackmailing Helen? Once the cops start digging, you know they won't stop. They might not be well bright, but you know as well as I do that when it comes to murder the bizzies don't ignore anything that looks like it might be a lead.'

I sighed. She was right. Coppers on murder inquiries are never satisfied till they've got somebody firmly in the frame. And if the obvious paths don't come up with a viable suspect, they start unravelling every loose end they can find. 'What's the second reason?' I asked.

'She had consulting rooms in Manchester. Sooner or later, somebody is going to notice she's not where she should be when she should be. And eventually, somebody's going to be emptying her filing cabinet. And if I know anything about people, whoever goes through those files isn't going to be dumping them straight in the bucket. It's only human nature to have a good root through. And then me and Chris are chopped liver, along with all the other dykes Helen Maitland has given babies to.' Alexis finished her cigarette and washed it down with a couple of gulps of her drink. 'We need you to find those files.'

I crossed my legs at the ankles and hugged my knees. 'You're asking a lot here. Interfering with a murder inquiry. Probably burglary, not to mention data theft.'

'I'm not asking for a *favour* here, KB. We'll pay you.'

I snorted with ironic laughter. 'Alexis, is this how you really think my professional life works? People walk in and ask me to break the law for money? I thought you knew me! When punters walk into my office and ask me to do things that are illegal, they don't stay in the room long enough to notice the colour of the carpet. When I have to break the law, I go out of my way to make sure my clients are the last to know. If I do this for you, it won't be because you're offering to *pay* me for it, it'll be because I decide it needs to be done.'

She had the grace to look abashed. 'I'm sorry,' she groaned. 'My head's cabbaged with all this. I know you're not some mad maverick burglar for hire. It's just that you're the only person I know who's got the skills to get us out from under whatever's going to happen now Helen Maitland's dead. Will you do the business for us?' The look of desperation that had temporarily disappeared was back.

'And what if the things I find out point to a conclusion you won't like?' I asked, stalling.

'You mean, if you uncover evidence that makes it look like one of her lesbian patients killed her?'

'That's exactly what I mean.'

Alexis covered her eyes and kneaded her temples. Then she looked up at me. 'I can't believe that's what you'll find. But even if you do, is that any reason why the rest of us have to have our lives destroyed too?'

Just call me the girl who can't say no.

7

The pleasant, caring atmosphere of the Compton Clinic hit me as soon as I walked through the door. Air subtly perfumed and temperature controlled, decor more like a country house than a medical facility, bowls of fresh flowers on every surface. I could almost believe they employed the only gynaecologists in the world who warm the speculums before plunging them deep into a woman's most intimate orifice. I made a mental note to ask Alexis about it later.

The clinic was in St John Street, a little Georgian oasis off Deansgate that pretends very hard to be Harley Street. The doctors who have their private consulting rooms there obviously figure that one of the most convincing ways of doing that is to charge the most outrageous prices for their services. From what I'd heard, you could make the down payment on one of the purpose-built yuppie flats round the corner on what they'd charge you to remove an unsightly blackhead. If Helen Maitland demanded that kind of price for her treatments, I couldn't imagine there were enough dykes desperate for motherhood and sufficiently well-heeled to make it worth her while. But then, what do I know? I'm the only woman I'm aware of who's been using the pill *and* demanding a condom since she was sixteen.

The Compton Clinic was about halfway down on the right-hand side, a three-storey terraced house with a plague of plaques arrayed on either side of the door. Interestingly, Helen Maitland's name didn't appear on any of them. Neither did Sarah Blackstone's. I opened the heavy front door and found myself in a short hallway with a large sign directing me left to the reception area. I noted a closed-circuit TV camera mounted above the outside door, pointing down the hall towards the door I was being encouraged to use. It was a considerable incentive not to go walkabout especially since I hadn't brought a tub of Vaseline to smear over the lens.

One of the many problems with my job is you do such a lot of different things in a day, you're seldom appropriately dressed. If I'd known what the carpet at the clinic was like, I'd have brought my snow shoes, but as it was, I just had to make do with wading through the deep pile in an ordinary pair of leather loafers. There were two other potential patients sitting a discreet distance from each other on deep, chintz-covered sofas, reading the sort of home and garden magazine the nouveaux riches need to copy to shore up their conviction that they've arrived and they belong.

A tip from the private-eye manual: magazines are one of the dead giveaways as to whether you're dealing with the NHS or the private sector. The NHS features year-old, dog-eared copies of slender weeklies that feature soap stars talking about their operations and TV personalities discussing their drink problems or their diets. The private sector provides this month's copies of doorstop glossies full of best-selling authors talking about their gardens and living with Prozac, and Holly-wood stars discussing their drink problems, their diets and living with Prozac.

I managed to reach the reception desk without spraining my ankle. It was pure English country-house library repro, right down to the fake tooled-leather top and the cottage-garden prints on the wall behind it. The middle-aged woman sitting at the desk had a pleasant face, the lines on it carved by comfortable optimism rather than adversity, an impression supported by her Jaeger suit and the weight of the gold chains at neck and wrist. Her eyes betrayed her, however. They were quick, sharp and assessing as they flicked over my smartest suit, the lightweight wool in grey and moss green. It felt like she was instantly appraising the likely level of my bank balance and the concomitant degree of politeness required.

'How may I help you?' she asked, her voice the perfect match for the house-and-garden images of the decor.

'I'd like to make an appointment with Dr Maitland,' I said,

deliberately lowering my voice so she'd think I didn't want the other two women to overhear.

'One moment,' she said, leaning to one side to stretch down and open one of the lower drawers in the desk. If Helen Maitland really was the murdered Dr Sarah Blackstone, the news hadn't made it to the Compton Clinic yet. The woman straightened up with a black A5 desk diary in her hand. She laid it on top of the larger diary that was already sitting open in front of her, and flicked through it to the following Sunday's date. Even I could see that every half-hour appointment was already filled up. If Alexis was right, there were going to be a lot of disappointed faces on Sunday.

I watched as the receptionist flicked forward a week. Same story. On the third attempt, I could see there were a couple of vacant slots. 'The earliest I can offer you is 3.30 on the twenty-fourth,' she said. There was no apology in her voice.

'Does it have to be a Sunday?' I asked. 'Couldn't I see her before then if I come during the week?'

'I'm afraid not. Dr Maitland only consults here on a Sunday.'

'It's just that Sundays are a little awkward for me,' I said, trying the muscularly difficult but almost invariably successful combination of frown and smile. I should have known it was a waste of time. Every medical receptionist since Hippocrates has been inoculated against sympathy.

The receptionist's expression didn't alter a millimetre. 'Sunday is the only day Dr Maitland consults here. She is not a member of the Compton partnership, she merely leases our facilities and employs our services in an administrative capacity.'

'You mean, you just make appointments on her behalf?'

'Precisely. Now, would you like me to make this appointment for you, Ms . . . ?'

'Do you know where else she works? Maybe I could arrange to see her there?'

Ms Country House and Garden was too well trained to let her facade slip, but I was watching for any signs, so I spotted the slight tightening of the skin round her eyes. 'I'm afraid we have no knowledge of Dr Maitland's other commitments,' she said, her voice revealing no trace of the irritation I was sure she was starting to feel.

'I guess I'll just have to settle for the twenty-fourth, then,' I said, pursing my lips.

'And your name is?'

'Blackstone,' I said firmly. 'Sarah Blackstone.'

Not a flicker. The receptionist wrote the name in the half-past-three slot. 'And a phone number? In case of any problems?'

I gave her my home number. Somehow, I don't think she had the same problems in mind as I did.

I had time to kill before I headed over to South Manchester to pick up Debbie for our prison visit, but I didn't want to go back to the office. I hate violence and I don't like putting myself in situations where GBH seems to be the only available option. I cut down through Castlefield to the canal and walked along the bank as far as Metz, a bar and Mittel European bistro on the edges of the city's gay village. Metz is so trendy I knew the chances of being spotted by anyone I knew were nil. I bought a bottle of designer mineral water allegedly flavoured with wild Scottish raspberries and settled down in a corner to review what little I knew so far.

I'd been taken aback when Alexis had revealed that she and Chris had been consulting Helen Maitland for six months. After all, we were best buddies. I had secrets from Richard, just as Alexis had from Chris. Show me a woman who doesn't keep things from her partner, and I'll show you a relationship on the point of self-destructing. But I was pretty certain I had no secrets from Alexis, and I'd thought that was mutual. Even though I understood her motives for not telling me about something so illegal, to discover she'd been hiding something this big made me wonder what else I'd been kidding myself about.

Alexis and Chris had been told about Dr Helen Maitland – in total confidence – by a close friend of theirs, a lesbian lawyer who'd been approached very cautiously by another couple who wanted to know the legal status of what they were planning to do. Because she knew about Alexis and

Chris's desire to have a child, their lawyer friend introduced them to her clients. I sincerely hoped the Law Society wasn't going to hear about this – even two years of a law degree was enough for me to realize that what was going on here wasn't just illegal, it was unethical too. And let's face it, there aren't enough lawyers around who act out of compassion and concern for the prospect of losing one of them to be anything other than bleak.

Alexis had phoned the Compton Clinic and made an appointment for her and Chris to see Dr Maitland the following Sunday. Obviously, the word had spread since then, judging by the delay I'd faced. She'd been told, as I had been, to go to the back door of the clinic, as the main part of the building was closed on Sundays. Alexis had told me that the initial consultation made interviewing bereft parents look as easy as finding a non-smoking seat on a train. Dr Maitland had offered nothing, instigated nothing. It had been Alexis and Chris who had to navigate through the minefield, to explain what they wanted and what they hoped she could do for them. According to Alexis, Helen Maitland had been as stiff and unyielding as a steel shutter.

In fact, she'd nearly thrown them out when she was taking their details and Alexis admitted to being a journalist. 'Why did you tell her?' I'd asked, amazed.

'Because I wanted her to work with us, soft girl,' Alexis had replied scornfully. 'She was obviously really paranoid about being caught doing what she was doing. That whole first consultation, it was like she was determined she wasn't going to say a word that would put her in the wrong if someone was taping the conversation. And then she was taking down all these details. Plus she insisted on leaving a three-week gap between the first and second appointments. I figured she must be checking people out. And I reckon that if what she found out didn't square with what she'd been told, you never got past that second appointment. So I had to tell her, didn't I?'

'How come she didn't throw you out then and there?'

The familiar crooked grin. 'Like I always say, KB, they don't pay me my wages for working a forty-hour week. They pay me for that five minutes a day when I persuade somebody who isn't going to talk to a living soul to talk to me. I can be very convincing when I really want something. I just told her that being a journalist didn't automatically make me a scumbag, and that I was a dyke before I was a hack. And that the best way to make sure a story never got out was to involve a journo with a bit of clout.'

I hadn't been able to argue with that, and I suspected that Helen Maitland hadn't either, especially since it would have been delivered with a hefty dollop of the Alexis Lee charm. So the doctor had agreed to work with them both to make Chris pregnant with their child. First, they each had to take courses of drugs that cost a small fortune and made both of them feel like death on legs. The drugs maximized their fertility and also controlled their ovulation so that on a particular Sunday, they'd both be at the optimum point for having their eggs harvested. Helen Maitland herself had carried out this apparently straightforward procedure. According to Alexis, who never forgets she's a journalist, the eggs were then transferred into a portable incubator which Helen Maitland could plug into the cigarette lighter of her car and transport to her lab, wherever that was. Another small detail I didn't have.

In the lab, one egg from Alexis would be stripped down to its nucleus and loaded into a micropipette one tenth the thickness of a human hair. Then one of Chris's eggs would be injected with Alexis's nucleus and hopefully the chromosomes would get it on and make a baby. This nuclear fusion was a lot less immediately spectacular than nuclear fission, but its implications for the human race were probably bigger. It was obvious why the doctor had chosen to use an alias.

I couldn't help wondering what would happen when men found out what was going on. If there was one thing that was certain, it was that sooner or later the world was going to know about this. It didn't seem possible that Helen Maitland was the only one who had worked out the practical means of making men redundant. I had this niggling feeling that all over California, women were making babies with women and doctors with fewer scruples than Helen Maitland were making a lot of money.

71

That was another thing that had become clear from Alexis's story. In spite of their desperation, Helen Maitland wasn't bleeding her patients dry. The prescriptions were expensive, but there was nothing she could do about that. However, her fees for the rest of the treatment seemed remarkably cheap. She was charging less per hour than I do. If the medical establishment had found out about that, she'd have been struck off a lot faster for undercharging than she ever would have been for experimenting on humans.

There was no other word for it. What she had been doing was an experiment, with all the attendant dangers. I didn't know enough about embryology to know what could go wrong, but I was damn sure that all the normal genetic risks a foetus faced would be multiplied by such an unorthodox beginning. If I'd been the praying sort, I'd have been lighting enough candles to floodlight Old Trafford on the off chance it would give Chris a better chance of bearing a healthy, normal daughter. Being the practical sort, the best thing I could do would be to find Helen Maitland's killer before the investigation led to my friends. Or worse. I couldn't rule out the possibility that someone had killed Helen Maitland because they'd discovered what she was doing and decided she had to die. Anyone with so fundamental a set of beliefs wasn't going to stop at seeing off the doctor who had set these pregnancies in motion. There was a lot to do, and the trouble was, I didn't really know where to start. All I had was an alias and a consulting room that I hadn't been able to get near.

I finished my drink and stared moodily at the dirty grey water of the canal. The city has screwed so much inner-city renewal money out of Europe that the banks of our canals are smarter than Venice these days. The water doesn't stink either. In spite of that, I figured I'd be waiting a long time before I saw a gondola pass. Probably about as long as it would take me to raise the money to buy Bill out of the partnership.

I couldn't bear the idea of just throwing in the towel, though. I'd worked bloody hard for my share of the business, and I'd learned a few devious tricks along the way. Surely I could think of *something* to get myself off the hook? Even if I could persuade the bank to lend me the money, working solo

I could never generate enough money to pay off the loan and employ Shelley, never mind the nonessentials like eating and keeping a roof over my head. The obvious answer was to find a way to generate more profit. I knew I couldn't work any harder, but maybe I could do what Bill had done and employ someone young, keen and cheap. The only problem was where and how to find a junior Brannigan. I could imagine the assorted maniacs and nerds who would answer a small ad in the *Chronicle*. Being a private eye is a bit like being a politician – wanting the job should be an automatic disqualification for getting it. I mean, what kind of person *admits* they want to spend their time spying on other people, lying about their identity, taking liberties with the law, risking life and limb in the pursuit of profit, and never getting enough sleep? I didn't have time to follow the path of my own apprenticeship – I'd met Bill when I was a penniless law student and he was having a fling with one of the women I shared a house with. He needed someone to serve injunctions and bankruptcy petitions, and I needed a flexible and profitable part-time job. It took me a year to realize that I liked the people I spent my time with when I was working for Bill a lot better than I liked lawyers.

I walked out of Metz and set off across town to where I'd parked my car. On my way through Chinatown, I popped into one of the supermarkets and picked up some dried mushrooms, five spice powder and a big bottle of soy sauce. There were prawns and char siu pork in the fridge already and I'd stop off to buy some fresh vegetables later. I couldn't think of a better way to deal with my frustrations than chopping and slicing the ingredients for hot and sour soup and sing chow vermicelli.

At the till, the elderly Chinese woman on the cash register gave me a fortune cookie to sample as part of a promotion they were running. Out on the street, I broke it open, throwing the shell into the gutter for the pigeons. I straightened out the slip of paper and read it. It was hard not to believe it was an omen. 'Sometimes, beggars can be choosers,' it said.

8

As my car rolled to a halt outside Debbie and Dennis's house on a modern suburban estate, the curtains started to twitch the length of the close. Before I could get out of the car and ring the bell, the front door was open and Debbie was coming down the drive of their detached home with gleaming blonde head held high for the benefit of the neighbours. She looked like a recently retired supermodel slumming it for the day. The dignified impression was only slightly diminished by the tiny stride imposed by the tightness of her skirt and the height of her heels. Debbie folded herself into the passenger seat of my car, her long legs gleaming with Lycra, and said, 'Nosy so-and-sos. Did you see them nets? Up and down like a bride's nightie. Imagine having nothing better to do all day than spy on everybody else. That Neighbourhood Watch scheme is just a licence to poke your nose into other people's business, if you ask me. Sad bastards.'

'How you doing, Debbie?' I asked in the first pause in the tirade.

She sighed. 'You don't want to know, Kate.'

She wasn't wrong. I'd had a brief taste of seeing the man I loved behind bars, and that had been enough for me to realize how hellish it must be to lose them to prison for months or years. 'You know you can always talk to me, Debbie,' I lied.

'I know, but it does my head in just thinking about it. Talking about it'd only make it worse.' Debbie flicked open the cover of the car's ashtray with a manicured nail. Seeing it was clean and empty, she closed it again and breathed out heavily through her nose.

'It's OK to smoke if you don't mind having the window open,' I told her.

She took a pack of Dunhills out of a handbag that I knew wasn't Chanel in spite of the distinctive gilt double C on the clasp. I knew it wasn't Chanel because I had an identical one in the same burgundy leather-look plastic. It had been a passing gift from Dennis about a year before, when he'd come by a vanload of counterfeit designer accessories. It had been good gear; Richard was still using the 'Cerruti' wallet. She managed to light up without smudging her perfect lipstick, then said, 'I flaming hate seeing him in there. I really appreciate you coming today. It'll do him good to see you. He always asks Christie if she's seen you and how you're doing.'

From anyone other than Debbie, that would have been a deliberate crack, a sideswipe aimed at triggering a major guilt trip. But given that her IQ and her dress size are near neighbours, I knew she'd meant exactly what she said, no more and no less. It didn't make any difference to me; I still got the stab of guilt. In the seven weeks Dennis had been inside, I'd only got along to see him once so far, and that had been the week after he went down. Sure, I'd been stretched at work, with Bill clearing his desk before Australia. But that was only half the story. Like Debbie, I hated seeing Dennis inside Strangeways. Unlike her, nobody was going to give me a bad time for not visiting him every week. Nobody except me.

'I'm sorry I've not managed more often,' I said lamely.

'Don't worry about it, love,' Debbie said. 'If I didn't have to go, you wouldn't catch me within a hundred miles of the place.'

I refrained from pointing out she lived only half a dozen miles from the red-brick prison walls; I like Debbie too much. 'How's he doing?'

'Not so bad now. You know how he is about drugs? Well, they've just opened this drug-free unit where you can get away from all the junkies and the dealers and he's got on it. The deal is if you stay away from drugs you get unlimited access to the gym. And if you work out daily, you get extra rations. So he's spending a lot of time on the weights. Plus the other blokes on this drug-free wing are mostly older like him, so it's not like being stuck on a wing with a load of drugged-up idiots.' Debbie sighed. 'He just hates being banged up. You know he can't be doing with anybody keeping tabs on him.'

I knew only too well. It was one of the things that united the two of us, superficially so different, but underneath disturbingly similar. 'And time passes a lot faster on the outside than it does behind those walls,' I said, half to myself.

'Don't you believe it,' Debbie said bitterly.

In silence, I navigated my way through the city centre, catching every red light on Deansgate before we passed the new Nynex arena. It's an impressive sight, towering over the substantial nineteenth-century edifice of Victoria Station. Unfortunately but predictably, it opened to a chorus of problems, the main one being that the seats are so steeply raked that people sitting in the top tiers have had to leave because they were suffering from vertigo.

I swung into the visitors' car park and stared up at another impressive sight – the new round-topped wall containing Her Majesty's Prison. The prisoners who destroyed half of Strangeways in a spectacular riot a few years ago ended up doing their successors a major favour. Instead of the horrors of the old Victorian prison – three men to a cramped cell without plumbing – they now have comfortable cells with latrines and basins. For once, the authorities listened to the people who have to run prisons, who explained that the hardest prisoners to deal with are the ones on relatively short sentences. A lifer knows he's in there for a long time, and he wants to make sure that one day he sees the outside again. A man who's got a ten-year sentence knows he'll only serve five years if he keeps his nose clean, so he's got a real incentive to stay out of trouble. But to some toerag who's been handed down eighteen months, it's not the end of the world to lose remission and serve the whole sentence. The short-term prisoners also tend to be the younger lads, who don't have the maturity to get their heads down and get through it. They're angry because they're inside, and they don't know how to control their anger. When cell blocks explode into anarchy and violence, nine times out of ten, it's the short-term men who are behind it.

So Strangeways has got a gym, satellite TV and a variety of other distractions. It's the kind of regime that has the rabid right-wingers foaming at the mouth about holiday camps for villains. Me, I've never been on a holiday where they lock you in your room at night, don't let you see your friends and family whenever you want to and never let you go shopping. Whatever else Strangeways is, a holiday camp it ain't. Most of the loudmouths who complain would be screaming for their mothers within twenty-four hours of being banged up in there. Just visiting is more than enough for me, even though one of the benefits of the rebuilding programme is the Visitors' Centre. In the bad old days, visitors were treated so atrociously they felt like they were criminals too. It's no wonder that a lot of men told their wives not to bring the kids to visit. It was easier to deal with the pain of missing them than to put them through the experience.

Now, they actually treat visitors like members of the human race. Debbie and I arrived with ten minutes to spare, and there wasn't even a queue to check in. We found a couple of seats among the other visitors, mostly women and children. These days, a Visiting Order covers up to three adults, and small children don't count. With every prisoner entitled to a weekly visit, it doesn't take long for a crowd to build up. Nevertheless, we didn't have to hang around for long. Five minutes before our visit time, we were escorted into the prison proper, our bags were searched by a strapping blonde woman prison officer who looked like a Valkyrie on her day off from Wagner's Ring Cycle. Then we were led through anonymous corridors and upstairs to the Visitors' Hall, a large, clean room with views across the city from its long windows. With its off-white walls, vending machines, no-smoking rule, tables laid out across the room and tense atmosphere, it was like a church hall ready for a whist tournament.

We found Dennis sitting back in his chair, legs stretched in front of him. As we sat down, he smiled. 'Great to see you both,' he said. 'Business must be slack for you to take the afternoon off, Kate.'

'Christie's got a cross-country trial,' Debbie said. 'Kate didn't want me coming in here on my own.' There was less bitterness in her voice than there would have been in mine in the same circumstances.

'I'm sorry, doll,' Dennis said, shifting in his seat and leaning forward, elbows on the table, eyes fixed on Debbie with all the appeal of a puppy dog. But Debbie knew only too well what that cute pup had grown into, and she wasn't melting.

'Sorry doesn't make it to parents' night, does it?' Debbie said.

Dennis looked away. 'No. But you're better off than most of this lot,' he added, gesturing round the room with his thumb. 'Look at them. Scruffy kids, market-stall wardrobes, you know they're living in shitholes. Half of them are on the game or on drugs. At least I leave you with money in the bank.'

Debbie shook her head, more in sorrow than in anger. 'Haven't you got it through your thick head yet that me and the kids wouldn't mind going without as long as we'd got you in the house?'

Time for me not to be here. I stood up and took the orders for the vending machines. There were enough kids milling around for it to take me a good ten minutes to collect coffees and chocolate bars, more than long enough for Dennis and Debbie to rehash their grievances and move on. By the time I got back, they were discussing what A levels Christie was planning on taking. 'She should be sticking with her sciences,' Dennis insisted forcefully. 'She wants to get herself qualified as a doctor or a vet or a dentist. People and animals are always going to get sick, that's the only thing that's guaranteed.'

'But she wants to keep up with her sport,' Debbie said. 'Three science A levels is a lot of homework. It doesn't leave her a lot of time for herself. She could be a PE teacher no bother.'

Dennis snorted. 'A teacher? You've got to be joking! Have you seen the way other people's kids are today? You only go into teaching these days if you can't get anybody else to give you a job!'

'What does Christie want to do?' I cut in mildly as I dumped the coffees in front of us.

Dennis grinned. 'What's that got to do with it?' He was only half joking. 'Anyway, never mind all this bollocks. No point us talking to each other when we've got entertainment on tap, is there, Debs? Tell us what you've been up to, Kate.'

Debbie sighed. She'd been married to Dennis too long to be bothered arguing, but it was clear that Christie's future was occupying all of her spare synapses. As Dennis turned the headlamp glare of his sparkling eyes on me, I could sense her going off the air and retreating into herself. Suited me, heartless bastard that I am. I didn't mind that Debbie was out of the conversation. That way I could get to the point without having to explain every second sentence. So I gave Dennis a blow-by-blow account of my aborted attempt to nail the gravestone scammers as a warm-up to asking for his help.

He loved the tale, I could tell. Especially the bit where Richard walked through the door with the takeaway and the Celtic cartoon characters. It was a short step from there to outlining Dan Druff's problems with the saboteurs. Dennis sat back again, linking his hands behind his chair with the expansive air of a man who knows his supplicant has come to the right place.

'Flyposting, isn't it?' he said as if delivering a profound pronouncement.

'Well, yeah, that's one of the problems they've been having,' I said, wondering if his spell behind bars was blunting Dennis's edge. I had already explained that the Scabby Heided Bairns's posters had been covered up by other people's.

'No, that's what it's all about,' he said impatiently. 'This whole thing is about staking out territory in the flyposting game.'

'You're going to have to give me a tutorial in this one, Dennis,' I said. Ain't too proud to beg, and there are times when that's what it takes.

Happy that he'd established his superiority despite his temporary absence from the streets, Dennis filled me in. 'Illegal flyposting is mega business in Manchester. Think about it. Everywhere you go in the city, you see fly posters for bands and events. The city council just don't bother prosecuting, so it's a serious business. The way it works is that people stake out their own territory and then they do exclusive deals with particular clubs and bands. The really clever ones set up their own printing businesses and do deals with ticket promoters as well. They'll do a deal with a club whereby they'll book bands for them, arrange the publicity and organize the ticket sales at other outlets. So for a band to get on and nail down a record deal, best thing they can do is get tied in with one of the boss operators. That way, they'll get gigs at the best venues, plenty of poster coverage on prime sites and their tickets get sold by all the key players.'

'Which costs what?'

Dennis shrugged. 'A big slice, obviously. But it's worth it to get noticed.'

'And you think what's going on here is something to do with that?'

'Must be, stands to reason. Looks like your lads have picked the wrong punter to do business with. They'll have chosen him because he's cheap, silly bastards. He's probably some kid trying to break into the market and your band's getting his kicking.'

I made the circular gesture with my hand that you do in charades when you're asking the audience to expand on their guesses. 'Gimme more, Dennis, I'm not seeing daylight yet,' I said.

'He'll have been papering somebody else's sites. If the person whose site he's been nicking doesn't know which chancer is behind the pirate flyposting, he'll go for the band or the venues the chancer's promoting. So your band are getting picked on as a way of warning off their cowboy promoter that he's treading on somebody else's ground.'

I understood. 'So if they want to get out from under, they need to get themselves a new promoter?'

He nodded. 'And they want to do it fast, before somebody gets seriously hurt.'

I gave a sardonic smile. 'There's no need to go over the top, Dennis. We're talking a bit of illegal flyposting here, not the ice-cream wars.'

His genial mask slipped and he was staring straight into my eyes in full chill mode, reminding me why his enemies call him Dennis the Menace. 'You're not understanding, Kate,' he said softly. 'We're talking heavy-duty damage here. The live-music business in Manchester is worth a lot of dosh. If you've got a proper flyposting business up and running with a finger in the ticket-sales pie, then you're talking a couple of grand a week tax free for doing not a lot except keeping your foot soldiers in line. That kind of money makes for serious enforcement.'

'And that's what my clients have been getting. Skinheads on super lager breaking up their gigs, their van being set on fire,' I reminded him. 'I'm not taking this lightly.'

'You've still not got it, Kate. You remember Terry Spotto?'

I frowned. The name rang vague bells, but I couldn't put a face to it.

'Little runty guy, lived in one of the Hulme crescents? Strawberry mark down his right cheek?'

I shook my head. 'I don't know who you mean.'

'Sure you do. They found him lying on the bridge over the Medlock, just down from your office. Somebody had removed his strawberry mark with a sawn-off shotgun.'

I remembered now. It had happened about a year ago. I'd arrived at work one Tuesday morning to see yellow police tapes shutting off part of the street. Alexis had chased the story for a couple of days, but hadn't got any further than the official line that Terry Spotto had been a small-time drug dealer. 'That was about flyposting?' I asked.

'Terry was dealing crack but he decided he wanted a second profit centre,' Dennis said, reminding me how expertly today's intelligent villains have assimilated the language of business. 'He started flyposting, only he didn't have the nous to stay off other people's patches or the muscle to take territory off them. He got warned a couple of times, but he paid no never mind to it. Since he wouldn't take a telling, or a bit of a seeing to, somebody decided it was time to make an example. I don't think anybody's seriously tried to cut in since then. But it sounds like your lads have made the mistake of linking up with somebody who's too new on the block to remember Terry Spotto.'

I took a deep breath. 'Hell of a way of seeing off the competition. Dennis, I need to talk to somebody about this. Get the boys off the hook before this gets silly. Gimme a name.'

'Denzel Williams,' Dennis said. 'Garibaldi's. Mention my name.'

'Thanks.' I hadn't been to Garibaldi's, but I'd heard plenty about it. If I'd had to guess where to find someone I could talk to about so dodgy a game, that's probably the place I'd have gone for.

'Anything else?'

I shook my head. 'Not in the way of business. Not unless you know somebody with a wad of cash to invest in a private-eye business.'

Dennis's eyebrows lowered. 'What's Bill up to?'

I told him. Debbie tuned back in to the conversation and the subject kept us going for the remainder of the visit. By the time I'd dropped Debbie back at the house, I had a list of a dozen or so names that Dennis reckoned had the kind of money to hand that they could invest in the business. Somehow, I didn't think I'd be following any of them up. I'm unpopular enough with the Old Bill as it is without becoming a money laundry for the Manchester Mafia.

Come five o'clock, I was parked down the street from Sell Phones. All I needed was a name and address on this pair of con merchants and I could hand the case over to the police as I'd already agreed with my clients. We had the names and addresses of nearly a dozen complainants, some of whom were bound to be capable of picking Will Allen or his female sidekick out of a line-up. I looked forward to handing the whole package over to Detective Chief Inspector Della Prentice, head honcho of the Regional Crime Squad's fraud task force. It wasn't exactly her bailiwick, but Della's one of the tightknit group of women I call friends, and I trusted her not to screw it up. There are coppers who hate private enterprise so much they'd let a villain walk rather than let a PI take an ounce of credit for a collar. Della isn't one of them. But before

I could have the pleasure of nailing these cheap crooks, I had to attach names and addresses to them. And I was damned if they were going to defeat me two nights running.

This time I was ready for them. When Allen swung left down the hill, I was right behind him. I stayed in close touch as we threaded through back streets flanked by decaying mills half filled with struggling small businesses and vacant lots turned into car parks, across the Rochdale Road and the Oldham Road, emerging on Great Ancoats Street just south of the black glass facade of the old Daily Express Building. I slipped into the heavy traffic with just one car separating me from the silver Mazda, and stayed like that right across town, past the mail-order warehouses and through the council estates.

In Hathersage Road, the car pulled up outside a general store opposite the old Turkish Baths, closed down by the council on the grounds that it cost too much to maintain the only leisure facility within walking distance for the thousands of local inner-city residents. As one of those locals, it made me fizz with fury every time I paid an instalment of my council tax. So much for New Labour. I carried on past the parked car as the woman jumped out and headed into the shop. I pulled into a parking space further down the street, hastily adjusting my rear-view mirror so I could see what was going on. A few minutes later, she emerged carrying a copy of the *Chronicle* and a packet of cigarettes.

As the Mazda passed me and headed for the traffic lights, I hung back. The lights were on red, and I wasn't going to emerge till they changed. On green, the Mazda swung left into Anson Road, the overhanging trees turning daylight to dusk like a dimmer switch. They turned off almost immediately into a quiet street lined with large Victorian houses. About halfway down on the left, the red brick gave way to modern concrete. Filling a space equivalent to a couple of the sprawling Victorians was a four-storey block of flats in a squared-off U. The Mazda turned into the block's car park and stopped. I cruised past, then accelerated, swung the car round at the next junction and drove back in time to see Allen and the woman from Sell Phones disappear through the block's entrance door. Even from this distance, I could see the entry phone. There must have been close on fifty flats in the block.

A whole day had trickled through my fingers and I didn't seem to be much further forward with anything. Maybe I should follow Shelley's advice and put my share of the business on the market. And not just as a ploy.

9

It was too early in the evening for me to have anything better to do, so I decided to keep an eye on the gravestone grifters. I figured that since they'd both gone indoors, the chances were that they were going to have a bite to eat and a change of clothes before heading out to hit the heartbroken, so I took fifteen minutes to shoot back to my house, pick up my copy of that night's *Chronicle* from the mat and throw together a quick sandwich of Dolcelatte and rocket that was well past its launch-by date. It was the last of the bread too, I mentally noted as I binned the wrapper. So much for a night of chopping and slicing and home-made Chinese. I tossed a can of Aqua Libra into my bag along with the film-wrapped sandwich and drove back to my observation post.

Just after seven, the woman emerged alone with one of those expensive anorexic girlie briefcases that have a shoulder strap instead of a handle. She made straight for the car. I waited until she was behind the wheel, then I started my engine and swiftly reversed into the drive of the house behind me. That way I could get on her tail no matter which direction she chose. She turned left out of the car park, and I followed her back to Anson Road and down towards the bottom end of Kingsway, past rows of between-the-wars semis where the vast assortment of what passes for family life in the nineties happened behind closed doors, a world we were completely cut off from as we drifted down the half-empty roads, sealed in our separate boxes.

Luckily we didn't have far to go, since I was acutely aware that there wasn't enough traffic around to cover me adequately. Shortly after we hit Kingsway, she hung a left at some lights and headed deep into the heart of suburban Burnage. Again, luck was on my side, a phenomenon I hadn't been experiencing much of lately. Her destination was on one of the long, wide avenues running parallel to Kingsway, rather than up one of the narrow streets or cul-de-sacs built in an era when nobody expected there would come a day when every household had at least one car. In those choked chicanes, she couldn't have avoided spotting me. When she did slow down, obviously checking out house numbers, I overtook her and parked a few hundred yards ahead, figuring she must be close to her target. I was right. She actually stopped less than twenty yards in front of me and walked straight up the path of a three-bedroomed semi with a set of flower beds so neat it was hard to imagine a dandelion with enough bottle to sprout there.

I watched her ring the bell. The door opened, but I couldn't see the person behind it. Three sentences and she was in. I flicked through my copy of that evening's *Chronicle* till I got to the death announcements and read down the column. There it was.

Sheridan. Angela Mary, of Burnage, suddenly on Tuesday at Manchester Royal Infirmary after a short illness. Beloved wife of Tony, mother of Becky and Richard. Service to be held at Our Lady of the Sorrows, Monday, 2 p.m., followed by committal at Stockport Crematorium at 3 p.m.

With that information and the phone book, it wouldn't be hard to identify the right address. And you could usually tell from the names roughly what age group you were looking at. I'd have guessed that Tony and Angela were probably in their middle to late forties, their kids late teens to early twenties. Perfect targets for the con merchants. Bereft husband young enough to notice an attractive woman, whether consciously or not. Probably enough money in the pot to be able to afford a decent headstone. The thought of it made me sick.

What was worse was the knowledge that even as I was working all this out, Will Allen's accomplice was giving the shattered widower a sales pitch designed to separate him from a large chunk of his cash. I couldn't just sit there and let it happen. On the other hand, I couldn't march up the path and unmask her unless I wanted her and her sleazy sidekick to cover their tracks and leave town fast. I couldn't call the cops; I knew Della was out of town at a conference, and trying to convince some strange officer that I wasn't a nutter fast enough to get them out here in time to stop it was way beyond my capabilities. I racked my brains. There had to be a way of blowing her out without blowing my cover.

There was only one thing I could come up with. And that depended on how well the Sheridans got along with their neighbours. If they'd had years of attrition over parking, teenage stereos and footballs over fences, I'd had it. Squaring my shoulders, I walked up the path of the other half of the Sheridans' semi. The woman who answered the door looked to be in her mid-thirties, thick dark hair pulled back into a ponytail, a face all nose, teeth and chin. She wore a pair of faded jeans, supermarket trainers and a Body Shop T-shirt demanding that some part of the planet should be saved. When she registered that it was a stranger on the doorstep, her cheery grin faded to a faint frown. Clearly, I was less interesting than whoever she'd been expecting. I handed her a business card. 'I'm sorry to bother you,' I started apologetically.

'Private investigator?' she interrupted. 'You mean, like on the telly? I didn't know women did that.'

Some days, you'd kill for an original response. Still, I was just grateful not to have the door slammed in my face. I smiled, nodded and ploughed on. 'I need your help,' I said. 'How well do you know Mr Sheridan next door?'

The woman gasped. 'He's never murdered her, has he? I know it were sudden, like, and God knows they've had their ups and downs, but I can't believe he killed her!'

I closed my eyes momentarily. 'It's nothing like that. As far as I'm aware, there's nothing at all suspicious about Mrs Sheridan's death. Look, can I come in for a minute? This is a bit difficult to explain.'

She looked dubious. 'How do I know you're who you say you are?'

I spread my hands in a shrug. 'Do I look the dangerous type? Believe me, I'm trying to prevent a crime, not take part in one. Mr Sheridan is about to be robbed unless you can help me here.'

She gasped again, her hand flying to her mouth this time. 'It's just like the telly,' she said, ushering me into a narrow hallway where there was barely room for both of us and the mountain bike that hung on one wall. 'What's going on?' she demanded avidly.

'A particularly nasty team of crooks are conning bereaved families out of hundreds of pounds,' I said, dressing it up in the tabloid style she clearly relished. 'They catch them at a weak moment and persuade them to part with cash for cut-price gravestones. Now, I'm very close to completing a water-tight case against them, so I don't want to alert them to the fact that their cover's blown. But I can't just sit idly by while poor Mr Sheridan gets ripped off.'

'So you want me to go and tell him there's a crook in his living room?' she asked eagerly.

'Not exactly, no. I want you to pop round in a neighbourly sort of way, just to see he's all right, and do what you can to prevent him parting with any money. Say things like, "If this is a respectable firm, they won't mind you sleeping on this and talking it over with your funeral director." Don't let on you're at all suspicious, just that you're a cautious sort of person. And that Angela wouldn't have wanted him to rush into anything without consulting other members of the family. You get the idea?'

She nodded. 'I've got you. You can count on me.' I didn't have a lot of choice, so I just smiled. 'I'll get round there right away. I was going to pop round anyway to see how Tony was doing. We got on really well, me and Angela. She was older than me, of course, but we played tenpin bowls in the same team every Wednesday. I couldn't get over it when I heard. Burst appendix. You never know the hour or the day, do you? You leave this to me, Kate,' she added, glancing at my card again.

We walked down the path together, me heading back to my car and her next door. As we parted, she promised to call me on my mobile to let me know what happened. I was on pins as I sat watching the Sheridans' house. My new sidekick was definitely a bit of a loose cannon, but I couldn't think of anything else I could have done that would have been effective without warning off Allen's partner in crime, particularly since they'd be on their guard after the earlier debacle at Richard's house. About half an hour passed, then the front door opened and my target emerged. Judging by the way she threw her briefcase into the car, she wasn't in the best of moods. I'd had my phone switched off all day to avoid communicating with the office, but I turned it back on as I pulled out behind the woman.

She was back inside the block of flats by the time my new confederate called. 'Hiya,' she greeted me. 'I think it went off all right. I don't think she was suspicious, just brassed off because I was sitting there being dead neg about the whole thing. I just kept saying to Tony he shouldn't make any decision without the kids being there, and that was all the support he needed, really. She realized she wasn't getting anywhere and I wasn't shifting, so she just took herself off.'

'You did really well. Do you know what she was calling herself?' I asked when I could get a word in.

'She had these business cards. Greenhalgh and Edwards. Tony showed me after she'd gone. Sarah Sargent, it says her name is. Will you need us to go to court?' she asked, the phone line crackling with excitement.

'Possibly,' I hedged. 'I really appreciate your help. If the police need your evidence to support a case, I'll let them know where to find you.'

'Great! Hey, I think your job's dead exciting, you know. Any time you need a hand again, just call me, OK?'

'OK,' I said. Anything to get out from under. But she insisted on giving me her name and phone number before I could finally disengage. I wondered how glamorous she'd find the job when she had to do a fifteen-hour surveillance in a freezing van in the dead of winter with a plastic bucket to pee in and no guarantee that she'd get the pictures she needed to avoid having to do the whole thing all over again the next day.

I started my engine. I didn't think the con merchants would be having another go tonight. But I still had miles to go before I could sleep. A little burglary, perhaps, and then a visit to clubland for a nightcap. Given that I wasn't dressed for either pursuit, it seemed like a good excuse to head for home. Maybe I could even squeeze in a couple of hours kip before I had to go about my nocturnal business.

Never mind mice and men. Every time I make a plan these days it seems to go more off track than a blindfolded unicyclist. I hadn't taken more than a couple of steps towards my bungalow when I heard another car door open and I saw a figure move in my direction through the dusk. I automatically moved into position, ready for fight or flight, arms hanging at my side, shoulder bag clutched firmly, ready to swing it in a tight arc, all my weight on the balls of my feet, ready to kick, pivot or run. I waited for the figure to approach, tensed for battle.

It was just as well I'm the kind who looks before she leaps into action. I don't think Detective Constable Linda Shaw would have been too impressed with a flying kick to the abdomen. 'DC Shaw?' I said, surprised and baffled as she stepped into a pool of sodium orange.

'Ms Brannigan,' she acknowledged, looking more than a little sheepish. 'I wonder if we might have a word?' Looming up in the gloom behind her, I noticed a burly bloke with more than a passing resemblance to Mike Tyson. I sincerely hoped we weren't going to get into the 'nice cop, nasty cop' routine. I had a funny feeling I wouldn't come off best.

'Sure, come on in and have a brew,' I said.

She cleared her throat. 'Actually, we'd prefer it if you came down to the station,' she said, her embarrassment growing by the sentence.

Now I was completely bewildered. The one and only time I'd met Linda Shaw, she'd been one of Detective Inspector Cliff Jackson's gophers on a murder case I'd been hired to investigate. There was a bit of history between me and Jackson that meant every time our paths crossed, we both ended up with sore heads, but Linda Shaw had acted as the perfect buffer zone, keeping the pair of us far enough apart to ensure that the job got done without another murder being added to the case's tally. I'd liked her, not least because she was her own woman, seemingly determined not to let Jackson's abrasive bull-headedness rub off on her. What I couldn't work out was why she was trying to drag me off to a police station for questioning. For once, I wasn't doing anything that involved tap-dancing over a policeman's toes. That might change once I got properly stuck in to the investigation of Alexis's murdered doctor, but even if it did, the detectives I'd be irritating were forty miles away on the other side of the Pennines. 'Why?' I asked mildly.

'We've got some questions we'd like to ask you.' By now, Linda wasn't even pretending to meet my eye. She was pointedly staring somewhere over my left shoulder.

'So come in, have a brew and we'll see if I can answer them,' I repeated. I call it the irregular verb theory of life; I am firm, you are stubborn, he/she is a pig-headed, rigid, anally retentive stick-in-the-mud.

'Like DC Shaw said, we'd like you to come down the station,' her oppo rumbled. It was like listening to Vesuvius by stethoscope. Only with a Liverpudlian accent instead of an Italian one.

I sighed. 'We can do this one of two ways. Either you can come into the house and ask me what you've got to ask me, or you can arrest me and we'll go down the station and I don't say a word until my brief arrives. You choose.' I gave the pair of them my sweetest smile, somehow choking down the anger. I knew whose hand was behind this. It had Cliff Jackson's sadistic fingerprints all over it.

Linda breathed out hard through her nose and compressed her lips into a thin line. I imagined she was thinking about the rocket Cliff Jackson was going to fire at her when she got back to base without me meekly following at her heels. That wasn't my problem, and I wasn't going to be guilt-tripped into behaving as if it was. When I made no response, Linda shrugged and said, 'We'd better have that brew, then.'

The pair of them followed me down the path and into the house. I pointed at the living room, told them they were having coffee and brewed up in the kitchen, desperately trying to figure out why Jackson had sent a team round to hassle me. I dripped a pot of coffee while I thought about it, laying milk, sugar, mugs and spoons on a tray at the same time. By the time the coffee was done, I was no nearer an answer. I was going to have to opt for the obvious and ask Linda Shaw.

I walked through the living-room door, dumped the tray on the coffee table in front of the detectives and took the initiative. 'This had better be good, Linda,' I said. 'I have had a bitch of a week, and it's only Tuesday. Tell me why I'm sitting here talking to you instead of running myself a long hot bath.'

Linda flashed a quick look at her partner, who was enjoying himself far too much to help her out. He leaned forward and poured out three mugs of coffee. Looking like she'd bitten into a pickled lemon, Linda said, 'We've received an allegation which my inspector felt merited investigation.'

'From whom? About whom?' I demanded, best grammar on show.

She poured milk into her coffee and made a major production number out of stirring it. 'Our informant alleges that you have engaged in a campaign of threats against the life of one Richard Barclay.'

I was beyond speech. I was beyond movement. I sat with my mouth open, hand halfway towards a mug of coffee, like a Damien Hirst installation floating motionless in formaldehyde.

'The complainant alleges that this harassment has included placing false death announcements in the local press. We have verified that such an advert has appeared. And now Mr Barclay appears to have gone missing,' the male detective asserted, sitting back in his seat, legs wide apart, arm along the back of the sofa, asserting himself all over my living room.

Anger kicked in. 'And this informant. It wouldn't be an anonymous tip-off, would it?'

He looked at her, his face puzzled, hers resigned. 'You know we can't disclose that,' Linda said wearily. 'But we have been trying without success to contact Mr Barclay since nine this morning, and as my colleague says, we have confirmed that a death announcement was placed in the *Chronicle* containing false information. It does appear that you have some explaining to do, Ms Brannigan.' Any more apologetic and you could have used her voice as a doormat.

I'd had enough. 'Bollocks,' I said. 'We both know what's really happening here. You get an anonymous tip-off and your boss rubs his hands with glee. Oh goody, a borderline legitimate excuse to nip round and make Brannigan's life a misery. You've got no evidence that any crime has taken place. Even if somebody did place a bullshit ad in the *Chronicle*, and *The Times* too for all I know or care, you've got nothing to indicate it's anything other than a practical joke or that it's anything at all to do with me.' My voice rose in outrage. I knew I was on firm ground; I'd paid for the *Chronicle* announcement cash on the nail, making sure I popped in at lunch time when the classified ads department is at its busiest.

'It's our duty to investigate serious allegations,' the Tyson lookalike rumbled. 'And so far you haven't explained why anyone would want to accuse you of a serious crime like this. I mean, it's not the sort of thing most people do unless they've got a good reason for it. Like knowing about some crime you've committed, Ms Brannigan.'

I stood up. I was inches away from really giving them something to arrest me for. 'Right,' I said, furious. 'Out. Now. Never mind finishing your coffee. This is bollocks and you know it. You want to talk to Richard, sit outside on your arses and waste the taxpayers' money until he comes home. The reason you haven't been able to contact him, soft lad, is because he's a rock journalist. He doesn't answer his phone to the likes of you, and right now, he's probably sitting in some dive listening to a very bad band desperate to attract his attention. He'll be in the perfect mood to deal with this crap when he gets home. Now you,' I added, leaning forward and pointing straight between his astonished eyes, 'are new in my life, so you probably don't know there's a hidden agenda here.'

I swung round to point at Linda, who was also on her feet and edging towards the door. 'But you should know better, lady. Now walk, before I have to drag Ruth Hunter away from her favourite TV cop to slap you with a suit for harassment.

Bugger off and bother some proper villains. Or don't you know any? Are you kicking your heels waiting for me to provide you with enough evidence to arrest some?'

Linda was halfway through the door by the time I'd finished my tirade. Her sidekick looked from me to her and back again before deciding that he'd better follow her and find out what the real story was here. I didn't bother seeing them out.

I couldn't believe Linda Shaw had let herself be sucked into Cliff Jackson's spiteful little game. But then, he was the boss, she had a career to think about, and women don't climb the career ladder in the police force by telling their bosses to shove their stupid vendettas where the perverts shove their gerbils. And as for their anonymous source – that cheeky, malicious little toad Will Allen was going to pay for ruining my evening. If he thought he could frighten me off with a bit of police harassment, he was in for the rudest shock of his life.

10

The front door closed on a silence so tremendous I could hear the blood beating in my brain. The last time I'd been this angry had nearly cost me my relationship with Richard, who had infuriated me to the point where violence seemed the most attractive option. This time it had been a police officer I'd nearly decked. The repercussions from that might have been less emotionally traumatic, but they would probably have cost me just as much in different ways. On the other hand, trying to sell a share in a business where the remaining partner is on bail for assault would present Bill with one or two problems . . . I nearly ran after Linda Shaw and begged her to wind me up again.

I rotated my head enthusiastically in a bid to loosen some of the knots the CID had put there and went through to the kitchen. I wasn't about to let Linda Shaw put me off the job I had planned for later that night, but I could allow myself the necessary indulgence of one stiff drink. I raked around in the freezer until I found the half-bottle of Polish lemon pepper vodka I'd been saving for a rainy day and poured the last sluggish inch into a tall slim tumbler. There was no freshly squeezed grapefruit juice in the fridge, which tells you all you need to know about the week I was having. I had to settle for a mixer bottle lurking behind the cheese. It needed the kind of shaking I'd wanted to give Linda Shaw. I'd barely swallowed the first mouthful when the silence gave up the ghost under the onslaught of the patio doors opening from the conservatory.

'Brannigan?' I heard.

Stifling a groan, I reached back into the fridge and pulled

out one of the bottles Richard periodically donates from his world beer collection so he doesn't have to walk all the way back to his kitchen when he's in my bed. Staropramen from Prague, I noted irrelevantly as I grasped the bottle opener, wishing I were there. 'Kitchen,' I called.

'Hullawrerrhen,' said another voice behind me. At least, that's what I think it said. I turned to see Dan Druff grinning warily in the doorway. Silently, I handed him the Czech beer and reached for the next bottle in line. Radeberger Pilsner. I popped the top just as Richard appeared alongside Dan.

'What the hell were Pinky and Perky after?' Richard demanded after the first half of the bottle had cleared his oesophagus.

'They spoke to you?'

He nodded. 'Weird as fuck. They were just getting into their motor when we pulled up. The brick shithouse got all excited and said, "That's him," to the Chris Cagney wannabe. She looked absolutely parrot and got out of the car.'

Richard paused to swallow again and Dan took up the tale. 'She comes across to us and says to your man, "Are you Richard Barclay?" and he goes, "Yeah, who's asking?" And she goes, "Police. Have you been the victim of any death threats?" And he looks at her as if she's just dropped off the planet Demented and shakes his head.'

'So she turns round and says, "Satisfied?" to her partner. She sounds dead narked, he looks as bemused as I feel, and off the pair of them go, little trotters twinkling all the way back to their unmarked pigsty,' Richard concluded. 'Now, I might not be Mastermind, but I reckon there's a higher chance of me winning the Lottery than there is of that little encounter being completely unconnected to you.'

'I cannot tell a lie,' I said.

Richard snorted. To Dan, he said, 'Do you know the story about the two Cretans? One could only tell lies, the other could only tell the truth. Guess which one is Brannigan?'

'Hey,' I protested. 'This man is my client.'

'That's right,' Dan said. 'Gonnae no' take the mince out of her?'

At last, something Richard and I could share, even if it was only total incomprehension. 'What?' we both chorused.

Dan looked like he was used to the reaction. 'Doesnae matter,' he sighed. 'When it does, I'll keep it simple enough for youse English, OK?'

I shooed the pair of them through to the living room and ran through my brief encounter. 'Obviously, that toerag who was here the other night decided to warn me off,' I concluded.

Richard frowned. 'But how did he know who you were? Presumably, you were just Mrs Barclay to him. How did he make the connection to Kate Brannigan? Isn't that a bit worrying?'

'It would be if you hadn't shouted "Brannigan" after me the other night when he was three steps in front of me,' I said drily.

'Which is not good news because if this guy knows your name, he's going to come after you. And then he'll be really sorry,' Dan chipped in, making a sideways chopping gesture with his hand. His faith was touching.

'I'm glad you dropped by,' I said. 'I've been making one or two inquiries about your problem. What I'm hearing as the most likely scenario is that it all comes down to flyposting. The person you're using is almost certainly invading somebody else's territory. Either by accident or deliberately.'

Dan pushed a hand through his long red fringe. He looked puzzled. 'It's kind of hard to get my head round that,' he said. 'The guy we're using isn't some new kid on the block. He's been knocking around the Manchester promotions scene for years. He did everybody when they were nobody.'

'You're sure about that?' I asked. 'He's not telling you porkies?'

Dan shook his head. 'No way. We checked him out before we came down here. Lice knows this guy that used to drive the van for the Inspiral Carpets when they were just starting out, and it was him that told us about Sean.'

'Sean?'

'Sean Costigan,' Dan said. 'The guy that does our promotions.'

'I need to talk to him. Can you give me his number?'

Dan pulled a face and looked to Richard for help. My lover

was too busy building a spliff that would have spanned the Mersey to notice. 'I'm not supposed to give his number out,' Dan finally said. Embarrassment didn't sit well on his ferocious appearance.

I took a deep breath. 'I need to talk to him, Dan. I'm sure that when he told you not to hand out his number, he didn't have people like me in mind.'

'I don't know,' Dan hedged. 'I mean, he's not going to be very happy when he finds there's a private polis on the end of his mobile, is he?'

Give me strength. 'Tell him I'm the people's pig,' I said, exasperated. 'Look, if you feel bad about giving me his number, you're going to have to set up a meet between us. I can't make any more progress until I talk to Sean Costigan myself. So if you don't want to waste the money you've clocked up on my meter so far, you'd better get something sorted.' I smiled sweetly. 'More beer, anyone?'

Brannigan's second rule of burglary: when in doubt, go home. I was already breaking rule number three, which states that you never burgle offices outside working hours because some nosey parker is bound to spot a light. One look at the back of the Compton Clinic told me that if I went ahead, I was going to be breaking the second rule too. Although the ginnel the clinic backed on to was only a narrow back alley, it was well lit. Never mind the block of flats behind me; any late-night carousers walking along Deansgate who happened to glance down the lane would immediately notice anything out of the ordinary.

And whatever means I used to get inside the clinic, ordinary wasn't on the menu. I'd already seen the closed-circuit video surveillance in the hall, which ruled out going in through the rear entrance and getting to the second-floor consulting room via the main staircase. Alexis had told me that when they went for their Sunday consultations, she and Chris followed instructions to approach by climbing a fire escape which led up to a heavy door which in turn gave on to a landing between the first and second floors. The only problem with that approach was the security floodlight mounted on the back of the building which would make me as visible as a bluebottle on a kitchen worktop. And even if I got past that, the chances were strong that I wouldn't be able to make it through the fire door which wasn't going to be conveniently wedged open for me as it had been for Alexis and Chris.

There was nothing else for it. I was going to have to brazen it out and hope there were no police cars cruising the quiet midnight streets. I walked round the block till I was looking at the front door of the clinic. Like a lot of people who spend a few grand on state-of-the-art security, they had neglected to spend fifty quid on serious locks. There were two mortices and a Yale, and just glancing at them, I knew I was only looking at ten minutes max with my lock picks. I undid the middle button on Richard's baggy but lightweight indigo linen jacket that was covering the leather tradesman's apron which houses my going-equipped-to-burgle kit, and took out my set of picks. I shoved my black ski cap up a couple of inches and switched on the narrow-beamed lamp I had strapped round my head. I studied the top lock for a few seconds, then chose a slender strip of metal and started poking around. Even with the handicap of latex gloves, I had both mortices open in less than six minutes. The Yale was the work of a couple of minutes. Now for the difficult bit.

I turned the handle and pushed the door open. I heard the electronic beep of a burglar alarm about to have hysterics as I closed the door firmly behind me. I set the timing ring on the diver's watch I was wearing. Locking the mortices should be slightly easier now I knew exactly which picks to use, but I'd be lying if I didn't admit that the wailing klaxon of the burglar alarm put me off my stride. Five minutes later, I was locked in with an alarm that was louder than the front row at a heavy-metal gig. I switched off my lamp, opened the inside door but didn't step into the hall just yet. There was still the small matter of the video camera. In the darkness, I strained my eyes to see if there were any dull glimmers, indicating sensors that would flood the hall with light. Nothing. I was going to have to chance it, and hope that the camera wasn't loaded with infrared film. Somehow, I doubted it.

Cautiously, I moved forward in the pitch black. Nothing

happened. No lights came on, no passive infrared sensors blossomed into red jewels recording the sequence of my journey. I was so intent on my surroundings, I misjudged the length of the hall and went sprawling over the bottom stair. Thank goodness the deep-pile carpet continued up the stairs otherwise I'd have been on the fast track to Casualty. I picked myself up and went up as fast as I could manage without breaking anything. I might be in a clinic but I didn't fancy my chances if the doctors arrived to find their burglar languishing on the stair carpet with a broken leg.

I made it round the turn of the stairs to the first floor and started to climb again. At the head of the stairs, I started groping down the hallway for door handles. The first one I came to opened and I stumbled inside. I took my heavy rubber torch out of my apron and risked a quick flash. I was in a consulting room. No hiding place. I backed out onto the landing and tried the next door. A bathroom. No hiding place apart from cubicles where any self-respecting security guard would check instantly. The third door was locked, as was the fourth, across the hall. Next came another consulting room, but this time the swift sweep of my torch revealed a kneehole desk with a solid side facing the door. I hurried round the desk and squeezed myself into the narrow space, wriggling until I was comfortable enough to stay still for a while. I checked my watch, which indicated that it had been twelve minutes since the alarm was triggered. That meant it should switch itself off automatically in eight minutes. With luck, I might still have some residual hearing left by then. I stuffed my thumbs in my ears and waited.

When the alarm stopped, it was like a physical blow, snapping my head back. Almost beyond belief, I unjammed my ears, struggling to accept that the ringing noise that remained was only inside my head. My watch said eighteen minutes had passed since the alarm had started its hideous cacophony. That meant a key holder had arrived. I felt myself sweat with nerves, clammy trickles in my armpits and down my spine. If I was caught now, there wasn't a lie in the world that was going to keep me out of a prison cell. Trying not to think about it, I started a mental replay of every note of the six minutes of Annie Lennox's 'Downtown Lights'. I was coming to the end when I heard a low murmur of voices that definitely wasn't part of my mental soundtrack. Then the door of my shelter swung open, casting a rectangle of light on the far wall opposite me.

'And this is the last one,' a man's voice said, sounding anxious. I made out two distorted shadows, one with a familiar peaked cap, before the light snapped on.

I sensed rather than heard a body moving nearer. Then a second voice, speaking from what seemed to be a couple of feet above my head, said, 'Your alarm must be on the blink, sir. No sign of forced entry, no one on the premises.'

'It's never done this before,' the first voice said, sounding irritated this time.

'Have it serviced regular, do you?'

'I don't know, it's not my area of responsibility,' the first voice said. 'So what do we do now?'

'I suggest we reset it, sir, and hope it's just a one-off.' The light died and the door closed. I exhaled slowly and quietly. I gave it five minutes, then I stepped out cautiously onto the landing. Nothing happened. I waved my arms around in a bizarre parody of a Hollywood babe work-out video. Still nothing.

I couldn't believe it. They'd spent a small fortune on perimeter security and a video camera, but they didn't have any internal tremblers or passive infrared detectors. And there I'd been, planning to keep setting the alarm off at five-minute intervals until they finally abandoned the building with an unset alarm. I almost felt cheated.

From what Alexis had told me, the second locked door I'd tried had been Helen Maitland's consulting room. I kneeled down in front of the door and turned on my headlamp. Interestingly, the lock on her consulting room had cost twice the total of all three front-door locks. A seven-lever deadbolt mortice. Just out of curiosity, I took a quick look at the other locked door. A straightforward three-lever lock that a ten-year-old with a Swiss Army knife could have been through in less time than it takes an expert to complete the first level of Donkey Kong. Helen Maitland hadn't been taking any chances.

It took nearly fifteen minutes of total concentration for me to get past the lock. I closed the door softly behind me and shone the torch in a slow arc round the room, like a bad movie. More wall-to-wall heavy-duty carpet in the same shade of champagne. Their carpet-cleaning bill must have been phenomenal. Curtained screen folded against the wall. Examination couch. Sink. Grey metal filing cabinet. Shredder. Printer table with an ink jet on it. Tall cupboard with drawers underneath. A leather chair with a writing surface attached to the right arm, set at an angle to a two-seater sofa covered in cream canvas. No pictures on the walls. No rugs, just basic hard-wearing, pale green, industrial-weight carpet. No desk. No computer. At least I knew it wasn't going to take me long to search. And by the look of things, nobody had been here before me.

I started on the filing cabinet. I was glad to see it was one of the old-fashioned ones that can be unlocked by tipping them back and releasing the lock bar from below. Filing-cabinet locks are a pig to pick, and I'd had enough fiddling with small pieces of metal for one night. I was doubly glad I hadn't had to pick it when I finally got to examine the contents. The bottom drawer contained photostats of articles in medical journals and offprints of published papers. A couple of the articles had Sarah Blackstone's name among the contributors, and I tucked them into the waistband of my trousers.

The next drawer up contained a couple of gynaecological textbooks and a pile of literature about artificial insemination. The drawer above that was partly filled with sealed packets of A4 printer paper. The top drawer held a kettle, three mugs, an assortment of fruit teas and a jar of honey. The cupboard held medical supplies. Metal contraptions I didn't want to be able to put a name to. Boxes of surgical gloves. Those overgrown lollipop sticks that appear whenever it's cervical smear time. The drawers underneath were empty except for a near-empty box of regular tampons. I love it when I'm snowed under with clues.

I sat back on my heels and looked around. The only sign that anyone had ever used this room was the shredder, whose bin was half full. But I knew there was no point in trying to get anything from that. Life's too short to stuff a mushroom and to reassemble shredded print-outs. But I couldn't believe that Helen Maitland had left nothing at all in her consulting room. That was turning paranoia into a fine art.

I knew from Alexis that the doctor worked with a laptop rather than a pen and paper, keying everything in as she went along. Even so, I'd have expected to find something, even if it was only a letterhead. I decided to have another look in the less obvious places. Under the examination couch: nothing except dust. Under the sofa cushions: not even biscuit crumbs.

It was taped to the underside of one of the drawers below the cupboard. A card-backed envelope containing three computer disks. I slid them out of the envelope and into the inside pocket of Richard's jacket. I checked my watch. I'd been inside the room getting on for twenty minutes and I didn't think there was anything more to learn here.

Back on the landing, I locked the door behind me. No point in telegraphing my visit to the world. I started off down the stairs, but just before I reached the first-floor landing, I realized there was a glow of light from downstairs. Cautiously, I crouched down, edged forward and peered through the bannisters. Almost directly below me, sitting on the bottom stairs was the unmistakable foreshortened figure of a police officer.

11

To be accused of one summary offence is unfortunate; to be accused of two within a twenty-four-hour period looks remarkably like carelessness. And since a reputation for carelessness doesn't bring clients to the door, I decided this wasn't a good time to attract the attention of the officer on the stairs. I shrank back from the bannisters and crept towards the upper flight of stairs. In the gloom, I noticed what I hadn't before. There actually were passive infrared sensors high in the corners of the stairwell; they were the ultra-modern ones that don't actually show a light when they're triggered. The reason nothing had happened when I'd waved my arms around on the upper landing earlier was that the alarm hadn't been switched on. Thank God for the need to impress clients with the luxury carpeting.

As I crouched at the foot of the second flight, I heard the crackle of the policeman's personal radio. I sidled forward again, trying to hear what he was saying. '. . . still here in St John Street,' I made out. '. . . burglar-alarm bloke arrives. The key holder's worried . . . Yeah, drugs, expensive equipment . . . should be here by now . . . OK, Sarge.'

Now I knew what was going on. The key holder had been nervous of leaving the building with what seemed to be a faulty alarm. Presumably, they had a maintenance contract that provided for twenty-four-hour call-out, and he'd decided to take advantage of it. It probably hadn't been difficult to pitch the Dibble into hanging around until the burglar-alarm technician arrived. It was a cold night out there, and minding a warm clinic had to be an improvement on cruising the early-morning streets with nothing more uplifting to deal with than nightclub brawls or drunken domestics.

I tiptoed back up to the top floor and considered my options. No way could I get past the copper. Once the burglar-alarm technician arrived and reset the system, I wasn't going to be able to get out without setting off the alarm again, and this time they'd realize it couldn't be a fault. OK, I'd be long gone, but with a murder investigation going on that might just lead back here, I didn't want any suspicious circumstances muddying the waters.

For all of five seconds, I considered the fire door leading off the half-landing below me. Chances were the hinges would squeak, the security lights would be on a separate system from the burglar alarm and I'd be spotlit on a fire escape with an apron full of exotica that I couldn't pretend was my knitting bag. Not to mention a pocketful of computer disks that might well tie me right into an even bigger crime. I could see only one alternative.

With a soft sigh, I got down on my knees again and started to unlock the door of Helen Maitland's consulting room.

I've slept in a lot less comfortable places than a gynaecologist's sofa. It was a bit short, even for me, but it was cosy, especially after I'd annexed the cotton cellular blanket from the examination couch and peeled off my latex gloves. I'd locked the door behind me, so I figured I was safe if anyone decided further investigations were necessary. Looking on the bright side, I'd managed to postpone a thrill-packed evening in Garibaldi's with some spaced-out rock promoter. And I'd used up every last bit of adrenaline in my system. I was too tired now to be scared. As I drifted off to sleep, I had the vague sense that I could hear electronic chirruping in the distance, but I was past caring.

I'd set my mental clock to waken me around nine. It was five to when my eyelids ungummed themselves. Six hours sleep wasn't enough, but it was as much as I usually squeezed in when I was chasing a handful of cases as packed with incident as my current load seemed to be. I unfolded my cramped body from the sofa and did some languid stretching to loosen my stiffened muscles. I peed in the sink, rinsed it out with paranoid care then splashed water over my face, dumping the used paper towels in the empty bin below. It looked like Helen Maitland had even taken her used bin liners home. Learning a lesson in caution from her, I used a paper towel to open cupboard and box and helped myself to a pair of her surgical gloves, then moved across to the door and listened. I couldn't hear a thing.

As quietly as possible, I unlocked the door. I opened it a crack and listened some more. Now I could hear the sort of noises that an occupied building gives off: distant murmurs of speech, feet moving on stairs and hallways, doors opening and closing. I didn't know how appointments were spaced at the Compton Clinic, but I reckoned that the best time to avoid coming into contact with too many other people was probably around twenty-five past the hour. I softly closed the door and checked myself over. I'd taken off the ski cap and headlamp, but I still looked a pretty unlikely private patient in my black hockey boots, leggings and polo-neck sweater. Even the fashionable bagginess of Richard's designer-label jacket didn't lift the outfit much. If anyone did see me, I'd have to hope they put me down as someone in one of those arty jobs never seen by the general public – radio producer, publisher's editor, novelist, literary critic.

I watched the second hand sweep round until it was time. Then I inched the door open. The landing was clear. I slipped out and pulled the door closed behind me, holding the handle so the catch wouldn't click into place. I carefully released it and stepped away smartly. The door was going to have to stay unlocked, but with luck, by the time it was discovered, the fault in the burglar alarm would be ancient history. I tripped down the stairs with the easy nonchalance of someone who's just been given some very good news by their gynae. I didn't see another soul. When I reached the foot of the stairs, I sketched a cheery wave at the video camera. Then I was out on the street, happily sucking in the traffic fumes of the city centre. Free and clear.

I walked up the street to the meter where I'd left the car the night before, expecting to pay the penalty for parking without payment for the first hour of the working day. This close to the traffic wardens' HQ just off Deansgate, it was practically inevitable. By some accidental miracle that the gods had obviously intended for some other mortal, I hadn't been wheel-clamped. I didn't even have a ticket.

The luck didn't last, of course. The phone was ringing as I got through the door and I made the mistake of answering it rather than letting the machine deal with the call. 'Your mobile has been switched off since this time yesterday,' Shelley stated without preamble.

'I know that,' I retorted.

'Have you lost the instruction manual? To turn it on, you depress the button marked "power".'

'I know that too.'

'Are you coming in today?'

'I doubt it,' I said briskly. 'Stuff to do. Clinkers to riddle, pots to side, cases to solve.'

'You are still working, then?' For once, Shelley's voice wasn't dripping sarcasm. It almost sounded like she was concerned about me, but that may have been my overactive imagination.

'I'm working on the gravestone scam, plus I have two other cases that are currently occupying significant amounts of my time,' I said, probably more abruptly than I intended.

'What other cases?' Shelley asked accusingly. Back to normal, thank God. Shelley as sergeant major I could cope with; Shelley as mother hen wasn't part of the deal.

'New cases. I'll let you have the paperwork just as soon as I get to it,' I said. 'Now I've got to go. There's a librarian out there waiting for me to make her day.' I cut the connection before Shelley could say anything more. I knew I was being childish about avoiding Bill, but until I could get my head straight about my future, I couldn't even bear to be in the office where we'd worked together so successfully.

I dumped my stale clothes in the laundry basket, left Richard's jacket by the door so I'd remember to take it to be dry-cleaned, and dived into the shower. Needles of water stung my flesh on the borderline of pain, stripping away my world-weariness. By the time I'd finished with the coconut shampoo, the strawberry body wash and the grapefruit body lotion, I must have smelled like a fruit salad, but at least I'd stopped feeling like chopped liver.

While I was waiting for the coffee to brew, I booted up my trusty PC and took a look at the disks I'd raided from Helen Maitland's consulting room. Each disk contained about a dozen files, all with names like SMITGRIN.DAT, FOS-THILL.DAT and EDWAJACK.DAT. When I came to one called APPLELEE.DAT my initial guess that the file names corresponded to pairs of patients was confirmed. I didn't have to be much of a detective to realize that this contained the data relating to Chris Appleton and Alexis Lee. The only problem was accessing the information. I tried various word-processing packages but whatever software Helen Maitland had used, it wasn't one that I had on my machine. So I tried cheating my way into the file, renaming it so my software would think it was a different kind of file and read it. No joy. Either these files were password protected, or the software was too specialized to give up its secrets to my rather crude methods.

I finished my coffee, copied the disks and sent Gizmo a piece of e-mail to tell him that he was about to find an envelope with three disks on his doormat and that I'd appreciate a print-out of the files contained on them. Then I went on a wardrobe mission for something that would persuade a doctor that I was a fit and proper person to talk to. Failing combat fatigues and a Kalashnikov, I settled for navy linen trousers, a navy silk tweed jacket and a lightweight cream cotton turtleneck. At least I wouldn't look like a drug rep.

I raided the cash dispenser again and stuffed some cash in an envelope with the originals of the disks and pushed the whole lot through Gizmo's letter box. I wasn't in the mood for conversation, not even Gizmo's laconic variety. Next stop was Central Ref. It was chucking it down in stair rods by then, and of course I hadn't brought an umbrella. Which made it inevitable that the nearest available parking space was on the far side of Albert Square down on Jackson's Row. With my jacket pulled over my head so that I looked like a strange, deformed creature from a Hammer Horror film, I sprinted through the rain-darkened streets to the massive circular building that manages to dominate St Peter's Square in spite of the taller buildings around it.

Under the portico, I joined the other people shaking themselves like dogs before we filed into the grand foyer with its twin staircases. I ignored the information desk and the lift and walked up to the reference room. Modelled on the British Museum reading room, the tables radiate out from the hub of a central desk like the spokes from a vast, literary wheel. Light filters down from the dome of the high ceiling, and everything is hushed, like a library ought to be. All these modern buildings with their strip lighting, antistatic carpets and individual carrels never feel like proper libraries to me. I often used to come and work in Central Ref. when I was a student. The atmosphere was more calm than the university law library, and nobody ever tried to chat you up.

Today, though, I wasn't after Halsbury's *Statutes of England*, or Michael Zander's analysis of the Police and Criminal Evidence Act. The first thing I wanted was Black's *Medical Directory*, the list of doctors licensed to practise in the UK, complete with their qualifications and their professional history. I'd used it before, so I knew where to look. Black's told me that Sarah Blackstone had qualified twelve years before. She was a graduate of Edinburgh University, a fellow of the Royal College of Obstetricians and Gynaecologists, and she had worked in Obs & Gynae in Glasgow, then one of the London teaching hospitals before winding up as a consultant at St Hilda's Infirmary in Leeds, one of the key hospitals in the north. It was clear from the information here plus the articles I'd taken from the consulting room that Dr Blackstone was an expert on sub-fertility, out there at the leading edge of an increasingly controversial field, a woman with a reputation for solid achievement. That explained in part why she'd chosen to operate under an alias.

Since the book was there in front of me, I idly thumbed forward. There was no reason why she should have chosen to use another doctor's name as an alias, except that Alexis had told me that Sarah Blackstone had written prescriptions in the name of Helen Maitland. While it wasn't impossible that she'd used an entirely fictitious name to do this, it would have been easier and safer to steal another doctor's identity. If she'd done that, uncovering the real Helen Maitland might just take me a step or two further forward.

Impatiently I ran my finger down the twin columns, past the Madisons, the Maffertys and the Mahons, and there it was. Helen Maitland. Another Edinburgh graduate, though she'd qualified three years before Sarah Blackstone. Member of the Royal College of Physicians. She'd worked in Oxford, briefly in Belfast, as a medical registrar in Newcastle, and now, like Sarah Blackstone, she was also a consultant at St Hilda's in Leeds, with research responsibilities. According to Black's, and the indices of the medical journals I checked afterwards, Helen Maitland had nothing to do with fertility treatment. She was a specialist in cystic fibrosis, and had published extensively on recent advances in gene replacement therapy. On the surface, it might seem that there was no point of contact between the two women professionally; but the embryologist who worked on Helen Maitland's patients' offspring in vitro might well be the same one who worked with Sarah Blackstone's subfertile couples. They'd certainly work in the same lab.

Even if I had all the files on the disks I'd recovered in the night, I still needed to make some more checks. The original computer files, of which I was sure these were only back-up copies, had to be on a computer somewhere. And I needed to check out whether the real Helen Maitland was sufficiently involved in Sarah Blackstone's fertility project to be a potential threat to Alexis and Chris, or whether she was simply an innocent victim of her colleague's deception.

Before I made the inevitable trip across the Pennines, I thought I'd make the most of being in Central Ref. Replacing the medical directory, I wandered across to the shelves where the city's electoral rolls are kept. I looked up the main index and found the volume that contained the street where 'Will Allen' and his partner 'Sarah Sargent' lived. I pulled the appropriate box file from the shelf and thumbed through the wards until I got to the right one. I found them inside a minute.

It's one of the truisms of life that when people pick an alias, they go for something that is easy for them to remember, so they won't be readily caught out. They'll opt for the same initials, or a name that has some connection for them. There, in Flat 24, was living proof. Alan Williams and Sarah Constable.

If I played my cards right, maybe I could get them done for wasting police time as well as everything else. That would teach them to mess with me.

12

I used the old flower-delivery trick on the real Helen Maitland. A quick call to St Hilda's Infirmary had established that Dr Maitland was doing an outpatients clinic that afternoon. A slow scan of the phone book had revealed that her phone number was ex-directory. Given the protective layers of receptionists and nurses, I didn't rate my chances of getting anywhere near her at work unless I'd made an appointment three months in advance. That meant fronting up at her home. The only problem with that was that I didn't know where she lived.

I headed for the hospital florist and looked at the flowers on offer. There were the usual predictable, tired arrangements of chrysanthemums and spray carnations. Some of them wouldn't have looked out of place sitting on top of a coffin. I suppose it saved money if your nearest and dearest seemed to be near death's door: one lot of flowers would do for bedside and graveside. Gave a whole new meaning to saying it with flowers. The only exception was a basket of freesias mixed with irises. When I went to pay for it, I realized why they only bothered stocking the one. It was twice the price of the others. I got a receipt. My client would never believe flowers could cost that much otherwise. I've seen the tired garage bunches she brings home for Chris.

The price included a card, which I didn't write out until I was well clear of the florist. 'Dear Doctor, thanks for everything, Sue.' Every doctor has grateful patients; the law of averages says some of them must be called Sue. Then I toddled round to the outpatients clinic and thrust the arrangement at the receptionist. 'Flowers for Dr Maitland,' I mumbled.

112

The receptionist looked surprised. 'Oh, that's nice. Who are they from?'

I shrugged. 'I just deliver them. Can I leave them with you?'

'That's fine, I'll see she gets them.'

A couple of hours later, a tall, rangy woman emerged from the outpatients department with a long loping stride. Given that she was in her mid- to late forties and she'd presumably done a hard day's work, she moved with remarkable energy. She was wearing black straight-leg jeans and cowboy boots, a blue and white striped shirt under a black blazer, and a trench coat thrown casually over her shoulders to protect her from the soft Yorkshire drizzle. In one hand, she carried a pilot's case. In the other, as if it were something that might explode, the basket of flowers. If this was Dr Helen Maitland, I had no doubt she wasn't the woman Alexis and Chris had seen. There was no way anyone could have confused her with the photograph in the paper by accident. This woman had fine features in an oval face, nothing like the strong, definite square face Alexis had shown me. Her hair was totally different too. Where Sarah Blackstone had a heavy mop of dark hair in a jagged fringe, this woman had dark blonde curls rampaging over the top of her head, while the sides and back were cropped short. I started my engine. Lucky I'd been parking in a 'consultants only' slot, really. Otherwise I might have missed her.

She stopped beside an old MGB roadster in British racing green and balanced the flowers on the roof while she unlocked the car. The case was tossed in, followed by the mac, then she carefully put the flowers in the passenger foot well. She folded her long legs under the wheel and the engine started with a throaty growl. The presumed Dr Maitland reversed out of her parking space and shot forwards towards the exit with the aplomb of a woman who would know exactly what to do if her car started fishtailing on the greasy Tarmac. More cautiously, I followed. We wove through the narrow alleys between the tall Victorian brick buildings of the old part of the hospital and emerged on the main road just below the university. She turned up the hill into the early-evening traffic and together we slogged up the hill, through

Hyde Park and out towards Headingley. Just as we approached the girls' grammar school, she indicated a right turn. From where I was, it was hard to see where she was going, but as she turned, I saw her destination was a narrow cobbled lane almost invisible from the main road.

I positioned myself to follow her, watching as she shot up the hill with a puff of exhaust. At the top, she turned right. Me, I was stuck on the main drag, the prisoner of traffic that wouldn't pause to let me through. A good thirty seconds passed before I could find a gap, long enough for her to have vanished without trace. Quoting extensively if repetitiously from the first few scenes of *Four Weddings and a Funeral*, I drove in her wake.

As I turned right at the top of the lane, I saw her put the key in the lock. She was standing in front of a tall, narrow Edwardian stone villa, the car tucked into a parking space that had been carved out of half of the front garden. I carried on past the house, turning the next available corner and squeezing into a parking space. A quick call to the local library to check their electoral register confirmed that Helen Maitland lived there. I always make sure these days after the time that the florist trick failed because the target was a hay-fever sufferer who passed the flowers on to her secretary.

I gave Dr Maitland ten minutes to feed the cat and put the kettle on, then I rang the bell set in stone to the right of a front door gleaming with gloss paint the same shade of green as the car. The eyes that looked questioningly into mine when the door opened were green too, though a softer shade, like autumn leaves on the turn. 'Dr Maitland? I'm sorry to trouble you,' I started.

'I'm sorry, I don't . . . ?' Her eyebrows twitched towards each other like caterpillars in a mating dance.

'My name is Brannigan, Kate Brannigan. I'm a private investigator. I wondered if you could spare me a few minutes.'

That's the point where most people look wary. We've all got something to feel guilty about. Helen Maitland simply looked curious. 'What on earth for?' she asked mildly.

'I'd like to ask you a few questions about Sarah Blackstone.' This wasn't the time for bullshit.

'Sarah Blackstone?' She looked surprised. 'What's that got to do with me?'

'You knew her,' I said bluntly. I knew now she did; a stranger would have said something along the lines of, 'Sarah Blackstone? The doctor who was murdered?'

'We worked in the same hospital,' Dr Maitland replied swiftly. I couldn't read her at all. There was something closed off in her face. I suppose doctors have to learn how to hide what they're thinking and feeling otherwise the rest of us would run a mile every time the news was iffy.

I waited. Most people can't resist silence for long. 'What business is it of yours?' she eventually added.

'My client was a patient of hers,' I said.

'I still don't see why that should bring you to my door.' Dr Maitland's voice was still friendly, but the hand gripping the doorjamb was tightening so that her knucklebones stood out in sharp relief. I hadn't been suspicious of her a moment before, but now I was definitely intrigued.

'My client was under the mistaken impression that she was being treated by one Dr Helen Maitland,' I said. 'Sarah Blackstone was using your name as an alias. I thought you might know why.'

Her eyebrows rose, but it was surprise rather than shock I thought I read there. I had the distinct feeling I wasn't telling her anything she didn't already know. 'How very strange,' she said, and I suspected it was my knowing that was the strange thing. I'd have expected any doctor confronted with the information that a colleague had stolen their identity to be outraged and concerned. But Helen Maitland seemed to be taking it very calmly.

'You weren't aware of it?'

'It's not something we doctors generally allow,' she said drily, her face giving nothing away.

I shrugged. 'Well, if you don't know why Dr Blackstone helped herself to your name, I'll just have to keep digging until I find someone who does.'

As I spoke, the rain turned from drizzle to downpour. 'Oh Lord,' she sighed. 'Look, you'd better come in before you catch pneumonia.'

I followed her into a surprisingly light hallway. She led me past the stairs and into a dining kitchen so cluttered Richard would have felt perfectly at home. Stacks of medical journals threatened to teeter over onto haphazard piles of cookery books; newspapers virtually covered a large table, themselves obscured by strata of opened mail. The worktops and open shelves spilled over with interesting jars and bottles. I spotted olive oil with chillis, with rosemary and garlic, with thyme, oregano, sage and rosemary, olives layered in oil with what looked like basil, bottled damsons and serried rows of jams, all with neat, handwritten labels. On one shelf, in an Art-Nouveau-style silver frame there was a ten-by-eight colour photograph of Helen Maitland with an arm draped casually over the shoulders of a pale Pre-Raphaelite maiden with a mane of wavy black hair and enough dark eye make-up to pass as an extra in the *Rocky Horror Show*. On one wall was a cork board covered with snapshots of cats and people. As far as I could see, there were no pictures of Sarah Blackstone.

'Move one of the team and sit down,' Dr Maitland said, waving a hand at the pine chairs surrounding the table. I pulled one back and found a large tabby cat staring balefully up at me. I decided not to tangle with it and tried the next chair along. A black cat looked up at me with startled yellow eyes, grumbled in its throat and leapt elegantly to the floor like a pint of Guinness pouring itself. I sat down hastily and looked up to find Helen Maitland watching me with a knowing smile. 'Tea?'

'Please.'

She opened a high cupboard that was stuffed with boxes. I remembered the filing-cabinet drawer in the consulting room. 'I've got apple and cinnamon, licorice, elderflower, peach and orange blossom, alpine strawberry . . .'

'Just plain tea would be fine,' I interrupted.

She shook her head. 'Sorry. I'm caffeine free. I can do you a decaff coffee?'

'No thanks. Decaff's a bit like cutting the swearing out of a Tarantino film. There's no point bothering with what's left. I'll try the alpine strawberry.'

She switched on the kettle and leaned against the worktop,

looking at me over the rim of the cup she'd already made for herself. Closer, the youthful impression of her stride and her style was undercut by the tired lines around the eyes. There was not a trace of silver in her hair. Either her hairdresser was very good, or she was one of the lucky ones. 'Dr Blackstone's death came as a shock to all her colleagues,' she said.

'But you weren't really colleagues,' I pointed out. 'You worked in different departments. You're medical, she was surgical.'

She shrugged. 'Hilda's is a friendly hospital. Besides, there aren't so many women consultants that you can easily miss each other.'

The kettle clicked off, and she busied herself with tea bag, mug and water. When she slid the mug across the table to me our hands didn't touch, and I had the sense that this was deliberate. 'She must have known you reasonably well to feel comfortable about pretending to be you. She was even writing prescriptions in your name,' I tried.

'What can I say?' she replied with a shrug. 'I had no idea she was doing it, and I have no idea why she was doing it. I certainly don't know why she picked on me.'

'Were there other doctors she was more friendly with? Ones who might be able to shed some light on her actions?' I cut in. It was the threat of going elsewhere that had got me across the threshold, not the rain. Maybe repeating it would shake something loose from Helen Maitland's tree.

'I don't think she was particularly friendly with any of her colleagues,' Dr Maitland said quickly.

That was an interesting comment from someone who was acting as if she were on the same footing as all those other colleagues. 'How can you be sure who she was and wasn't friendly with? Given that you work in different departments?'

She smiled wryly. 'It's very simple. Sarah lived under my roof for a while when she first came to Leeds. She expected to sell her flat in London pretty quickly, so she didn't want to get into a formal lease on rented property. She was asking around if anyone had a spare room to rent. I remembered what that felt like, so I offered her a room here.'

'And she was here long enough for you to know that she

didn't have particular friends in the hospital?' I challenged.

'In the event, yes. She was here for almost a year. Her London flat proved harder to shift than she imagined. We seemed not to get on each other's nerves, so she stayed.'

'So you must have known who her friends were?'

Dr Maitland shrugged again. 'She didn't seem to need many. When you've got a research element in your job and you have to work as hard as we do, you don't get a lot of time to build a social life. She went away a lot at weekends, various places. Bristol, Bedford, London. I didn't interrogate her about who she was visiting. I regarded it as none of my business.'

Her words might have been cool, but her voice remained warm. 'You haven't asked what she was doing with your identity,' I pointed out.

That wry smile again. 'I presumed you'd get round to that.'

There was something irritatingly provocative about Helen Maitland. It undid all my good intentions and made my interview techniques disappear. 'Did you know she was a lesbian when you offered her your spare room?' I demanded.

A small snort of laughter. 'I presumed she was. It didn't occur to me she might have changed her sexuality between arriving in Leeds and moving in here.'

She was playing with me, and I didn't like it at all. 'Did she have a lover when she was living here?' I asked bluntly. Games were over for today.

'She never brought anyone back here,' Dr Maitland replied, still unruffled. 'And as far as I know, she did not spend nights in anyone else's bed, either in Leeds or elsewhere. However, as I have said, I can't claim to have exhaustive knowledge of her acquaintance.'

'Don't you mind that she was using your name to carry out medical procedures?' I demanded. 'Doesn't it worry you that she might have put you at professional risk by what she was doing?'

'Why should it? If anyone ever claimed that I had carried out inappropriate medical treatment on them, they would realize as soon as we came face to face that I had not been the doctor involved. Besides, I can't imagine Sarah would involve herself, or me, in anything unethical. I never thought of her as a risk taker.'

'Why else would she be using your identity?' I said forcefully. 'If it was all above board, she wouldn't have needed to pretend to be someone else, would she?'

Dr Maitland suddenly looked tired. 'I suppose not,' she said. 'So what exactly was she doing that was so heinous?'

'She was working with lesbian couples who wanted children,' I said, picking my words with care. If I'd learned anything about Helen Maitland, it was that it would be impossible to tell where her loyalties lay. The last thing I wanted was to expose Alexis and Chris accidentally.

'Hardly the crime of the century,' she commented, turning to put her cup in the sink. 'Look, I'm sorry I can't help you,' she continued, facing me and running her hands through her curls, giving them fresh life. 'It's three years now since Sarah moved out of here. I don't know what she was doing or who she was seeing. I have no idea why she chose to fly under false colours in the first place, nor why she chose to impersonate me. And I really don't know what possible interest it could be to anyone. According to the newspapers, Sarah was murdered by a burglar whom she had the misfortune to interrupt trying to find something he could sell, no doubt to buy drugs. That had nothing to do with anything else in her life. I don't know what your client has hired you to do, but I suspect that he or she is wasting their money. Sarah's dead, and no amount of raking into her past is going to come up with the identity of the crackhead who killed her.'

'As a doctor, you'll appreciate the burdens of confidentiality. Even if I wanted to tell you what I've been hired to do, I couldn't. So I'll have to be the judge of whether I'm wasting my time or not,' I said, staking out the cool ground now I'd finally raised Helen Maitland's temperature a degree or two.

'Be that as it may, you're certainly wasting mine,' she said sharply.

'When did you see Sarah last?' I asked, taking advantage of the fact that our conversation had become a subtlety-free zone.

She frowned. 'Hard to say. Two, three weeks ago? We bumped into each other in the lab.'

'You didn't see each other socially?'

'Not often,' she said, biting the words off abruptly.

'What? She shared your house for the best part of a year because the two of you got along just fine, then she moves out and the only time you see each other is when you bump into each other in hospital corridors? What happened? You have a row or what?'

Helen Maitland glowered at me. 'I never said we were friends,' she said, enunciating each word carefully. 'All I said was that we didn't get on each other's nerves. After she moved out, we didn't stay in close touch. But even if we had fallen out, it would still have nothing to do with the fact that Sarah Blackstone was murdered by some junkie burglar.'

I smiled sweetly as I got to my feet. 'You'll get no argument from me on that score,' I said. 'What it might explain, though, is why Sarah Blackstone was hiding behind your name to commit her crimes.'

I started for the door. 'What crimes?' I heard.

Half turning, I said, 'Obviously nothing to do with you, Dr Maitland, since you had nothing to do with her. Thanks for the tea.'

She didn't follow me down the hall. I opened the door and nearly walked into a key stabbing towards me at eye height. I jumped backwards and so did the woman wielding the key. She was the original of the photograph in the kitchen. With her cascade of dark hair, skin pale as marble and a long cape-shouldered coat, she looked as extreme as a character in an Angela Carter story. 'God, I'm sorry,' she gasped. 'You look like you've seen a ghost!'

No, just an extra from Francis Ford Coppola's *Dracula*, I thought but didn't say. 'You startled me,' I said, putting a hand on my pounding heart.

'Me too!' she exclaimed.

From behind me, I heard Helen Maitland's voice. 'Ms Brannigan was just leaving.'

The other woman and I skirted round each other, swapping places. ''Bye,' I said brightly as the door closed behind me.

Trotting down the stone steps leading to the garden, I told myself off for being childish enough to give away my secrets to Helen Maitland just to score a cheap point because she'd made her way under my skin. It was hard to resist the conclusion that she had learned more from our interview than I had.

I didn't think she had lied to me. Not in so many words. Over the years, I've developed a bullshit detector that usually picks up on outright porkies. But I was fairly sure she wasn't telling me anything like the whole story. Whether any of it was relevant to my inquiries, I had no idea. But I had an idea where I might find some of the facts lurking behind her smoke screen of half-truths. When I got back to the car, I switched on my mobile and left a message for Shelley on the office answering machine. An urgent letter needed to go off to the Land Registry first thing in the morning. The reply would take a few days, but when it came, I had a sneaky feeling I'd have some bigger guns in my armoury to go after Helen Maitland with.

13

In these days of political correctness, it's probably an indictable offence to say it, but Sean Costigan didn't have to open his mouth to reveal he was Irish. I only had to look at him, even in the sweaty laser-split gloom of the nightclub. He had dark hair with the sort of kink in it that guarantees a bad hair life, no matter how much he spent on expensive stylists. His eyes were dark blue, his complexion fair and smooth, his raw bones giving him a youthful, unformed look that his watchful expression and the deep lines from his nostrils to the corners of his mouth denied.

I'd got home around nine after fish and chips in Leeds's legendary Bryan's, making the mistake I always do of thinking I'm hungry enough for a jumbo haddock. Feeling more tightly stuffed than a Burns Night haggis, I'd driven back with the prospect of an early night all that was keeping me going. I should have known better, really. Among the several messages on my machine – Alexis, Bill, Gizmo and Richard, just for a kickoff – there was one I couldn't ignore. Dan Druff had called to say he'd set up a meet at midnight in Paradise. Why does nobody keep office hours any more?

I've never been able to catnap. I always wake up with a thick head and a mouth that feels like it's lined with sheepskin. I don't mean the sanitized stuff they put in slippers – I mean the stuff you find in the wild, still attached to its smelly owner. I rang Alexis, but she didn't want to talk in front of Chris, whom she was keeping in the dark about Sarah Blackstone's murder on account of her delicate condition. Richard was out – his message had been to tell me he wouldn't be home until late. We'd probably meet on the doorstep as we both staggered home in the small hours. Bill I still wasn't talking to, and Gizmo doesn't do conversation. So I booted up the computer and settled down for a serious session with my football team. Not many people know this, but I'm the most successful manager in the history of the football league. In just five seasons, I've taken struggling Halifax Town from the bottom of the Conference League up through the divisions to the Premier League. In our first season there, we even won the Cup. This game, Premier Manager 3, is one of my darkest secrets. Even Richard doesn't know about my hidden nights of passion with my first-team squad. He wouldn't understand that it's just fantasy; he'd see it as an excuse to buy me a Manchester United season ticket for my next birthday so I could sit next to him in the stands every other week and perish from cold and boredom. He'd never comprehend that while watching football sends me catatonic, developing the strategies it takes to run a successful team is my idea of a really good time. So I always make sure he's out when I sit down with my squad.

Around half past eleven, I told the boys to take an early bath and grabbed my leather jacket. When I stepped outside the door, I discovered the rain had stopped, so I decided to leave the car and walk to the Paradise. It's only fifteen minutes on foot, and the streets of central Manchester are still fairly safe to walk around late at night. Especially if you're a Thai boxer. Besides, I figured it wouldn't do me any harm to limber up for looking chilled out.

The Paradise Factory considers itself Manchester's coolest nightclub. The brick building is on the corner of Princess Street and Charles Street, near Chinatown and the casinos, slightly off the beaten track of clubland. It used to house Factory Records, the famous indie label that was home to Joy Division and lots of other bands less talented but definitely more joyful. When Factory failed, a casualty to the recession, an astute local businesswoman took over the building and turned it into a poser's heaven. Officially, it's supposed to be an eclectic mix of gay and hetero, camp and straight, but it's the only club where I've been asked on the door to verify that I'm not a gender tourist by listing other Manchester gay and lesbian venues where I've drunk and danced.

As soon as I went through the door, I was hit by a bass rhythm that pounded stronger in my body than my heart ever had. It was hard to move without keeping the beat. I found Dan and Lice propped against a wall near the first bar I came to as I walked into the three-storey building. The guy I knew without asking was Sean Costigan stood slightly to one side, his wiry body dwarfed by his fellow Celts. His eyes were restless, constantly checking out the room. He let me buy the drinks. Both rounds. That wasn't the only way he made it plain he was there on sufferance. The sneer was another dead giveaway. It stayed firmly in place long after the formal introductions were over and he'd given me the kind of appraising look that's more about the labels and the price tags on the clothes than the body inside them.

'I don't know what the boys have been saying to you, but I want to make one thing absolutely plain,' he told me in a hard-edged Belfast whine. 'We are the victims here, not the villains.' He sounded like every self-justifying Northern Irish politician I'd ever heard. Only this one was leaning over me, bellowing in my ear, as opposed to on a TV screen I could silence with one blast of the remote control.

'So how do you see what's been happening?' I asked.

'I've been in this game a very long time,' he shouted over the insistent techno beat. 'I was the one put Morrissey on the map, you know. And the Mondays. All the big boys, I've had them all through my hands. You're talking to a very experienced operator here,' he added, wetting his whistle with a swig of the large dark rum and Coke he'd asked for. Dan and Lice nodded sagely, backing up their man. Funny how quickly clients forget whose side you're on.

I waited, sipping my extremely average vodka and bottled grapefruit juice. Costigan lit a Marlboro Light and let me share the plume of smoke from his nostrils. Sometimes I wonder if being a lawyer would really have been such a bad choice. 'And I have not been trespassing,' he said, stabbing my right shoulder with the fingers that held the cigarette. 'I am the one trespassed against.'

'You're telling me that you haven't been sticking up posters on someone else's ground?' I asked sceptically.

'That's exactly what I'm telling you. Like I said, we're the victims here. It's my ground that's getting invaded. More times than I can count in the past few weeks, I've had my legitimate poster sites covered up by cowboys.'

'So you've been taking revenge on the guilty men?'

'I have not,' he yelled indignantly. 'I don't even know who's behind it. This city's always been well regulated, you know what I mean? Everybody knows what's what and nobody gets hurt if they stick to their own patch. I've been doing this too long to fuck with the opposition. So if you're trying to lay the boys' trouble at my door, you can forget it, OK?'

'Is there any kind of pattern to the cowboy flyposting?' I asked.

'What do you mean, a pattern?'

'Is it always the same sites where they're taking liberties? Or is it random? Are you the only one who's being hit, or is it a general thing?'

He shrugged. 'It's all over, as far as I can tell. It's not the sort of thing you talk about, d'you understand? Nobody wants the opposition to think they're weak, you know? But the word on the street is that I'm not the only one suffering.'

'But none of the other bands are getting the kind of shit we're getting,' Dan interjected. God knows how he managed to follow the conversation. He must have trained as a lip-reader. 'I've been asking around. Plenty other people have had some of their posters covered up, but nobody's had the aggravation we've had.'

'Yeah, well, it's nothing to do with me, OK?' Costigan retorted aggressively.

There didn't seem to be anything else to say. I told Dan and Lice I'd be in touch, drained my drink and walked home staring at every poster I passed, wondering what the hell was going on.

I dragged my feet up the stairs to the office just after quarter past nine the next morning. I felt like I was fourteen again,

Monday morning before double Latin. I'd lain staring at the ceiling, trying to think of good excuses for not going in, but none of the ones that presented themselves convinced either me or Richard, which gave them no chance against Shelley or Bill.

I needn't have worried. There was news waiting that took Bill off the front page for a while. I walked in to find Josh Gilbert perched on the edge of Shelley's desk, one elegantly trousered leg crossed casually over the other. I could have paid my mortgage for a couple of months easily with what the suit had cost. Throw in the shirt, tie and shoes and we'd be looking at the utility bills too. Josh is a financial consultant who has managed to surf every wave and trough of the volatile economy and somehow come out so far ahead of the field that I keep expecting the Serious Fraud Office to feel his collar. Josh and I have a deal: he gives me information, I buy him expensive dinners. In these days of computerization, it would be cheaper to pay Gizmo for the same stuff, but a lot less entertaining. Computers don't gossip. Yet.

Shelley was looking up at Josh with that mixture of wariness and amusement she reserves for born womanizers. When he saw me, he broke off the tale he was in the middle of and jumped to his feet. 'Kate!' he exclaimed, stepping forward and sweeping me into a chaste embrace.

I air-kissed each cheek and stepped clear. The older he got, the more his resemblance to Robert Redford seemed to grow. It was disconcerting, as if Hollywood had invaded reality. Even his eyes seemed bluer. You didn't have to be a private eye to suspect tinted contacts. 'I don't mean to sound rude,' I said, 'but what are you doing here at this time of the morning? Shouldn't you be blinding some poor innocent with science about the latest fluctuations of the Nikkei? Or persuading some lucky Lottery winner that their money is safe in your hands?'

'Those days are behind me,' he said.

'Meaning?'

'I am thirty-nine years and fifty weeks old today.'

I wasn't sure whether to laugh or cry. Ever since I've known him Josh has boasted of his intention to retire to some tax haven when he was forty. Part of me had always taken this with a pinch of salt. I don't move in the sort of circles where people amass the kind of readies to make that a realistic possibility. I should have realized he meant it; Josh will bullshit till the end of time about women, but he's never less than one hundred per cent serious about money. 'Ah,' I said.

'Josh has come to invite us to his fortieth birthday and retirement party.' Shelley confirmed my bleak fear with a sympathetic look.

'Selling up and selling out, eh?' I said.

'Not as such,' Josh said languidly, returning to his perch on Shelley's desk. 'I'm not actually selling the consultancy. Julia's learned enough from me to run the business, and I'm not abandoning her entirely. I might be going to live on Grand Cayman, but with fax machines and e-mail, she'll feel as though I've only moved a few miles away.'

'Only if you don't have conversations about the weather,' I said. 'You'll get bored, Josh. Nothing to do all day but play.'

The smile crinkled the skin round his eyes, and he gave me the look Redford reserves for Debra Winger in *Legal Eagles*. 'How could I be bored when there are still beautiful women on the planet I haven't met?'

I heard the door open behind me and Bill's voice said, 'Are we using "met" in the biblical sense here?'

Bill and Josh gave each other the usual once-over, a bit like dogs who have to sniff each other's bollocks before they decide a fight isn't worth the bother. They'd never been friends, probably because they'd thought they were competitors for women. Neither had ever realized how wrong they were; Bill could never have bedded a woman without brains, and Josh never bedded one with an IQ greater than her age except by accident. Shelley had her pet theories on their respective motivations, but life's too short to rerun that seminar.

'So it's all change then,' Bill said once Josh had brought him up to speed on his reasons for visiting. 'You off to Grand Cayman, me off to Australia.'

'I thought you'd only just come back,' Josh said.

'I'm planning to move out there permanently. I'm marrying an Australian businesswoman.'

'Is she pregnant?' Josh blurted out without thinking. Seeing my face, he gave an apologetic smile and shrug.

'No. And she's not a rich widow either,' Bill replied, not in the least put out. 'I'm exercising free will here, Josh.'

I swear Josh actually changed colour. The thought of a man as dedicated as he was to a turbo-charged love life finally settling down, and from choice, was like suddenly discovering his body was harbouring a secret cancer. 'So because of this woman, you're going to get married and live in *Australia*? My God, Bill, that's worse than moving to Birmingham. And what about the business? You can keep a finger on the financial pulse from anywhere you can plug in a PC, but you can't run an investigation agency from the other side of the globe.'

'The game plan is that I'll sell my share of the agency here and start up again in Australia.'

Josh's eyebrows rose. 'At your age? Bill, you're only a couple of years younger than me. You're really planning to start from ground zero in a foreign country where you don't even speak the language? God, that sounds too much like hard work to me. And what about Kate?'

I'd had enough. 'Kate's gotta go,' I said brusquely. 'People to be, places to see. Thanks for the invite, Josh. I wouldn't miss it for the world.' I wheeled round and headed back out of the door. I wasn't sure where I was going, and I didn't care. I knew I was behaving like a brat, but I didn't care about that either. I stood on the corner outside the office, not even caring about the vicious northeasterly wind that was exfoliating every bit of exposed skin. A giggling flurry of young women in leg warmers and tights accompanied by a couple of well-muscled men enveloped me, waiting for the lights to change as they headed for rehearsals at the new dance theatre up the street, one of the handful of tangible benefits we got from being UK City of Drama for a year. Their energy and sense of direction shamed me, so I followed briskly in their wake and collected my car from the meter where I'd left it less than twenty minutes before. Given that I'd planned to be in the office for a couple of hours, somebody was going to get lucky.

One quick phone call and fifteen minutes later, I was walking round the big Regent Road Sainsbury's with Detective Chief Inspector Della Prentice. When I'd called and asked her if she could spare half an hour, she'd suggested the supermarket. Her fridge was in the same dire straits as mine, and this way we could both stock up on groceries while we did the business. We took turns pushing the trolley, using our packs of toilet rolls as a convenient Maginot line between our separate purchases. I filled her in on the headstone scam in the fruit and veg. department, handing over a list of victims who should be able to pick out Williams and Constable in an identity parade. She promised to pass it on to one of her bright young things.

The outrageous tale of Cliff Jackson's waste of police time kept us going as far as the chill cabinets. By the time we hit the breakfast cereals, I'd moved on to the problems at Mortensen and Brannigan, which lasted right up to hosiery and tampons. Della tried an emerald green ruffle against her copper hair. I nodded agreement. 'I can see why Shelley suggested you putting your share of the business on the market too,' Della said. 'But that could present you with a different set of problems.'

'I know,' I sighed. 'But what else can I do?'

'You could talk to Josh,' she said. Sometimes I forget the pair of them were at Cambridge together, they're such different types. It's true that they were both fascinated by money but while Josh wanted to make as much of it as possible, Della wanted to stop people like him doing it illegally. She was too bright for him to fancy, so he gave her his respect instead, and a few years ago he did me the biggest favour he's ever managed when he introduced us.

'What good would that do? Josh deals with multinational conglomerates, not backstreet detective agencies. I can't believe he knows anyone with investigative skills and enough money to buy Bill out that he hasn't already introduced me to. Besides, investigative skills never seem to go hand in hand with the acquisition of hard cash. You should know that.'

Della reached for a tin of black olives then turned her direct green eyes on me. 'You'd be surprised at what Josh knows about,' she said, giving a deliberate stage wink.

'I'm not even going to ask if the Fraud task force is about to lose its major inside source,' I said. 'Besides, Josh is too busy extricating himself from business right now. He's not about to get involved in setting up a whole new partnership for me. Did you know he's retiring in a couple of weeks?'

Della nodded, looking depressed. 'He's been saying he was going to retire at forty since he was nineteen.'

'I wouldn't worry about it, Della. He'll never retire. Not properly. He'll die of boredom in a week if he's not spreading fear and loathing in global financial institutions. He'll always have fingers in enough pies to keep you busy.'

Whatever I'd said, it seemed to have deepened Della's gloom. Then I twigged. If Josh was about to hit the big four zero, it couldn't be far off for Della. And she wasn't a multi-millionaire with the world her oyster. She was a hard-working, ferociously bright woman in what was still a man's world, a woman whose career commitment left her no space for relationships other than a few close friendships. I stopped the trolley by the spirits and liqueurs, put a hand on her arm and said, 'He might have made the money, but you've made the difference.'

'Yeah, and everything at the agency is going to work out for the best,' she said grimly. We looked at each other, registering the self-pitying misery that was absorbing each of us. Then, suddenly and simultaneously, we burst out laughing. Nobody could get near the gin, but we didn't give a damn. Like the song says, girls just wanna have fun.

14

If you think it's embarrassing to get a hysterical fit of the giggles with one of your best friends in Sainsbury's wines and spirits department, try having your mobile phone ring in the middle of it. Now that's *really* excruciating. At least when it's someone as laconic as Gizmo, you don't have to destroy your street cred totally by having a conversation. A series of grunts signifying 'yes' and 'no' will do just fine. I gathered he'd got the stuff I wanted and he was about to stuff it through my letter box unless I had any serious objections. I didn't. Even if it was Police Harassment Week and Linda Shaw and her sidekick were back on my doorstep, they could hardly arrest Gizmo for impersonating a postman.

Being midweek and mid-morning, we were through the checkouts in less time than it takes to buy a newspaper in our local corner shop. Della and I hugged farewell in the car park and went our separate ways, each intent on making some criminal's life a misery. 'Talk to Josh,' were her final words.

Gizmo had done me proud. Not only had he translated the files into a format I could easily read on my computer, but he'd also printed out hard copies for me. As far as her patient notes were concerned, Sarah Blackstone's passion for secrecy had been superseded by a medical training that had instilled the principle of always leaving clear notes that another doctor could follow through should you be murdered by a burglar between treatments. I flicked through until I found the file relating to Alexis and Chris. Not only were their names correct on the print-out, but so also were their phone numbers at home and work, address and dates of birth. Which meant the chances were high that all the other patients' details were accurate. If ever I needed to interview any of them, I knew where to start looking.

At one level, the job Alexis had hired me to do was now complete. I had checked out the consulting rooms and removed any evidence that might lead back to Sarah Blackstone's patients. But what I had were only backup copies. The originals were still out there somewhere, presumably sitting on the hard drive of the laptop that the doctor had used throughout her consultations. If Gizmo had cracked their file protection, it was always possible that the police had someone who could do the same thing. It was also possible that whoever had killed Sarah Blackstone had stolen her computer and was sitting on the best blackmail source since Marilyn Monroe's address book. Women who could afford this treatment could afford payoffs too. The game was a long way from being over.

What I needed now was more information. I understood very little of the patient notes sitting in front of me and I understood even less of the fertility technology that I was dealing with here. I needed to know what technical backup Sarah Blackstone had needed, and just how difficult it was to achieve what she had done. I also needed to know if this was something she could do alone, or if she'd have had to involve someone else. Time to beg another favour from someone I already owed one to. Dr Beth Taylor is one of the legion of women who have been out with Bill Mortensen without managing to accomplish what an Australian boutique bimbo had pulled off. Beth works part time in an inner-city group practice where nobody's had to pay a prescription charge in living memory. The rest of the time she lectures on ethics to medical students who think that's a county in the south of England. If she feels like a bit of light relief, she does the odd bit of freelance work for us when we're investigating medical insurance claims.

I tracked Beth down at the surgery. I didn't tell her about Bill's planned move. It wasn't that I thought it would hurt her feelings; I just couldn't bear to run through it yet again.

Once we'd got the social niceties out of the way, I said, 'Test-tube babies.'

She snorted. 'You've been reading too many tabloids. IVF, that's what you call it when you want a bit of respect from the medical profession. Subfertility treatment, when you want to impress us with your state-of-the-art consciousness. What are you after? Treatment or information?'

'Behave,' I said scathingly.

'I know someone at St Mary's. He used to be a research gynaecologist, now he works part time in the subfertility unit. I bring him in to do a seminar on my course on the ethics of interference with human fertility.'

'Would he talk to me?' I asked.

'Probably. He likes to show off what a new man he is. Nothing he loves more than the chance to demonstrate to a woman how sensitive he is to our reproductive urges. What is it you want to know, and why?'

'I need the five-minute crash course in IVF for beginners and a quick rundown on where the leading edge is right now. What can and can't be done. I'm not asking for anything that isn't readily available in the literature, I just need it in bite-sized pieces that a lay person can understand.'

'Gus is your man, then. You didn't mention why this sudden interest?'

'That's right, I didn't. Is he going to want a reason?'

Beth thought for a moment. 'I think it might be as well if you were a journalist. Maybe looking for nonattributable background for a piece you're doing following women's experiences of being treated for subfertility?'

'Fine. How soon can you fix it?'

'How soon do you need it?'

'I'm free for lunch today,' I said. The devil finds work for idle hands; if you can't manage any other exercise, you can always push your luck.

'So I'll lie. I'll tell him you're young, gorgeous and single. Gus Walters, that's his name. I'll get him to call you.'

Ten minutes later, my phone rang. It was Gus Walters. Young, gorgeous and single must have worked. I hoped he wouldn't be too disappointed. Two out of three might not be bad, but none ain't good. 'Thanks for getting back to me so quickly,' I said.

'No problem. Besides, I owe Beth a favour.'

'Are you free for lunch today? I know it's short notice . . .'

'If you can meet me at half past twelve at the front entrance, I can give you an hour and you can buy me a curry,' he said.

'Deal. How will I know you?' I asked.

'Oh, I think I'll know you,' he said, voice all dark brown smoothness. Definitely a doctor.

It's a constant source of amazement to me that the staff at Manchester's major hospital complex don't all have serious weight problems. They're only five minutes' walk from the Rusholme curry parade, as serious a selection of Asian restaurants as you'll find anywhere in the world. If I worked that close to food that good, cheap and fast, I couldn't resist stuffing my face at least twice a day. Richard might be convinced that the Chinese are the only nation on earth with any claim to culinary excellence, but for me, it's a dead heat with the chefs of the subcontinent. Frankly, as soon as I had sat down at a window table with a menu in front of me, I was a lot more interested in the range of pakoras than in anything Gus Walters could possibly tell me.

He was one of the non-rugby-playing medics: medium height, slim build, shoulders obviously narrow inside the disguise of a heavy, well-cut tweed jacket. His hands were long and slender, so pale they looked as if they were already encased in latex. Facially, he had a disturbing resemblance to Brains, the *Thunderbirds* puppet. Given that he'd opted for the identical haircut and very similar large-framed glasses, I wondered if he had enough sense of irony to have adopted them deliberately. Then I remembered he was a doctor and dismissed the idea. He probably thought he looked like Elvis Costello.

On the short walk to the nearest curry house we'd done the social chitchat about how long we'd lived in Manchester and what we liked most and least about the city. Now I wanted to get the ordering done with so we could cut to the chase. I settled for chicken pakora followed by karahi gosht with a garlic nan. Gus opted for onion bhajis and chicken rogan josh. He grinned across the table at me and said, 'The orifice I get closest to doesn't bother about garlic breath.' It rolled out with the smoothness of a line that never gets the chance to go rusty.

I smiled politely. 'So tell me about IVF,' I said. 'For a start, what kind of technology do you need to make it work?'

'It's all very low tech, I'm afraid,' he replied, his mouth turning down at the corners. 'No million-pound scanners or radioactive isotopes. The main thing you need is what's called a Class II containment lab which you need to keep the bugs out. Clean ducted air, laminar flow, temperature stages that keep things at body temperature, an incubator, culture media. The only really specialized stuff is the glassware – micropipettes and micromanipulating equipment and of course a microscope. Also, when you're collecting the eggs, you need a transvaginal ultrasound scanner, which gives you a picture of the ovary.'

He was off and running. All I needed to do was provide the odd prompt. I was glad I wasn't his partner; I could just imagine how erotic his bedroom conversation would be. 'So what are the mechanics of carrying out an IVF procedure?' I asked.

'OK. Normally, women release one egg a month. But our patients are put on a course of drugs which gives us an optimum month when they'll produce five or six eggs. The eggs are in individual sacs we call follicles. You pass a very fine needle through the top of the vagina and puncture each follicle in turn and draw out the contents, which is about a teaspoonful of fluid. The egg is floating within that. You stick the fluid on the heated stage of the microscope, find the egg, and strip off some of the surrounding cells, which makes it easier to fertilize. Then you put it in an individual glass Petri dish with a squirt of sperm and culture medium made of salts and sugars and amino acids – the kind of soup that would normally be around in the body to nourish an embryo. Then you leave them overnight in a warm dark incubator and hope they'll do what opposite genders usually do in warm dark places at night.' He grinned. 'It's very straightforward.'

The food arrived and we both attacked. 'But it doesn't always work, does it?' I asked. 'Sometimes they don't do what comes naturally, do they?'

'That's right. Some sperm are lazy. They don't swim well and they give up the ghost before they've made it through to the nucleus of the egg. For quite a few years, when we were dealing with men with lazy sperm, there wasn't a lot we could do and we mostly ended up having to use donor sperm. But that wasn't very satisfactory because most men couldn't get over the feeling that the baby was a cuckoo in the nest.' He gave a smile that was meant to be self-deprecating but failed. Try as he might, you didn't have to go far below the surface before Old Man reasserted itself.

'So what do you do now?' I asked.

But he wasn't to be diverted. He'd started so he was going to finish. 'First they developed a technique where they made a slit in the "shell" of the harvested egg,' he said, waggling his fingers either side of his head to indicate he was using inverted commas because he was unable to use technical terms to a mere mortal. 'That made it easier. Twenty-five per cent success rate. But it wasn't enough for some real dead-leg sperm. So they came up with SUZI.' He paused expectantly. I raised my eyebrows in a question. It wasn't enough. Clearly I was supposed to ask who Suzie was.

Disappointed, he carried on regardless as the impassive waiter delivered our main courses. 'That involves passing a very fine microneedle through the "shell" and depositing two or three sperm inside, in what you could call the egg white if you were comparing it to a bird's egg. And still some sperm just won't make the trip to the nucleus of the egg. Twenty-two per cent success rate is the best we've managed so far. So now, clinics like ours out on the leading edge have started to use a procedure called ICSI.'

'ICSI?' I thought I'd better play this time. Even puppies need a bit of encouragement.

'Intracytoplasmic Sperm Injection,' he said portentously. 'One step beyond.'

I wished I hadn't bothered. 'Translation?'

'You take a single sperm and strip away its tail and all the surrounding gunge until you're left with the nucleus. Then the embryologist takes a needle about a tenth the thickness of a human hair and pushes that through the "shell", through the equivalent of the egg white right into the very nucleus of the egg itself, the "yolk". Then the nucleus of the sperm is injected into the heart of the egg.'

'Wow,' I said. It seemed to be what was expected. 'So is it you, the doctor, who does all this fiddling around?'

He smiled indulgently. 'No, no, the micromanipulation is done by the embryologist. My job is to harvest the eggs and then to transfer the resulting embryo into the waiting mother. Of course, we keep a close eye on what the embryologist does, but they're essentially glorified lab technicians. I've no doubt I could do what they do in a pinch. God knows, I've watched them often enough. See one, do one, teach one.' It's hard to preen yourself while you're scoffing curry, but he managed.

'So, does the lab have to be on twenty-four-hour stand-by so you're ready to roll the minute a woman ovulates?' I'd been presuming that Sarah Blackstone did her fiddling with eggs and microscopes in the watches of the night when the place was deserted, but I needed to check that hypothesis.

'We don't just leave it to chance,' Gus protested. 'We control the very hour of ovulation with drugs. But big labs like ours do offer seven days a week, round-the-clock service so we can fit in with the lives of our patients. There's always a full team on call: embryologist, doctor and nurse.'

'But not constantly in the lab?'

'No, in the hospital. With their pagers.'

'So anybody could walk into the lab in the middle of the night and wreak havoc?' I asked.

He frowned. 'What kind of article are you researching here? Are you trying to terrify people?'

Furious with myself for forgetting I wasn't supposed to be a hard-nosed detective, I gave him a high-watt smile. 'I'm sorry, I get carried away. I read too much detective fiction. I'm sure people's embryos are as safe as houses.' And we all know how safe that is in 1990s Britain.

'You're right. The lab's always locked, even when we're

working inside. No one gets in without the right combination.' His smile was the smug one of those who never consider the enemy within.

'I suppose you have to be careful because you've got to account to the Human Fertilisation and Embryology Authority,' I said.

'You're not kidding. Every treatment cycle we do has to be documented and reported to the HFEA. Screw up your paperwork and you can lose your licence. This whole area of IVF and embryo experimentation is such a hot potato with the God squad and the politically paranoid that we all have to be squeaky clean. Even the faintest suggestion that we were doing any research that was outside the scope of our licence could have us shut down temporarily while our lords and masters investigated. And it's not just losing the clinic licence that's the only danger. If you did mess around doing unauthorized stuff with the embryos that we don't transfer, you'd be looking at being struck off and never practising medicine again. Not to mention facing criminal charges.'

I tore off another lump of nan bread and scooped up a tender lump of lamb, desperately trying not to react to his words. 'That must put quite a bit of pressure on your team, if you're always having to look over your shoulder at what the others are doing,' I said.

Gus gave me a patronizing smile. 'Not really. The kind of people employed in units like ours aren't mad scientists, you know. They're responsible medical professionals who care about helping people fulfil their destiny. No Dr Frankensteins in our labs.'

I don't know how I kept my curry down. Probably the thought of being tended by the responsible medical professional opposite me. Either that or the fact that I wasn't paying much attention because I was still getting my head round what he'd said just before. If I was short of a motive for terminating Dr Sarah Blackstone, Gus Walters had just handed me one on a plate.

15

A few days before, I'd have reckoned that as motives for murder go, the prospect of losing your livelihood was a pretty thin one. That had been before Bill's bombshell. Since then, I'd been harbouring plenty of murderous thoughts, not just against a business partner who'd been one of my best friends for years, but also against a blameless Australian woman I'd barely met. For all I knew, Sheila could be Sydney's answer to Mother Teresa. Somehow, I doubted it, but I'd been more than ready to include her in the homicidal fantasies that kept slipping into my mind. Like unwanted junk mail, I always intended to throw them straight in the bin, but every time I found myself attracted by some little detail that sucked me in. If a well-adjusted crime fighter like me felt the desire to kill the people I saw as stealing my dream, how easy it would be for someone who was borderline psychotic to be pushed over the edge by the prospect of losing their professional life. What Gus Walters told me handed motive on a plate to everyone Sarah Blackstone had worked with at St Hilda's, from the professor who supervised the department to the secretary who maintained the files.

There was nothing I could do now about pursuing that line of inquiry. By the time I'd got home and driven to Leeds, it would be the end of the medical working day. I made a mental note to follow it up, which freed my brain to gnaw away at the problem which had been uppermost there since Bill's return. Never mind murderers, never mind rock saboteurs, what I wanted the answer to was what to do about Mortensen and Brannigan. The one thing I was sure about was that I didn't intend to roll over and die, waiting for Bill to find the buyer of his choice. As I walked back through the red-brick streets dotted with grass-filled vacant sites that lie between Rusholme and my home, I was plagued by the question of whether I could find a way to generate enough income to pay off a loan big enough to buy Bill out while managing to remain personally solvent.

The key to that was to find a way to make the agency work more profitably. There was one obvious avenue that might prove lucrative, but I'd need an extra pair of hands. Back when I'd started working for Bill, I'd done bread-and-butter process-serving. Every week, I'd abandon the law library and turn up at the office where Shelley would hand me a bundle of court papers that had to be served a.s.a.p. Domestic-violence injunctions, writs and a whole range of documents relating to debt. My job was to track down the individuals concerned and make sure they were legally served with the court documents. Sometimes that was as straightforward as cycling to the address on the papers, ringing the doorbell and handing over the relevant bumf. Mostly, it wasn't. Mostly, it involved a lot of nosing about, asking questions of former colleagues, neighbours, drinking cronies and lovers. Sometimes it got heavy, especially when I was trying to serve injunctions on men who had been persistently violent to wives who took out injunctions one week and were terrorized, bullied, sweet-talked or guilt-tripped into taking their battering men back the next. The sort of men who see women as sexually available punchbags don't usually take kindly to being served papers by a teenager who barely comes up to their elbow.

In spite of the aggravation, I'd really got into the work. I'd loved the challenge of tracking down people who didn't want to be found. I'd enjoyed outwitting men who thought that because they were bigger and stronger than me, they weren't going to accept service. I can't say I took any pleasure slapping some of the debtors with bankruptcy papers when all they were guilty of was believing the propaganda of the Thatcher years, but even that was instructive. It gave me a far sharper awareness of real life than any of my fellow law students. So I'd quit to work for Bill full time as soon as the opportunity arose.

But I hadn't joined the agency to be a process-server. In the medium to long term, Bill wanted a partner and he was prepared to train me to do everything he could do. I learned about surveillance, working undercover, doing things with computers that I didn't know were possible, security systems, white-collar crime, industrial sabotage and espionage, and subterfuge. I learned how to use a video camera and how to bug, how to uncover bugs and how to take photographs in extreme conditions. I'd also picked up a few things that weren't on the syllabus, like kick boxing and lock picking.

Of course, as my skills grew, the range of jobs Bill was prepared to let me loose on expanded too. The end result of that was that we'd been content to let most of the process-serving fall into the laps of other agencies in the city. Maybe the time had come to snatch back that work for ourselves.

What I needed was a strategy and a body to serve the papers.

Shelley sipped her glass of white wine suspiciously, as if she were checking it for drugs, and glanced around her with the concentration of a bailiff taking an inventory. She had only been in my house a couple of times before, since we tended to do our socializing on the neutral ground of bars and restaurants. That way, when Richard reached screaming point we could make our excuses and leave. It's not that he doesn't like Shelley's partner Ted, a former client who opted for a date with her instead of a discount for cash and ended up moving in. It's just that Ted has the conversational repertoire of a three-toed sloth and is about as quick on the uptake. Nice bloke, but . . .

'You can't stay out of the office forever,' she said. A woman who's never been afraid to state the obvious, is Shelley.

'Call it preventative medicine. I'm trying to get a plan in place before I have to confront Bill,' I said. 'At the moment, every time I'm within three yards of him, I feel an overwhelming desire to cave his head in, and I don't fancy spending the next twenty years in prison. Besides, I do have some cases that I'm working on.' I picked up the microcassette recorder on the table and flipped the cassette out of it. 'I dictated some reports this afternoon. That brings me up to date. I've included the new client details.'

Shelley leaned across and picked up the tape. 'So why am I here? I don't guess it's because you couldn't go without my company for a whole day.'

I explained my idea about generating more income by reclaiming process-serving work. Shelley listened, a frown pulling her eyebrows closer together. 'How are you going to get the business? All the solicitors who used to put the work our way have switched to somebody else, and presumably they're satisfied with the service they're getting.'

This was the bit I was slightly embarrassed about. I leaned back and looked at the ceiling. 'I thought I could do a Charlie's Angel and try some personal visits.'

I risked a look. Shelley had a face like thunder. Jasper Charles runs one of the city's biggest firms of criminal solicitors. The primary qualification for employment as a clerk or legal executive there is having terrific tits and long legs. The key role of these women, known in legal circles as Charlie's Angels, is to generate more business for the firm. Every day, one or more of the Angels will visit remand clients in prison, often for the slenderest of reasons. They'll get the business out of the way then sit and chat to the prisoner for another half-hour or so. All the other prisoners who are having visits from their briefs see these gorgeous women fawning all over their mates, and a significant proportion of them sack their current lawyers and shift their business to Jasper Charles. Every woman brief in Manchester hates them. 'You've done some cheesy things in your time, Kate, but this is about as low as it gets,' she eventually said.

'I know. But it'll work. That's the depressing thing.'

'So you go out and prostitute yourself and you snatch back all this business. How you going to find the time to do it?'

'I'm not.'

Shelley's head tipped to one side. Unconsciously, she drew herself in and away from me. 'Oh no,' she said, shaking her head vigorously. 'Oh no.'

'Why not? You'd be great. You're the biggest no-shit I know.'

'Absolutely not. There isn't enough money printed yet to make me want to do that. Know what you're good at and stick to it, that's my motto, and what I'm good at is running that office and keeping you in line.' She slammed her drink down on the table so hard that the wine lurched in the glass like the contents of a drunk's stomach.

So far, it was going just like I'd expected it to. 'OK,' I said with a small sigh. 'I just thought I'd give you first refusal. So you won't mind me hiring someone else to do it?'

'Can we afford it?' was her only concern.

'We can if we do it on piecework, same as Bill did with me.'

Shelley nodded slowly and picked up her glass again. 'Plenty of students out there hungry for a bit extra.'

'Tell me about it,' I said. 'Actually, I've got someone provisionally lined up.'

'You never did hang about,' Shelley said drily. 'How did you find somebody so fast? How d'you know they're going to be able to cut it?'

I couldn't keep the grin from my face. Any minute now, there was going to be the kind of explosion that Saddam could have used to win the Gulf War if there had been a way of harnessing it. 'I think he'll fit in just fine,' I told her. 'You know how wary I am of involving strangers in the business, but this guy is almost like one of the family.' I got up and opened the door into the hall. 'You can come through now,' I called in the direction of the spare room that doubles as my home office.

He had to stoop slightly to clear the lintel. Six feet and three inches of lithe muscle, the kind you get not from pumping iron but from actually exercising. Lycra cycling trousers that revealed a lunchbox like Linford's and quads to match, topped with a baggy plaid shirt. He moved lightly down the hall, his Air Nikes barely making a sound. I stepped back to let him precede me into the living room and put my fingers in my ears.

'Donovan? What you doing here?' Shelley's thunderous roar penetrated my defences, no messing. The volume she can produce from her slight frame is a direct contradiction of the laws of physics. Don half turned towards me, his face pleading for help.

'I've hired him to do our process-serving, as and when we need him. We pay him a flat fee of –'

'No way,' Shelley yelled. 'This boy has a career in front of him. He is going to be an engineer. Not a private eye. No child of mine. No way.'

'I quite agree, Shelley. He's not going to be a private eye –'

'You're damn right he's not,' she interrupted.

'He's not going to be a private eye, any more than students who work in Burger King three nights a week are going to be stuffing Whoppers for the rest of their working lives. All he's doing is a bit of work on the side to relieve the financial pressures on his hard-working single mother. Because that's the kind of lad he is,' I said quietly.

'She's right, Mam,' Don rumbled. 'I don't wanna do what she does. I just wanna make some readies, right? I don't wanna ponce off you all the time, OK?' He looked as if he was going to burst into tears. So much for muscle man. Forget valets; no man is a hero to his mother.

'He's not a kid any more,' I said gently. For a long moment, mother and son stared at each other. Hardest thing in the world, letting kids go. This was worse than the first day at school, though. There was nothing familiar or safe about the world she was releasing him into.

Shelley pursed her lips. 'About time you started acting like a man and took some of the responsibility for putting food on the table,' she said, trying to disguise the pain of loss with sternness. 'And if it stops you wasting your time with that band of no-good losers that call themselves musicians, so much the better. But all you do is serve papers, you hear me, Donovan?'

Don nodded. 'I hear you, Mam. Like I said, I don't want to do what she does, right?'

'And you don't neglect your studies either, you hear?'

'I won't. I *want* to be an engineer, OK?'

'Why don't you two discuss the details on the way home?' I inserted tactfully. I had the feeling it was going to take a while for the pair of them to be reconciled at any level beyond the purely superficial, and I had a life to get on with.

When I said 'life', I'd been using the term loosely, I decided as I tagged on to the tail end of a bunch of girl Goths and scowled my way past the door security. If this was life, it only had a marginal edge on the alternative. Garibaldi's was currently the boss night spot in Manchester. According to the *Evening Chronicle*'s yoof correspondent, it had just edged past the Hacienda in the trendiness stakes with the acquisition of Shabba Pilot, the hottest DJ in the north. In keeping with its status, the door crew were all wearing headsets with radio mikes. They're supposed to make them look high tech and in control; I can never see them without remembering all those old black-and-white movies where little old dears ran old-fashioned telephone exchanges and eavesdropped on all the calls.

I'd dressed for the occasion. I couldn't manage the paper white, hollow-eyed *Interview with the Vampire* look adopted by the serious fashion victims, not without a minor concussion. So I'd opted for the hard-case pretentious-philosopher image. Timberland boots, blue jeans, unbleached cotton T-shirt that told the world that Manchester was the Ur-city, and a leather jacket with the collar turned up. Plus, of course, a pair of fake Ray-Bans, courtesy of Dennis's brother Nick. The look got me past the door no bother and didn't earn me a second glance as I walked into the main part of the club.

Garibaldi's belongs to a guy called Devlin. I've never met anybody who knows what his other name is. Just Devlin. He materialized in Manchester in the late seventies with a Cumbrian accent and more money than even the resident gangsters dared question. He started small, buying a couple of clubs that had less life in them than the average geriatric ward. He spent enough on the interior, the music and the celebs who could be bought for a case of champagne to turn the clubs into money machines. Since when Devlin has bought up every ailing joint that's come on the market. Now he owns half a dozen pubs, a couple of restaurants known more for their clientele than their cuisine, and four city-centre clubs.

Garibaldi's was the latest. The building used to be a warehouse. It sat right on the canal, directly opposite the railway arches that raise Deansgate Station high above street level. When Devlin bought it, the interior was pretty bare. Devlin hired a designer who took Beaubourg as his inspiration. An inside-out Beaubourg. Big, multi-coloured drainage pipes curved and wove throughout the building, iron stairs like fire escapes led to iron galleries and walkways suspended above the dancers and drinkers. The joys of post-modernism.

I climbed up steps that vibrated to the beat of unidentifiable, repetitive dance music. At the second level, I made my way along a gallery that seemed to sway under my feet like a suspension footbridge. It was still early, so there weren't too many people around swigging designer beers from the bottle and dabbing whizz on their tongues. At the far end of the gallery, a rectangular structure jutted out thirty feet above the dance floor. It looked like a Portakabin on cantilevers. According to Dennis, this was the 'office' of Denzel Williams, music promoter and, nominally, assistant manager of Garibaldi's.

I couldn't see much point in knocking, so I simply stuck my head round the door. I was looking at an anteroom that contained a pair of battered scarlet leather sofas and a scarred black ash dining table pushed against the wall with a couple of metal mesh chairs set at obviously accidental angles to it. The walls were papered with gig posters. In the far wall, there was another door. I let the door close behind me and instantly the noise level dropped enough for me to decide to knock on the inner door.

'Who is it?' I heard.

I pushed the door open. The noise of the music dropped further, and so did the temperature, thanks to an air-conditioning unit that grunted in the side wall. The man behind the cheap wood-grain desk stared at me with no great interest. 'Who are you?' he demanded, the strong Welsh vowels immediately obvious. Call me a racist, but when it comes to the Welsh, I immediately summon my irregular verb theory of life. In this instance, it goes, 'I have considered opinions; you are prejudiced; he/she is a raging bigot.' And in my considered opinion, the Welsh are a humourless, clannish bunch whose contribution to the sum total of human happiness is on the negative side of the ledger. The last time I said that to a Welshman, he replied, 'But what about Max Boyce?' QED.

I had the feeling just by looking at him that Denzel Williams wasn't going to redeem my opinion of his fellow countrymen. He was in his middle thirties, and none of the deep lines that scored his narrow face had been put there by laughter. His curly brown hair was fast losing the battle with his forehead and the moustache he'd carefully spread across as much of his face as possible couldn't hide a narrow-lipped mouth that clamped meanly shut between sentences. 'Do I know you?' he said when I failed to reply before sitting in one of the creaky wicker chairs that faced his desk.

'I'm a friend of Dennis O'Brien's,' I said. 'He suggested I talk to you.'

He snorted. 'Anybody could say that right now.'

'You mean because he's inside and it's not easy to check me out? You're right. So either I am a genuine friend of Dennis's or else I'm a fake who knows enough to mention the right name. You choose.'

He looked at me uncertainly, slate-grey eyes narrowing as he weighed up the odds. If I was telling the truth and he booted me out, then when Dennis came out, Williams might be eating through a straw for a few weeks. Hedging his bets, he finally said, 'So what is it you want? I may as well tell you now, if you're fronting a band, you're about ten years too old.'

I'd already had a very bad week. And if there's one thing that really winds me up, it's bad manners. I looked around the shabby room. The money he'd spent on that mandarin-collared linen suit would probably have bought the office furnishings three times over. The only thing that looked remotely valuable in any sense was the big tank of tropical fish facing Williams. I stood up and felt in my pocket for my Swiss Army knife. As I turned away from him and appeared to be making for the door, I flipped the big blade open, side-stepped and picked up the loose loop of flex that fed power to the tank. Without a heater and oxygenation, the fish wouldn't last too long. Tipped on to the floor, they'd have an even shorter life span.

I turned and gave him my nastiest grin. 'One wrong move and the fish get it,' I snarled, loving every terrible B-movie moment of it. I saw his hand twitch towards the underside of his desk and grinned even wider. 'Go on, punk,' I said, all bonsai Clint Eastwood. 'Hit the panic button. Make my day.'

16

I wouldn't have hurt the fish. I knew that, but Denzel Williams didn't. 'For fuck's sake!' he yelled, starting up from his seat.

'Sit down and chill out,' I growled. 'I only wanted to ask you a couple of questions, but you had to get smart, didn't you?'

He subsided into his chair and scowled at me. 'Who the fuck are you? Who sent you here?'

'Nobody sent me. Nobody *ever* sends me anywhere,' I said. I was beginning to enjoy playing the bastard. I couldn't remember the last time I'd had so much fun. No point in lying, though. He could find out who I was easily enough if he cared enough to make trouble later. 'The name's Brannigan. Kate Brannigan. I'm a private eye.'

He looked shaken but not stirred. 'And what do you think you're going to see here?' he sneered.

I shook my head wonderingly. 'I can't believe Dennis said you were worth talking to. I've met coppers with better manners.'

The reminder of who had recommended Williams to me worked wonders. He swallowed his surliness and said, 'OK, OK, ask your questions, but don't piss about. I've got some people coming shortly, see?'

I saw only too well. Threatening the fish might hold Williams at bay, but it would cut no ice with his sidekicks. He'd also be very unhappy at anybody else witnessing his humiliation. Held to ransom by a midget with a Swiss Army knife. Regretfully I waved my posturing farewell and cut to the chase. 'Flyposting,' I said. 'My client's been having some problems. Obviously nobody likes admitting they're being had over, but somebody is definitely taking liberties. All I'm trying to do is to check out whether this is a personal vendetta or if everybody in the business is feeling the same pain.'

'Who's your client, then?'

'Dream on, Denzel. Just a simple yes or no. Has anybody been papering over your fly posters? Has anybody been fucking with your venues? Has anybody been screwing up gigs for your bands?'

'What if they have?' he demanded.

'If they have, Denzel, you just got lucky, because you will reap the benefit of the work I'm doing without having to part with a single shilling. All I'm concerned about is finding out who is pouring sugar in the petrol tank of my client's business, and getting them to stop. Now, level with me before I decide to have sushi for dinner. Have you been getting agg?'

'There's been one or two incidents,' he grudgingly admitted.

'Like?'

He shrugged. 'Yeah, some of my posters have been papered over.' He took a deep breath. He'd obviously decided that since he'd started talking, he might as well spill the lot. Funny how the ones that seem the hardest often turn out the gobbiest. 'The fresh paperwork has always been promoting out-of-town bands, so I'm pretty sure it's a stranger who doesn't know the way things work here. We've had one or two problems with tickets too. Some of the agents that sell tickets for our gigs have had phone calls saying the gig's a sellout, not to sell any more tickets. We've even had some scumbag pretending to be me ringing up and saying the gig was cancelled. It's got to be somebody from out of town. Nobody else would dare to mess with me.' His tone of voice left me in no doubt that when he got his hands on the new kid in town, the guy would be sorry he'd been born.

'Where specifically?'

He rattled of a list of names and venues. I hoped I'd be able to remember them later, because I didn't have a spare hand for note taking. 'Any ideas who's behind it?' I asked.

He gave me the look I suspected he normally reserved for

traffic wardens who thought that giving him a ticket would discourage him from parking on double yellow lines. 'If I had any ideas, do you think he'd still be out there walking around?'

Ignoring the sarcasm, I persisted. 'Anybody else been hit that you know of?'

'Nobody's boasting about it. But I know Sean Costigan's taken worse shit than I have. The Crumpsall firm's been hit, so has Parrot Finnegan. And Joey di Salvo.'

'Collar di Salvo's lad?' I asked, surprised. I hadn't known the family of the local godfather were involved in flyposting. Whoever was muscling in on the patch was treading on the kind of toes that hand out a proper kicking.

'That's right.'

'That's serious.'

'We're talking war,' Williams said. He wasn't exaggerating. People who deprive the di Salvos of what they regard as their legitimate sources of income have an unfortunate habit of winding up silenced with extreme prejudice.

'So are you all supposed to take your bats and balls and go home? Does the new team expect everybody to back down so they can pick up the business?'

Williams shrugged. 'Who knows? But some of the boys that put the nod-and-a-wink record-company business our way are starting to get a bit cheesed off, see? They pay us to do a job and they're not too happy when their fancy posters get covered up the night after they've appeared. And one or two of the bigger managers are starting to mutter too. You're not the only one wanting to put a stop to this.'

Before I could ask more, I heard the telltale sequence of sounds that revealed the outer door to the anteroom opening and closing. I dropped the electric cable and opened the office door. As I walked swiftly past a trio of sharp-suited youths who looked like flyweight boxers, I heard Williams shouting, 'Fucking stop her.'

By the time they got their brains to connect with their legs, I was out the door and sprinting down the gallery, head down, tanking past the bodies leaning over the railings and surveying the dancers down below. I could feel the rhythmic thud of the pursuing feet cutting across the beat as I swung onto the stairs and hurtled down as fast as I could go.

I had the advantage. I was small enough to weave through the bodies on the stairs and landings. My pursuers had to shove curious people out of the way. By ground level, I was hidden from my followers by the turn of the stair. I slid into the press of bodies on the dance floor, pulling off my shades and my jacket. I squirmed through the dancers till I was at the heart of the movement, imitating their blank-eyed stares and twitching movements. I couldn't even glimpse the three toughs who had come after me. That meant they probably couldn't see me either. That was just the way I wanted to keep it.

There was one salt-and-pepper chicken wing left. My heart said yes, my head said no. It would be a lot easier to enlist Richard's help if he wasn't harbouring a grudge. 'There you go,' I said, shoving the foil container towards him. There was none of that false politesse about Richard. No, 'Oh no, I couldn't possibly.' I filled my bowl with spicy vermicelli and added a crab cake wrapped in sesame seeds and a couple of Szechuan king prawns. 'I was at Garibaldi's earlier on,' I said casually.

Richard's teeth stopped their efficient stripping job. 'For fun?' he asked incredulously.

'What do you think?'

'Not,' he said with a grin.

'You'd be right. You know Denzel Williams?'

He went back to his chicken wing, sucking it noisily as he nodded. 'I know the Weasel,' he said eventually. 'So called because of his ability to worm his way out of any deal going. Doesn't matter how tight you think you've got him tied up. Doesn't even matter if you've got your lawyer to draw up the paperwork. If Weasel Williams wants out, he'll get out.'

'Does he do the business for his bands?'

Richard shrugged noncommittally, filling his bowl again. 'I've not heard many complaints. He seems to have a deal going with Devlin – he does the flyposting for all of the man's venues, and he has a ticket agency going on the side as well.

He bought a jobbing printer's last year, so now he prints all his own posters and a lot of the band merchandising as well. T-shirts, posters, programmes, flyers. And, of course, he manages bands as well. He's one of the serious players.'

'He's been having a taste of the same agg as Dan and the boys.'

Richard looked surprised. 'Weasel has? You must be looking at some operator, then. With Devlin's muscle to call on, I can't see the Weasel taking it from some street punk.'

'That's what I figured. I need to find out who is behind it, and I don't think Denzel Williams knows. But somebody must.' There was a short silence while we ate and digested what we'd been saying. 'I need your help, Richard,' I said.

He stopped eating. He actually stopped eating to look at me and consider what I'd just said. When Richard and I first got together, we'd both been wary, like experimental mice who have learned that certain activities result in pain and damage. Somehow, we'd managed to build a relationship that felt equal. We gave each other space, neither preventing the other from doing the things we felt were important. It had taken real strength from both of us not to interfere with the other's life when we felt we knew better, but mostly we'd managed it. Then a year before, I'd had to call in every favour anybody ever owed me to get him out of jail. He'd been stripped of power, reliant on me, my skills and my contacts. Since then, our relationship had been off balance. His last attempt to square things between us had nearly cost us the relationship and driven me into someone else's arms. Maybe I finally had a real opportunity to let him take the first step towards evening the scores. 'What is it you think I can do for you?' he asked, his voice giving nothing away.

'You know everybody in the rock business in this town. Half of them must owe you. I need you to call in a couple of favours and get me some kind of a lead into who's pulling the strings here.'

He shrugged and started eating again. 'If the Weasel doesn't know, I don't know who will. He's got the best grapevine in town.'

'I can't believe it's better than yours,' I said, meaning it.

'Besides, there must be people who wouldn't lose any sleep at the thought of Devlin and the Weasel getting a hard time. They might be keeping their mouths shut out of pure *Schadenfreude*.'

'Or fear,' Richard pointed out.

'Or fear. But they're not necessarily going to be afraid of talking to you off the record, are they? If they trust you as much as you seem to think, they'll have slipped you unattributable stuff before without any comebacks. So they know in advance that you're not going to drop them in the shit with the Weasel or with Devlin himself.'

Richard ran a hand along his jaw and I heard the faint rasp of the day's stubble. Normally, it's a sound I find irresistibly erotic, but for once it had no effect. There was too much going on under the surface of this conversation.

'Sure, I've covered their backs before. But I've never asked questions like this before. It's a bit different from getting the latest goss on who's signing deals with whom. Nosing into stuff like this is your business, not mine. If I put the word around that I'm looking for info on the cowboy fly posters, I'm the one the finger will point at when you clear up the shit. I need to keep people's confidence or I don't get the exclusive stories and if I don't get the stories, I don't eat.'

'You think I don't understand about keeping contacts cultivated? Look, based on what I've dug up so far, I've drawn up a list of places and people who have been hit. You must know somebody on the list who trusts you enough to tell you what they know about who's behind this business.' I took the paper out of my pocket, unfolded it and proffered it across the table. It was so tense between us that if a car had backfired outside, we'd both have hit the deck.

Without taking it from me, Richard read the list. He tapped one name with a chopstick. 'Manassas. I've known the manager there for years. We were muckers in London together before we both came up here. Yeah, I could talk to him. He knows I won't drop him in it.' He took a deep breath and let it out in a slow sigh. 'OK, Brannigan, I'll talk to him tomorrow.'

'I'll come along.'

He scowled. 'Don't you trust me? He's not going to open up if I've got company, you know.'

'Of course I trust you. But I need to hear what he's got to say for myself. Like you said, these are my kind of questions, not yours. Treat me like a bimbo all you want, but you have to take me with you.'

Richard looked at me for a long minute, then he nodded gravely. 'OK. I'll be happy to help.' He grinned and the tension dissipated so suddenly it was hard to believe how wound up we'd both been moments earlier.

'I appreciate it.' I put down my bowl and chopsticks and leaned forward to kiss him deeply, running my hands up the insides of his thighs. For an unheard of second time in the same Chinese meal, Richard lost interest in food. This time, for rather longer.

Later, we lay, too comfortable to move from the sofa. I reached over and pulled the throw over our sweaty bodies so we wouldn't get chilled too soon. My head in the crook between Richard's strong shoulder and his jaw, I told him about my decision to hire Don and claw back enough process-serving business to keep him busy. I didn't mention the Charlie's Angels ploy; the moment was too sweet for that, and besides, one lecture a day is more than enough for me.

'Will that be enough?' Richard asked dubiously.

'No,' I said. Sometimes I wish I didn't have such a strong streak of realism. There are times when it would be a blessing to be afflicted with blind optimism.

'So what are you going to do?' he asked, gently stroking my back to show there was nothing aggressive in the question.

'I'm not entirely sure yet,' I admitted. 'Hiring Don is just a starting point. What I'm really worried about is if Bill goes we're going to lose a lot of the computer-security business. He's spent a lot of time and energy playing games with the big boys to establish his credentials in the field of computer security. Now, when it comes to making your system secure in the first place, or tracking down the creeps who are trying to steal your secrets or your money via your computer,

Mortensen and Brannigan is right up there alongside some of the really big companies,' I said proudly.

'And that's all tied in to Bill's name, right?' Richard chipped in, shoving me back on track.

'Give the boy a coconut,' I said. 'Most of the people Bill deals with don't even know who Brannigan is. They're fully paid up members of the laddish tendency. Not the sort of men who are going to be convinced that a woman knows her RAM from her ROM.'

'Least of all a cute redhead with the best legs in Man-chester,' Richard said, reaching round me to check the accuracy of his comment with the hand that wasn't holding me.

'So the problem is twofold,' I continued, trying to ignore the sensations his touch was triggering off. 'First, I don't have the credibility. Secondly, if I'm being brutally honest –'

'Be brutal, be brutal,' Richard interrupted with a mock moan.

' – I don't have the expertise either,' I said firmly, wriggling away from his wandering fingers.

'You could learn,' he murmured, refusing to be evaded. 'You're a very quick learner.'

'Only when I'm motivated,' I said sternly, squirming down and away. 'I can't get excited enough to put in the hours it takes to develop the skills. And I haven't got the patience to devote days to finding a leak and plugging it.'

'So don't. Do what you've done with Don. GSI.'

'GSI?'

'Get somebody in.'

'Like who?' I asked sarcastically. 'People with those kind of skills don't grow on trees. If they're straight, they're already earning far more than I could afford to pay them. And if they're dark-side hackers, they don't want to do anything as straight as work for me.'

'Set a thief to catch a thief, isn't that what they say? Didn't you mention that Telecom had just given Gizmo the "Dear John" note?'

I could have kissed him. But frankly, he didn't need the encouragement.

17

Private eyes should have the same motto as boy scouts: 'Be Prepared'. If I had to pass on one secret to any aspiring PI, that's what it would be. With that in mind, I settled down in my half of the conservatory with breakfast and the printed version of Sarah Blackstone's case notes. I needed to look more closely at the idea of her former colleagues having a motive for murder. If I was going to grip them by the lapels of their lab coats, thrust them against the wall and apply the red-hot pincers to treasured parts of their anatomy, I wanted to be sure I was asking the right questions.

Armed with the background information I'd picked up from the boy wonder of St Mary's, this time I was able to make a lot more sense of what I was reading. And it was the kind of sense that made the hairs on the back of my neck stand up. I flicked back through the pages to check that I wasn't misunderstanding what I saw in front of me. But there was no mistake. If I'd been short of motives for Sarah Blackstone's murder before, I was awash with them now.

Women tend to assume that it's only male doctors who are sufficiently arrogant, overbearing and insensitive to ride roughshod over their patients' lives. Wrong. Overexposure to these charming traits during training obviously rubs off on a lot of the women who go the distance too. However pleasant, supportive and discreet Dr Blackstone might have appeared to the women who consulted her, it seemed they hadn't so much been patients as the subjects of her experiments. That was the message that came through loud and clear from her notes.

It wasn't enough for her that she'd been breaking new

ground by performing miracles that women had never had the chance to experience before; she wanted a different kind of immortality. What her notes told me was that she'd been playing a kind of Russian roulette to achieve it. She had been harvesting her own eggs for as long as she'd been treating other women. The notes were there. She'd persuaded one of her colleagues to do the egg collection, on the basis that Sarah was going to donate the eggs to women who couldn't produce fertile ones of their own. I knew now from my own research that because of the courses of fertility drugs involved in producing half a dozen eggs at once, she'd only have been able to harvest her own eggs two or three times a year. But that had been enough. Although she couldn't use her own eggs exclusively in the mix, she had been including one of her own eggs with each couple's batch. She'd have been growing on four or five embryos for each couple, and returning three of them to the womb. For every woman she'd successfully impregnated, there was a one-in-four or -five chance that the baby was not the child of the mother and her partner. Instead, it would be the result of a genetic mixture from the mother and Sarah Blackstone. And Chris was pregnant.

It was a nightmare, and one that I absolutely couldn't share with my client. And if I couldn't tell my best friend, there was nobody else I could dump on either. Certainly not Richard. After the recent rockiness of our road, the last thing he needed to hear about was a testosterone-free tomorrow. But it wasn't just the implications for Chris's pregnancy that bothered me. It was the long-term dangers within the gene pool. Judging by what I knew from Alexis, a lot of lesbian mothers in Manchester formed a close-knit social group, for obvious reasons. Their kids played together, visited each other's houses, grew up together. Chances were by the time they were adults, two women making babies together would be accepted medical practice, not some hole-in-the-corner criminal activity. What would happen if a couple of those girls fell in love, decided they wanted to make babies and they were half-sisters because they'd both come from Sarah Blackstone's eggs? Either they'd find out in preliminary genetic tests. Or even worse, they'd start a cycle of inbreeding whose consequences could poison the future for children not yet imagined, never mind conceived. It was a terrifying thought. But it didn't surprise me that it was a possibility on the horizon. When society sets things up so that the only way people can achieve their dreams is to go outside the law, it automatically loses any opportunity to control the chain reaction.

It was also an experiment that wasn't hard to unravel. Any of the couples who were looking at a child who didn't look a bit like either of them but had a striking resemblance to their doctor wasn't likely to be handing out the benefit of the doubt. It's not hard to have private DNA testing done these days, and at around five hundred pounds, not particularly expensive either, compared to the cost of IVF treatment and the expense of actually having a child. A few weeks and the couple would have their answer. And if the mother's partner wasn't the biological coparent, you wouldn't have to be a contender on *Mastermind* to work out that the chances were that the other egg had come from the person most concerned with the procedure.

The more I found out, the more the idea of a random burglar sounded as likely as Barry Manilow duetting with Snoop Doggy Dog. Forget her colleagues in Leeds. They'd still be there tomorrow. Right now, I needed to check whether there was a murderer on my own doorstep.

Lesley Hilton was Sarah Blackstone's first experimental mother. According to the files, she lived with her partner on the edge of the Saddleworth moors, where the red-brick terraced slopes of Oldham yield to the Yorkshire stone villas built by those of the Victorians who managed to get rich on the backs of the ones toiling in the humid spinning mills. It was far from the nearest address to me, but Lesley's daughter Coriander must be around eighteen months old by now, and if she was Blackstone's baby, it might be obvious. It was as good a place to start as any, and better than most.

The house was one of a group of three cottages set at the foot of a steep field where sheep did the job I'd have cheerfully paid a gardener to do. Anything's preferable to having a herd of wild animals at the back door. The original tawny colour of the stone was smudged with more than a century's worth of grime. So much for the clean country air. I yanked an old-fashioned bell pull and heard a disproportionately small tinkle.

The woman who opened the door looked like a social worker in her fisherman's smock, loose cotton trousers and the kind of sensible leather sandals that make Clarks Startrite look positively dashing. She was short and squarely built, with dark blonde hair cut spiky on top. She peered at me through granny glasses, her chubby face smiling tentatively. 'Yes?' she said.

I'd been working on a decent cover story all the way out along the Oldham Road. What I had was pitifully thin, but it was going to have to do. 'I wonder if you could spare me a few minutes?' I started. 'This isn't easy to talk about on the doorstep, but it concerns a Dr Sarah Blackstone.'

Either Lesley Hilton had never heard the name before, or she had more acting skills than a family outing of Redgraves. She looked blank and frowned. 'Are you sure you've got the right house?'

'You are Lesley Hilton?'

She nodded, her head cocked in what I recognized as the classic pose of a mother listening for a toddler who is probably dismantling the TV set as we speak.

'I think you probably knew Dr Blackstone as Dr Helen Maitland,' I said.

This time the name got a reaction. Her cheekbones bloomed scarlet and she stepped back involuntarily, the door starting to close. 'I think you'd better go,' she said.

'I'm no threat to you and Coriander. I'm not from the authorities, I swear,' I pleaded, fishing out a card that simply said 'Kate Brannigan, Confidential Consultant', with the office address and phone number. I gave her the card. 'Look, it's important that we talk. Dr Blackstone or Dr Maitland, whatever you prefer to call her, is dead and I'm trying to –'

The door closed, shutting off the expression of panic that had gripped Lesley Hilton's features. Cursing myself for my clumsiness, I walked back to my car. At least I hadn't blown it with someone who knew that Dr Helen Maitland was really

Sarah Blackstone. I'd have put money on that. And if she wasn't aware of that, chances were she hadn't killed her.

I fared better with Jude Webster, another of the early births. According to the files, she'd been a self-employed PR copywriter when she became pregnant. Judging by the word processor whose screen glowed on the table next to the pack of disposable nappies, she was still trying to earn some money that way. She had glossy chestnut hair which, considering the depth of the lines round her eyes, owed more to the bottle than to nature. Even though little Leonie was at the child minder, the buttons on Jude's cardigan had been done up in a hurry and didn't match the appropriate buttonholes, but I didn't feel it would help our rapport if I pointed that out.

The news of Sarah Blackstone's real identity and her death had got me across the threshold. I hadn't even needed a business card. Maybe she assumed I was another of the lesbian mothers come to bring the bad news. 'I'm sorry,' she now said, settling me down with the best cup of tea I'd had in weeks. 'I didn't catch your connection to Dr Maitland . . . Dr Blackstone, I mean.'

Time for the likeliest story since Mary told Joseph it was God's. 'As you know,' I started, 'Sarah was a real pioneer in her field. I'm representing women who are concerned that her death doesn't mean the end of her work. What we're trying to do is to put together a sort of case book that those who follow in her footsteps will be able to refer to. But we want it to be more than just her case notes. It's an important piece of lesbian history. The experience of the women who led the way mustn't be lost.'

Jude was nodding sympathetically. She was going for it, all the way. Pity she had acted totally blankly when I'd first mentioned the name Sarah Blackstone. 'You're so right,' she said earnestly. 'So much of women's achievements and contributions just get buried because the books are written by men. It's vital that we reclaim our history. But –'

'I know, you're concerned about confidentiality,' I cut in. 'And let me tell you, I can fully appreciate why. Obviously, the last thing my clients want is for people's privacy to be compromised, especially in circumstances like these. It wouldn't serve anyone's interests for that to happen. But I can assure you that there will be nothing in the finished material to identify any of the mothers or the children.'

We danced around the issue of confidentiality for a bit, then she capitulated. My Granny Brannigan always remarked that I had an honest face. She said it made up for my devious soul. Within an hour, Jude had told me everything there was to tell about the consultations that she and her partner Sue had had with Dr Blackstone. And it was all a complete waste of time. The first two minutes with the photograph album revealed a child that was the image of Sue, right down to an irrepressible cowlick above the right eye that wouldn't lie down and die. This time, Sarah Blackstone had missed.

By late afternoon, I knew the laws of probability had been on the doctor's side. But then, aren't they always? Ask anybody who's ever tried to sue a surgeon. At least two of the kids I'd seen bore more than a passing resemblance to the dead doctor. I was astonished the parents didn't seem to notice. I suppose people have always looked at their children and seen what they wanted to see. Otherwise there would be even more divorces than there are already.

At ten to five, I decided to hit one more and then call it a day. Jan Parrish and Mary Delaney lived less than a mile away from me in a red-brick semi on what had once been one of the city's smarter council housing estates. When the Tories had introduced a right-to-buy scheme so loaded with inducements that anyone in employment would have had to be crazy to say no, this estate had fallen like a line of dominoes. Now finding a resident who still paid rent to the council was harder than finding food in Richard's fridge.

Porches, car ports and new front doors had sprouted rampantly with no regard to any of their neighbours, each excrescence an indicator of private ownership, like a dog pissing on its own gatepost. Jan and Mary were among the more restrained; their porch was a simple red-brick and glass affair that actually looked as if it were part of the house rather than bolted on as a sad afterthought. I rang the bell and waited.

The woman who answered the door had an unruly mop of flaming red hair. It matched perfectly the small girl wrestling for freedom on her hip. I went through the familiar routine. When I got to the part where I revealed the doctor's real identity, Jan Parrish looked appalled. 'Oh my God,' she breathed. 'Oh my God.'

It was the first time I'd struck anything other than cracked plastic with that line. And that was even before I'd told her Sarah Blackstone was dead. 'It doesn't get any better,' I said, not sure quite how to capitalize on her state. 'I'm afraid she's dead. Murdered, in fact.'

I thought she was going to drop the baby. The child took the opportunity to abseil down her mother's body and stumble uncertainly towards me. I moved in front of her, legs together and bent at the knees like a hockey goalkeeper and blocked her escape route. Jan picked her up without seeming to be aware of it and stepped back. 'You'd better come in,' she said.

The living room was chaos. If I'd ever considered motherhood for more than the duration of a movie, that living room would have put me off for life. It made Richard's mess look structured. And this woman was a qualified librarian, according to her medical record. Worrying. I shoved a pile of unironed washing to one end of a sofa and perched gingerly, carefully avoiding a damp patch that I didn't want to think too closely about. Jan deposited the child on the carpet and sat down heavily on a dining chair with a towel thrown over it. I was confused; I couldn't work out what Jan Parrish's excessive reaction to my exposure of her doctor's real identity meant. It didn't fit my expectation of how a killer would react. I couldn't see Jan Parrish as a killer, either. She didn't seem nearly organized enough. But she had been horrified and panicked by what I'd said and I needed to find out why. Playing for time, I gave her the rigmarole about lesbian history. She was too distracted to pay much attention. 'I'm sorry it's been such a shock,' I said finally, trying to get the conversation back on track.

'What? Oh yes, her being murdered. Yes, that's a shock, but it's the other thing that's thrown me. Her not being who she said she was. Oh my God, what have I done?'

That's exactly what I was wondering too. It wasn't that I was too polite to say so, only too cautious. 'Whatever it was, I'm sure it had nothing to do with her death,' I said soothingly.

Jan looked at me as if I was from the planet Out To Lunch. 'Of course it didn't,' she said, frowning in puzzlement. 'I'm talking about blowing her cover with the letter.'

I knew the meaning of every word, but the sentence failed to send messages from my ears to my brain. 'I'm sorry . . . ?'

Jan Parrish shook her head as if it had just dawned on her that she had done something so stupid that even a drunken child of two and a half would have held fire. 'We were all paranoid about security, for obvious reasons. Dr Maitland always impressed on us the importance of that. She told us never to write to her at the clinic, because she was afraid someone might open the letter by mistake. She said if we needed to contact her again, we should make an appointment through the clinic. But we were so thrilled about Siobhan. When she had her first birthday, we both decided we wanted Dr Maitland to know how successful she'd been. I'm a librarian, I'm back at work part time, so I looked her up in Black's. The *Medical Directory*, you know? And it said she was a consultant at St Hilda's in Leeds, so we sent her a letter with a photograph of Siobhan with the two of us and a lock of her hair, just as a sort of keepsake. But now you're telling me she wasn't Dr Maitland at all? That means I've exposed us all to a terrible risk!' Her voice rose in a wail and I thought she was going to burst into tears.

'When was this?' I asked.

'About three months ago,' she said, momentarily distracted by Siobhan's sudden desire to commune with the mains electricity supply via a plug socket. She leapt to her feet and scooped up her daughter, returning her to the carpet but facing in the opposite direction. Showing all the stubbornness of toddlers everywhere, Siobhan immediately did a five-point turn and crawled back towards the skirting board. This time, I took a better look at her face. The hair might be Jan Parrish's but the shape of her face was unmistakable. I wondered whether Helen Maitland had also noticed.

'Well, if you haven't heard anything by now, I'd think

you're all safe,' I reassured her. 'What did the letter actually say?'

She frowned. 'I can't remember the exact wording, but something like, "We'll never be able to thank you enough for Siobhan. You made a dream come true for us, that we could really share our own child." Something along those lines.'

'I wouldn't worry about it,' I said. 'That could mean anything. It certainly wouldn't make anyone jump to the conclusion that something so revolutionary was going on. And it doesn't give any clue as to who was actually treating you, does it? Unless the real Helen Maitland knew Sarah Blackstone was using her name, she's got no way of guessing. And if she did know, then presumably she was in on the secret too. I really don't think you should worry about it, honestly,' I lied. I wanted to grab her by the shoulders and shake her for her stupidity. With a secret that held so much threat for her and her daughter, she should never have taken such an outrageous risk. Given that her mother faced a lifetime of discretion, I didn't rate little Siobhan's chances of making it to adulthood without being taken into care and treated like an experimental animal in a lab. Instead, I made my excuses and left.

I hadn't found a serious suspect yet among the women who had been Sarah Blackstone's patients. I hoped I'd still be able to say that when I'd finished interviewing them. I cared far too much for Alexis and Chris to want to take responsibility for the hurricane of official and media attention that would sweep through their lives if I had to open that particular corner of Sarah Blackstone's life to public scrutiny.

Sometimes I think Alexis is psychic. I'd driven home thinking about her, and there she was on my doorstep. But it only took one glimpse of her face to realize she hadn't popped round to say how gratified she was at my concern for her. If looks could kill, I'd have been hanging in some psychopath's dungeon praying for the merciful end that death would bring.

18

Ask people what they think of when they hear the name 'Liverpool' and they'll tell you first about the Scouse sense of humour, then about the city's violent image. Tonight, Alexis definitely wasn't seeing the funny side. I'd barely got out of my car before she was in my face, the three inches she has on me suddenly seeming a lot more. Her tempestuous bush of black hair rose round her head like Medusa on a bad hair day and her dark eyes stared angrily at me from under the lowering ledges of her brows. 'What in the name of God are you playing at?' she demanded.

'Alexis, please stop shouting at me,' I said quietly but firmly. 'You know how it winds me up.'

'Winds you up? Winds *you* up? You put me and Chris in jeopardy and you expect me to care about winding you up?' She was so close now I could feel the warmth of her breath on my mouth.

'We'll talk about it inside,' I said. 'And I mean talk, not shout.' I ducked under the hand that was moving towards my shoulder, swivelled on the balls of my feet and walked smartly up the path. It was follow me or lose me.

Alexis was right behind me as I opened the inside door and marched into the kitchen. Mercifully, she was silent. Without asking, I headed for the fridge freezer and made us both stiff drinks. I pushed hers down the worktop towards her and after a long moment, she picked it up and took a deep swallow. 'Can we start again?' I asked.

'I hired you to make some discreet inquiries and cover our backs, not stir up a hornet's nest,' Alexis said, normal volume resumed.

'My professional opinion is that talking to other women in the same position as you is not exposing you to any danger, particularly since I have not identified you as my client to any of the women I have spoken to,' I said formally, trying to take the heat out of the situation. I knew it was fear not fury that really lay behind her display. In her stressed-out place, I'd probably have behaved in exactly the same way, best friend or not. 'I had a perfectly credible cover story.'

'Yeah, I heard that load of toffee about lesbian history,' Alexis said derisively, lighting a cigarette. She knows I hate smoking in my kitchen, but she clearly reckoned this was one time she was going to get away with it. 'No flaming wonder you set off more alarm bells than all the burglars in Greater Manchester. It's not on, girl. I asked you to make sure we weren't going to be exposed because of Sarah Blackstone's murder. I didn't expect you to go round putting the fear of God into half the lesbian mothers in Manchester. What the hell did you think you were playing at?'

It was a good question, and one I didn't have an answer for yet. The one thing I knew for sure was that this wasn't the right time to tell Alexis that Sarah Blackstone had added her mystery ingredient to the primordial soup. I was far from certain there was ever going to be a right time, but I know a wrong one when I see it. 'Who told you anyway?' I stalled.

'Jude Webster rang me. She assumed that because you had the names and addresses of all the women involved that you were kosher. But she thought she'd better warn me in case I didn't want Chris bothered in her condition. So what's the game?'

Inspiration had provided me with an attempt at an answer. 'I wanted to make sure none of them knew Blackstone's real identity,' I said. 'If they had, they might have contacted her at her home under her real name, and there could be a record of that. A letter, an entry in an address book. I need to be certain that there isn't a chink in the armour that could lead the police back to this group of women if they get suspicious about the burglar theory and start routine background inquiries.' I spread my hands in front of me and tried for wide-eyed innocence.

Alexis looked doubtful. 'But they're not going to, are they? I've been keeping an eye on the local papers, and there's no sign the police are even thinking it might have been anything more than a burglary that went wrong. What makes you think it was?'

I shrugged. 'If anybody she worked with had found out what she was up to, they had a great motive for getting rid of her. A scandal like this associated with the IVF unit at St Hilda's would have the place closed down overnight.' This was thinner than Kate Moss, but given what I couldn't tell Alexis, it was the best I could do.

'Hey, I know it's hard getting a decent job these days, but I can't get my head round the idea of somebody knocking off a doctor just to avoid signing on,' Alexis protested. Her anger had evaporated now I had anaesthetized her fears and her sense of humour had kicked in.

'Heat of the moment? She's arguing with somebody? They grab a knife?'

'I suppose,' Alexis conceded. 'OK, I accept you did what you did with the best of motives. Only it stops here, all right? No more terrorizing poor innocent women, all right?'

That's the trouble when friends become clients. You lose the power to ignore them.

Midnight, and we were arranged tastefully round the outer office of Mortensen and Brannigan. As soon as Richard had mentioned the f-word to Tony Tambo, the manager of Manassas had insisted that we meet somewhere nobody from clubland could possibly see him talking to a woman who'd already been publicly asking questions on the subject. Otherwise, flyposting was definitely off the agenda. He'd vetoed a rendezvous in a Chinese restaurant, a casino, an all-night caff in the industrial zone over in Trafford Park and the motorway services area. Richard's house was off limits because it was next door to mine. But the office was OK. I couldn't work out the logic in that until Richard explained.

'Now they've converted the neighbouring building into a student hall of residence, if anybody sees Tony coming out of your building, they'll assume he's been having a leg-over with some teenage raver,' he said.

'And I bet he wouldn't mind that,' I said drily.

'Show me a man over thirty who'd object to people making that assumption and I'll show you a liar,' Richard replied wistfully.

So we were sitting with the blinds drawn, the only light coming from the standard lamp in the corner and Shelley's desk lamp. Tony Tambo was hunched into one corner of the sofa, somehow managing to make his six feet of muscles look half their usual size. Although it was cold enough in the office for me to have kept my jacket on, the slanting light revealed a sheen of sweat on skin the colour of a cooked chestnut that covered Tony's shaved skull. He was wearing immaculate taupe chinos, black Wannabes, a black silk T-shirt that seemed moulded to his pectorals and a beige jacket whose soft folds revealed it was made of some mixture of natural materials like silk and cashmere.

It's a mystery to me, silk. For centuries it was a rare, exotic fabric, worn only by the seriously rich. Then, almost overnight, somewhere around 1992, it was everywhere. From Marks and Spencer to market stalls, you couldn't get away from the stuff. Kids on council estates living on benefits were suddenly wearing silk shirts. What I want to know is where it all came from. Were the Chinese giving silkworms fertility drugs? Had they been stockpiling it since the Boxer rebellion? Or is there some deeper, darker secret lurking behind the silk explosion? And why does nobody know the answer? One of these days, I'm going to drive over to Macclesfield, grip the curator of the Silk Museum by the throat and demand an answer.

I was sitting in an armchair at right angles to the opposite end of the sofa from Tony. Richard was in Shelley's chair, his feet on the desk. The pool of light illuminated him to somewhere around mid-thigh, then he disappeared into darkness. The whole scenario looked like a straight lift from a bad French cop movie. I decided pretty quickly that there weren't going to be any subtitles to help me out. The questions were down to me.

'I really appreciate you talking to me, Tony,' I said.

'Yeah, well,' he mumbled. 'I ain't said nothing yet. It's edgy out there right now, you know? Stability's gone, know what I mean? It's not a good time to stick your head above the parapet, people are too twitchy.'

'Anything you tell me, nobody's going to know it came from you,' I tried.

He snorted. 'So you say. But if some bruiser's got you up against the wall, how do I know you ain't going to give him me?'

'You don't know for sure.' I gestured round the office, which we've spent enough on to impress corporate clients. 'But I didn't get a gaff like this by dropping people in the shit. Anyway, in my experience, if some bruiser's got you up against the wall, he's going to do what he's going to do. So there's not a lot of point in giving him any more bodies. It doesn't save you any grief.'

He gave me a long, slow, head-to-toe look. 'What's your interest?' he eventually said.

'I'm working for Dan Druff and the Scabby Heided Bairns.' Sometimes you need to give a bit to get a lot.

'They got well unlucky,' Tony observed.

'How do you mean? What have they done to deserve what they're getting?'

'Nothing. Like I said, they just got unlucky. Any war of attrition, somebody always has to be made an example of. To keep the rest in line. Dan and the Bairns just drew the short straw, that's all. Nothing personal. Least, I don't think it is. I haven't heard anything that says it is.'

'So who's making the example of the boys?'

Tony took a packet of Camels out of his pocket and lit up without asking permission. I said nothing, but walked through into my office, took the saucer out from under a mother-in-law's tongue that wasn't ever going to dish out any more lip and pointedly slid it down the coffee table so it was in front of Tony. Richard took that as a sign and straightened up in the chair, using the desk top to roll a joint. Shelley was going to be well pleased in the morning to find tobacco shreds all over her paperwork. 'So what's happening in the music business?' I asked, getting bored with all this mannered posturing we were playing at. 'Who's making a bid for a piece of the action?'

'I don't think it's a piece of the action they want,' Tony said in a sigh of smoke. 'I think they want the lion's share.'

'Tell me about it,' I said.

'It started a couple of months ago. There was a wave of cowboy flyposting. Nobody seemed to know who was behind it. It wasn't the usual small-time gangsters trying to muscle in. So one or two of the major players decided to have a go at the bands and the venues who were having their posters put up by the cowboys. The intention was to find out who was behind it, but also to put the frighteners on the bands and the venues, so they'd come back to heel and abandon this new team.'

Tony paused, staring into the middle distance. 'So what happened?' I asked.

'They got a coating,' he said simply.

'What happened?'

'They sent a team of enforcers along to one of the gigs. They found themselves staring down the barrels of half a dozen sawn-off shotguns. Not the kind of thing you argue with. So they went off to get tooled up themselves. By the time they came back, the Old Bill were waiting and the whole vanload got a nicking. And not a one of the door crew got lifted.' Tony shook his head, as if he still couldn't quite comprehend it.

I was taken aback. I couldn't remember a time when Manchester villains had ever called the police in to sort out an internal matter. Whoever was trying for a takeover bid was so far outside the rules it must be impossible for the resident villains to know what the hell was coming round the next corner. 'So what happened?' I asked.

'There were a lot of unhappy people around. I don't have to draw pictures, do I? So they decided they'd go down one of the venues mob-handed. Out of working hours, so the door crew wouldn't be around. They figured a good wrecking job would sort things out. They'd hardly got the door broken down when the Old Bill arrived even more mob-handed and nicked the fucking lot of them. They couldn't believe it. I mean, you're talking people who've got coppers on their teams. Where do you think they get the extra door muscle on Friday and Saturday nights? But there they were being faced down by a fucking busload of coppers in riot gear. You can't get that kind of a turnout when it all goes off in the Moss on a hot summer's night!' Tony crushed out his cigarette and pulled another one out of the pack.

'So, whoever is behind all of this has got a bit of pull?' It was more of a statement than a question.

'You could say that.'

'Who is it, Tony?' I asked.

A drift of smoke from Richard's joint hid Tony's face for a moment. When it passed, his dark eyes met mine. I could see worry, but also a kind of calculation. I felt like I was being weighed in the balance. I'd wondered why Tony had agreed to talk to me. It hadn't seemed enough that he was an old mate of Richard's. Now I realized what the hidden agenda was. Like his buddies, Tony had been comfortable with the way things were run in the city. Like a lot of other people, he wasn't comfortable with what was happening now. They'd tried to sort it out themselves in the conventional ways, and that hadn't worked. Now Tony was wondering if he'd found a cleaner way of getting the new team off the patch. 'Somebody came to see me a couple of weeks ago,' he said obliquely. 'A pair of somebodies, to be precise. Very heavy-duty somebodies. They told me that if I wanted Manassas to carry on being a successful club, I should hand my promotions over to them. I told them I didn't negotiate with messengers and that if they wanted my business, the boss man had better get off his butt and talk face to face.'

I nodded. I liked his style. It was a gamble, but he was on his own turf, so it wasn't likely to have been too expensive. 'And?'

'They went away. Two nights later, I was walking from my car to my front door when three guys jumped me. They put a sack over my head and threw me in the back of a van. They drove me around for a while. Felt like we were going in circles. Then they tipped me out in a warehouse. And I met the boss.'

'Who is it, Tony?' I asked softly. He wasn't talking to me any more. He was talking to himself.

'Peter Lovell. Detective Inspector Peter Lovell. Of the Vice Squad. He's due to retire next year. So he's setting himself up in business now to make sure he can replace all his back-handers with a nice little earner.'

There was a long pause. Then eventually I said, 'What's he like, this Lovell?'

'You ask the plod, they'll probably tell you he's a model copper. He's got commendations, the lot. The top brass don't want to know the truth, do they? Long as their cleanup rate looks OK to the police committee, everything's hunky-dory. But this Lovell, he's a real bastard. He's on the pad with all the serious teams that really run the vice in this city. The faces behind the class-act brothels, the boss porn men, the mucky-movie boys, they're all paying Lovell's wages. But he makes it look good by picking up plenty of the small fry. Street girls, rent boys, any small-time operators that think they can live off the crumbs from the top lads' tables. When-ever Lovell needs a good body, they're his for the taking, there to make him look like a hero in the *Chronicle*. But he never touches anybody serious.' Tony's voice was bitter with contempt.

'What about his private life? He married?'

'Divorced. No kids.'

'Girlfriend?'

Tony shook his head, his mouth twisting in a grimace. 'Word is, he likes fresh meat. And his paymasters know it. Soon as they get some nice new recruit who's managed to avoid being raped, they give her to Lovell to break her in. Not too young, though. Not below about fourteen. He wouldn't like people to think he was a pervert.' He spat out the word as if it tasted as unpleasant as Lovell himself.

I took a deep breath. It was going to be a real pleasure to nail this bastard. 'How many people know he's the face behind the flyposting invasion?'

'Not many,' Tony said. 'It's not common knowledge, take

it from me. One or two of the big players on the music scene, not more than that. That's the only reason there's not a war on the streets right now. They're keeping the lid on it, because as long as Lovell's still on the force, he can screw us all one way or another. But somebody's got to put a stop to him. Or else there's going to be blood and teeth on the floor.'

I stood up. 'I'm going to have to think about this, Tony,' was all I said. We all knew what I meant.

He lit his cigarette and jammed it into the corner of his mouth.'Yeah,' he muttered, unfolding his body from the sofa and making for the door.

'I'll be in touch,' I said.

He jerked to a stop and half turned. 'No way,' he said. 'You want to talk, get Richard to call me and we'll set something up. I don't want you anywhere near Manassas, you hear?'

I heard. He walked out the door and I moved over to the window, snapping the standard lamp off as I went. I pulled the blind back a couple of inches and gazed down three storeys to the shiny wet street below. A taxi sat at the traffic lights, its diesel ticking noisily above the background hum of the city. The lights changed and the taxi juddered off.

'I've never worked for gangsters before,' I remarked as I watched Tony dodge out of the front door and double back past the student residence.

'It can't be that different. Some of your other clients have been just as dodgy, only they were wearing suits.'

'There's one crucial difference,' I said. 'With straight clients, if you succeed, they pay. With gangsters, unless you succeed, *you* pay. I'm not sure I can afford the price.'

Richard put an arm round my shoulders. 'Better not fail then, Brannigan.'

19

Even I don't know many people whose doors I can knock on just after one in the morning in the absolute certainty I won't be waking them up. But I didn't have any qualms about this particular door. I pressed the bell and waited, leaning up against the doorjamb to shelter from the persistent night rain.

After Tony had sloped off into the groovy world of nightclub Manchester, I'd felt too wired to go home to bed. Richard had tried to talk me into a Chinese followed by cool jazz in some Whalley Range cellar known only to a handful of the true faith. It hadn't been hard to say no. I've always thought jazz was for anoraks who think they're too intellectual for train spotting, and my stomach already felt like it had been stir-fried. Besides, I knew exactly how I could profitably fill the time till sleep ambushed me.

The door opened suddenly and, caught unawares, I tipped forward. I almost fell into Gizmo's arms. I don't know which of us was more appalled by the prospect, but we both jumped back like a pair of fifties teenagers doing the Bunny Hop. 'You don't believe in office hours, do you?' Gizmo demanded belligerently.

'No more than you do. You going to let me in? It's pissing it down out here,' I complained.

I followed him back upstairs to the computer room, where screens glowed softly in the dim interior and REM reminded me that night swimming deserves a quiet night. 'Tell me about it,' I muttered, shaking the raindrops from my head well out of range of any hardware.

'Gimme a minute,' he said. There were only two chairs in the room, both of them leather desk chairs. I sat in the one

Gizmo wasn't occupying and waited patiently while he finished whatever he'd been in the middle of doing. After ten minutes, I began to wish I'd brought my own games software with me. I cleared my throat. 'Be right there,' he said. 'This is crucial.'

A few more minutes passed and I watched the headlights on Stockport Road sneak round the edge of the blinds and send slender beams across the ceiling, an activity that could give counting sheep a run for its money. Then Gizmo hit a bunch of keys, pushed his chair away from the desk and swivelled round to face me. He was wearing an elderly plaid dressing gown over jeans that were ripped from age not fashion and an unironed granddad shirt. Eat your heart out, corporate man. 'Got some work for me, then?' he asked.

'Depends. You found another job yet?'

He snorted. 'Come round to take the piss, have you? Like I said, Kate, I'm too old to be a wunderkind any more. Nobody believes in you if you're old enough to vote and shave unless your name's Bill Gates. No, I haven't got another job yet.'

I took a deep breath. 'You make a bit of money on the side, don't you? Doing bits and pieces for people like me?'

'Yeah, but not enough to support a habit like this,' he said wryly, waving a hand round at the computers and their associated software and peripherals.

'But you're good at finding the weak points in systems and worming your way in, aren't you?'

He nodded. 'You know I'm the best.'

'How do you fancy working the other side of the street?'

He frowned suspiciously. 'Meaning what, exactly?'

'Meaning going straight. At least in normal working hours. Meaning, coming to work for me.'

'Thought you had a partner who did all the legit security stuff?' he demanded. 'I don't want charity, you know. I either want a proper job or nothing.'

'My partner is taking early retirement due to ill health,' I said grimly.

'What's the matter with him?'

'Delusional psychosis. He thinks he's in love and wants to live in Australia.'

Gizmo grinned. 'Sounds like an accurate diagnosis to me. So what's the job description?'

'We do a lot of corporate computer security work, liaising with their software engineers and consultants to make their systems as unbeatable as we can get them. We also work with people whose systems have been breached, both plugging the holes and trying to track what's been raided and where it's gone. We've done a little bit of work with banks and insurance companies tracking money that's been stolen by breaching Electronic Fund Transfers. I know enough about it to pitch for the business, but not enough to do the work. That's where I'm going to need to replace Bill. Interested?'

He spun round on his chair a couple of times. 'I think I might be,' he said. 'Are you talking a full-time job or ad hoc consultancy?'

'I'll be honest, Giz. Right now, I can't afford to take you on full time. Initially, it would have to be as and when I can bring the work in. But if you're as good as you say you are, we'll generate a lot of word-of-mouth business.'

He nodded noncommittally. 'When would you want me to start?'

'Mutually agreed date in the not-too-distant?'

'Dosh?'

'Fifty per cent of the net? Per job?'

'Gross.'

I shook my head. 'Net. I'm not a charity. Shelley has to put the pitch document together and she has to do all the admin. Her time comes off the fee. Plus phone expenses, faxes, photocopying. Most jobs, it's not big bucks. But sometimes it starts to run into money. Net or nothing.'

'I can live with it. Net it is. Six-month trial, see how we both go on?'

'Suits me. There is one thing though, Giz . . . ?' His red-rimmed eyes narrowed in suspicion. 'Well, two things,' I continued. 'A haircut and a smart suit.' I held a hand up to stem the protest I knew was coming. 'I know it breaks your heart to spend money on a suit that could be better spent on a new genlock adapter. And I know you think that anything more sophisticated than a number one all over once a year is for girlies, but these are deal breakers. If you like, I'll even come with you and make the process as painless as possible, but it's got to be done.'

Gizmo breathed out heavily through his nose. 'Fuck it, who do you think you are? I've managed to avoid that kind of shit working for Telecom, why should I do it for you?'

'Telecom have just fired you, Giz. Maybe corporate image had something to do with it, maybe not. Bottom line is, Telecom were a necessary evil for you. Working for me is going to be fun, and you know it. So get the haircut, get the suit.'

He scowled like a small boy who's been told to wash behind his ears. 'Yeah, well,' he growled, scuffing his heels on the floor. 'You drive a hard bargain.'

I smiled sweetly. 'You'll thank me for it one day. Let me know when you want to shop till you drop.'

I walked downstairs alone, leaving Gizmo staring at a screen. I still didn't know where the money was going to come from to buy Bill out. But at least I was starting to feel like it might be possible for the agency to earn enough to pay it back.

Rasul and Lal's sandwich bar is one of Manchester's best kept secrets. Nestled under the railway arches at the trendy rather than the glossy end of Deansgate, it produces some of the finest butties in town. They like to name sandwiches after their regular customers, and I'm proud to reveal there's a Brannigan Butty up there on the board – tuna and spring onion in mayo with black olives and tomatoes in crusty French bread. Strictly speaking, it's a takeaway, but in the room behind the shop some of us get to perch and munch. I'm not sure of the criteria Rasul and Lal apply for admission to the back shop, but I've found myself sharing the privileged space with doctors, lawyers, Equal Opportunities Commission executives and TV technicians. The one thing we all have in common is that we're refugees, hiding from our lives for as long as it takes to scoff a sandwich and swallow a coffee.

When I arrived in the back shop the following morning, Della was already there. She'd opted for an egg mayonnaise sandwich. I was feeling less traditional, going for a paratha with a spicy omelette on top. There was no one else around apart from the brothers. There seldom is around ten, which was why I'd chosen it for our meeting. This was one time I absolutely didn't want to be seen publicly with Della.

We gave each other as much of a hug and kiss as our breakfasts would allow. She looked like she'd had more sleep than me, her skin glowing, her green eyes clear, copper hair pulled back into the kind of chignon that never stayed neat for more than five minutes on me when I had the hair for it. On Della, there wasn't a stray hair to be seen. I couldn't quite work out why, but Della was getting better looking with every passing year. Maybe it had something to do with cheekbones her whole body seemed to hang from. 'Mysterious morning call,' she remarked as we cosied up in the corner between the fridge and the back door.

'You'll understand why when I tell you what I've got for you.'

'Goodies?' she inquired enthusiastically.

'Not so's you'd notice.' I bit into my sandwich. Anything to postpone the moment when I delivered the bad news.

Realizing I needed to work up to this one, Della said, 'We lifted your headstone con artists yesterday morning before their eyes were open. We'd fixed up an ID parade with some of the names you gave us, and we got enough positive identifications to persuade them that they might as well put their hands up and admit to the lot. Turns out they'd pulled the same routine in Birmingham and Plymouth before they turned up here. Nice work, Kate.'

'Thanks. By the way, on the subject of those two, something occurred to me which you've probably thought of already.'

'Mmm?'

'I was thinking about the business they're in. Mobile phones. I just wondered how straight the company is that they're working for. Given how many ways there are to make an illegal buck out of mobies, and given that this pair are cool as Ben and Jerry's in the way they operate, I wondered if it might be worth a poke about at Sell Phones.'

'You know, that might not be such a bad idea. I was so busy with my own team this week, I never gave it a thought.

But Allen and Sargent's arrest gives me the perfect excuse to get a search warrant on Sell Phones. Thanks for the thought,' Della said, looking slightly embarrassed that she hadn't worked it out for herself. I knew just how she felt; I've been there too many times myself.

'No problem. However I don't think you're going to be quite as thrilled about today's bulletin, somehow.'

'Come on, get it over with. It can't be as bad as all that. The only news that deserves a face like yours is that Josh is a serial killer.'

'What about a bent DI?' I said gloomily.

The smile vanished from Della's eyes. 'I don't have to ask if you're sure, do I?'

'It's possible somebody's setting me up, but I don't think so. It fits the facts too well.'

Della's mouth tightened into a grim line and she looked past me into the middle distance. 'I absolutely hate corrupt police officers,' she said bitterly. 'They've always got some pathetic piece of self-justification, and it never ever justifies the damage they do. So, who are we talking about here? Just tell me it's not one of mine.'

'It really isn't one of yours,' I said, knowing it was pretty bleak as reassurances go. 'It's a DI in Vice. Peter Lovell? Heard of him?'

Della's answer had to wait. Rasul came through to the fridge for another tray of sliced ham. 'All right?' he asked cheerfully, far too polite to indicate that the expressions on our faces showed the exact opposite.

'Fine,' we chorused.

When he'd left, Della said, 'I know who you mean. I've never had anything to do with him directly, never met him socially, but I have heard the name. He's supposed to be a good copper. High body count, keeps his patch clean. What's the story?'

'I'm not too sure of the exact wording on the charge sheet, but it goes something like threatening behaviour, assault, illegal possession of firearms, conspiracy, incitement to cause an affray, obtaining money with menaces, improper use of police resources . . . Oh, and illegal billposting.'

'If I didn't know you better, I'd say you were winding me up,' Della said wearily. She looked at her half-eaten sandwich. 'I just lost my appetite.' She was about to bin it, but I stopped her. For some reason I was ravenous this morning. I had the last mouthful of my paratha and started on her leftovers. Ignoring every environmental health regulation from Brussels to Baltimore, Della pulled out her cigarettes and Zippo and sucked on a Silk Cut. 'Details, then,' she said.

Lal stuck his head round the door into the shop. 'Can you crack the window if you're smoking, Del?' he asked. I was astonished. I'd never heard anyone contract Della's name and live. Not only did she ignore his liberty-taking, she even opened the window a couple of inches. Either Della was in a state of shock or there was something going on between her and Lal that I knew nothing about.

'It all started when Richard came home with Dan Druff and the Scabby Heided Bairns,' I began. By the time I'd finished, Della looked like she was about to have a second close encounter with the half-sandwich she'd already eaten. 'So right now, Lovell's winning,' I finished up. 'He's got the muscle to get what he wants, and the gangsters can't beat him the usual way because every time they make a move, their shock troops end up behind bars.'

'I can't believe he'd be so stupid,' she said. 'He must be looking at having his thirty in when he retires. That's a good pension, and he's young enough to pull something decent in private security. And he's risking the lot.'

I helped myself to a Kit Kat from an open box on a shelf behind me. 'He's risking a hell of a lot more than that,' I pointed out as I stripped the wrapper off. 'He's risking his life. The people he's dealing with can't afford to lose that much face. If the normal ways of warning someone off aren't working with Lovell, somebody is going to shell out the requisite five grand.'

'And then there *will* be a war. It doesn't matter how bent a bobby is, when he's dead, he's a hero. And when we lose one of our own, the police service doesn't stop till somebody has paid the price.'

'I think they realize that,' I said quietly. 'They'll have to be desperate before they go for a hit. But every week that goes by where money goes into Lovell's pocket instead of theirs is a week when the ratchet gets screwed a notch tighter. I don't know how far away desperation is for the likes of Collar di Salvo's lad, but I know some of the other players are really hurting.'

Della thumbed another cigarette out of the packet. 'So Greater Manchester Police has to put a stop to Lovell on humanitarian grounds? Is that what you're saying?'

'Something like that. But I'm not talking GMP, I'm talking DCI Della Prentice and a small hand-picked team. If Lovell's been on the force this long, he must have a fair few in his corner, and I don't see how you can be sure who they all are. You need outsiders like you've got in the Regional Crime Squad.'

Della did the time-wasting thing that smokers do to buy some space: fiddling with the cigarette, rolling the lighter round in her hand, examining the filter for holes. 'So what do you suggest?' she asked.

'An undercover operation?'

'Nice of you to volunteer.'

I shook my head. 'No way. I'm not sticking my head above the trench on this one. Remember, I'm the one who doesn't believe in private health insurance, and the waiting list for key organ transplants is too long for my liking.'

Della took another hit of nicotine then said, 'Bottle gone?'

'Cheeky bastard,' I growled. 'My bottle's as sound as it's ever been.'

'Really?' she drawled. God, I hate Oxbridge graduates. They learn that sarcastic drawl at their first tutorial and they never forget it. Those of us who grew up in the backstreets shadowed by the dreaming spires never got past the snarl.

'Yeah, really,' I snarled. 'You're the police, it's your job to catch criminals, remember?'

'Problem is, you're not bringing me any hard evidence,' Della said.

'So mount your own undercover operation. Leave me out of it.'

'It's hard for us, Kate. We don't have any way into an

undercover. We haven't got some tame club manager who's going to roll over and help us. And from what you've said, your contacts are not going to welcome Officer Dibble with open arms. They might well think it's better to deal with the devil they know. Whereas you . . .'

'Call yourself my friend, and you want me to go up against an animal like Lovell with his army of hard cases?'

Della shrugged. 'You know you'll have all the back up you need. Besides, from what you tell me, there's been a lot of mouth but not a lot of serious action. Nobody's been killed, nobody's even had a serious going-over. Mr Lovell's merry men seem to specialize in violence against property. When it comes to sorting people out, he seems to go for remarkably law-abiding means. He calls the police. I think you'd be perfectly safe.'

'Gee thanks,' I said.

Della put a hand on my arm. Her eyes were serious. 'I'm not asking you to do anything I wouldn't do myself. I'll hand-pick the back up team.'

'You think that makes me feel any better? Everybody knows you're an even madder bastard than I am!' I pointed out bitterly, knowing I was beaten.

'So you'll do it?'

'I'll call you when I've got the setup sorted,' I said resignedly. 'I'm not a happy camper, I want you to know that.'

'You won't regret this,' Della said, pulling me into a hug.

'I better not.'

Della paid for the Kit Kat on the way out.

I thought it was about time I showed my face in the office lest Bill got to thinking he could start the revolution without me. With luck, he would still be busy showing Sheila the delights of the NorthWest.

I don't know why I indulged myself with the notion that luck might be on my side. It had been out of my life so long I was beginning to think it had run off to sea. When I walked in Bill was sitting on Shelley's desk, going through a file with her. Given that I wasn't speaking to Bill and Shelley wasn't speaking to me, it looked like an interesting conversation might be on the cards. 'Kate,' Bill greeted me with a cheerful boom. 'Great to see you.' And I am Marie of Romania.

'Hi,' I said to no one in particular. 'Has anything come for me from the Land Registry?'

'If you checked your in-tray occasionally, you'd know, wouldn't you?' Shelley said acidly. It probably wasn't the time to tell her I'd gone through it at one that morning. Not if I wanted to keep my office manager.

'Have you thought any more about the implications of my move?' Bill asked anxiously.

I stopped midway to my office door, threw my hands up in mock amazement and said, 'Oh dearie me, I *knew* there was something I was supposed to be thinking about. Silly me! It just slipped my mind.' I cast my eyes up to the ceiling and marched into my office. 'Of course I've bloody thought about it,' I shouted as I closed the door firmly behind me. People who ask asinine questions should expect rude answers.

The letter from the Land Registry was sitting right on top of my in-tray. Their speed these days never ceases to amaze me. What I can't work out is why it still takes solicitors two months to convey a house from one owner to another. I flipped through the photocopied sheets of information that came with the covering letter. It confirmed the suspicion that had jumped up and down shouting, 'See me, Mum, I'm dancing!' when I'd interviewed Helen Maitland.

I might have been warned off talking to Sarah Blackstone's former patients. But Alexis hadn't said anything about her former lover.

20

I'd gone into my first interview with the real Dr Helen Maitland without enough background information. I wasn't about to make the same mistake twice. After a late lunch in a Bradford curry café that cost less than a trip to McDonald's, I parked up in a street of back-to-back terraced houses that spilled down a hill on the fringe of the city centre. Half a dozen Asian lads and a couple of white ones were playing cricket on a scrap of waste ground where one of the houses had been demolished. When I didn't get out of the car at once, they stopped playing and stared curiously at me. I wasn't interesting enough to hold their attention for long, and they soon returned to their game.

I sat staring at a house halfway down the street. It looked well kempt, its garden free of weeds and its paintwork intact. It was a door I hadn't knocked on for a few years, and I had no idea what kind of welcome I'd get. Even so, it still felt like a more appealing prospect than quizzing Sarah Blackstone's medical colleagues. I'd first come here in search of a missing person. Not long after I'd found her, she ended up murdered, with her girlfriend the prime suspect. My inquiries had cleared the girlfriend, but in the process, I'd opened a lot of wounds. I hadn't spoken to Maggie Rossiter, the girlfriend, since the trial. But she was still on the office Christmas card list. Not because I ever expected her to put work our way, but because I'd liked her and hadn't been able to come up with a better way of saying so.

Maggie was a social worker and a volunteer worker at a local drug rehab unit, though you wouldn't suspect either role on first encounter. She could be prickly, sharp tongued and fierce. But I'd seen the other side. I'd seen her tenderness and her grief. Not everyone can forgive that sort of knowledge. I hoped Maggie was one who could.

I sat for the best part of an hour, listening to the rolling news programme on Radio Five Live to fight the boredom. Then an elderly blue Ford Escort with a red offside front wing drew up outside Maggie's house. As the car door opened, a small calico cat leapt from the garden to the wall to the pavement and wove itself round the legs of the woman who emerged. Maggie had had her curly salt-and-pepper hair cropped short at the back and sides, but otherwise she looked pretty much the same as when I'd seen her last, right down to the extra few pounds round the middle. She bent to scoop up the cat, draped it over her shoulder and took a briefcase and an armful of files out of the car. I watched her struggle into the house and gave it five more minutes.

One of my rules of private investigation is, always try to leave an interviewee happy enough that they'll talk to you a second time. I was about to find out how well I'd practised what I preached. When the door opened, hostility replaced interested curiosity so fast on Maggie's face that I wondered whether I'd imagined the first expression. 'Well, well, well,' she said. 'If it isn't Kate Brannigan, girl detective. And whose life are you buggering up this week?'

'Hello, Maggie,' I said. 'I don't suppose you'd believe me if I said I was just passing?'

'Correct,' she said sarcastically. 'I'd also tell you that next time you're passing, just pass.'

'I know you blame me for Moira's death . . .'

'Correct again. You going for three in a row?'

'If I hadn't brought her back, he'd just have hired somebody else. Probably somebody with even fewer scruples.'

'It's hard to believe people with fewer scruples than you exist,' Maggie said.

'Don't you ever listen to *Yesterday in Parliament*?'

In spite of herself, Maggie couldn't help cracking a smile. 'Give me one good reason why I shouldn't close the door,' she said.

'Lesbians will suffer?' I tried, a half-grin quirking my mouth.

'I don't think so,' she sighed. The door started to close.

'I'm not joking, Maggie,' I said desperately. 'My client's a lesbian who could be facing worse than a murder charge if I don't get to the bottom of the case.'

The door stopped moving. I'd hooked her, but she wasn't letting me reel her in too easily. 'Worse than a murder charge?' she asked, her face suspicious.

'I'm talking about losing her child. And not for any of the conventional reasons.'

Maggie shook her head and swung the door open. 'This had better be good,' she warned me.

I followed her indoors and aimed for a rocking chair that hadn't been there the last time I'd visited. The shelves of books, records and tapes looked the same. But she'd replaced the big Klimt with a blue-and-white print from Matisse's *Jazz* sequence. It made the room cooler and brighter. 'I know I've got a cheek asking you for help, but I don't care how much I have to humiliate myself to do the business for my clients.' I tried for the self-effacing look.

'Ain't too proud to beg, huh?' Maggie said sardonically.

'I'm hoping you won't make me. But I am going to have to ask you to promise me one thing.'

'Which is?' she asked, sitting on the arm of the sofa, one foot on the seat, the other still on the floor.

'That you'll treat what I have to tell you with the same degree of confidence you'd offer to one of your own clients.'

'If you want confidentiality, you can afford to pay a therapist for it. My clients don't have that option. But if that's the price for hearing this tale of yours, consider it paid. Nothing you tell me goes beyond these four walls, unless I think people are going to come to harm if I keep silence. Is that fair enough?'

'That'll do me. Did you know a doctor called Sarah Blackstone?'

The way her face closed down gave me the answer. 'Tell me your tale. Then we'll see about questions,' Maggie said, her voice harsh.

Time to rearrange the truth into a well-known phrase or saying. 'My client and her partner were patients of Dr Blackstone. She was using them as human guinea pigs in an experiment to see if it's possible to make babies from two women. It is. And my client's partner is currently a couple of months pregnant.' Maggie's attitude had melted like snow on a ceramic hob. She was staring at me with the amazement of a child who's just had Christmas explained to her. Then she remembered.

'But Sarah Blackstone's just been murdered,' she breathed. 'Oh my God.'

'Exactly. Publicly, the police are saying she was killed by a burglar she disturbed. It's only a matter of time before the words "drug-crazed" start showing up in their press briefings. My client is concerned that they have uncovered what Dr Blackstone was really doing, but they're keeping quiet about it while they carry out their investigations.'

'So why are you here?'

Good question. This time, I'd had plenty of time to think about the interview so I had my lies ready. 'I'm trying to get as much background on Sarah Blackstone as I possibly can. If there was more to her killing than meets the eye, I want to find out who was behind it. That way, I can hand the information to the police on a plate, which might stop any kind of investigation into what Sarah was really up to.'

'Sounds plausible. But then, you always did,' Maggie commented. She didn't appear to be overwhelmed with the desire to help me out.

'I don't have any contacts on the lesbian scene this side of the Pennines except you,' I said. 'Believe me, if there had been any other way of getting into this, I'd have gone for it. Being here under these circumstances probably thrills me about as much as it does you. But I need help, Maggie. If what Sarah Blackstone was doing gets into the public domain, there's going to be more than just an outcry. There's going to be a witch-hunt.'

Maggie wasn't meeting my eyes. She looked like she was giving the matter serious thought and she didn't want to be distracted by any more passion from me. Eventually, she glanced across at me and said, 'I might be able to help you with some aspects of your inquiry.'

'Did you know Sarah Blackstone?'

Maggie shrugged. 'Not well. We met through Women's Aid. I'm involved with the refuge in Leeds as well as the one here. Sarah used to run an informal clinic at the refuge in Leeds. She was also one of the doctors they call out to provide medical evidence when they get emergency admissions of women and children who have been badly beaten. We were both on the management committee up until a couple of years ago when Sarah resigned. She said she didn't have the time to give it the energy it demanded.'

'What was she like?'

A smile ghosted on Maggie's face. 'She was exhausting. One of those women who's always full of bounce, never doing anything by halves. Ambitious, clever, committed. She gave up a lot of her time for the causes she believed in. Passionate about the women she dealt with professionally. A great sense of humour. She could be a real clown sometimes.'

'You make her sound like Mother Teresa.'

Maggie gave a bark of laughter. 'Sarah Blackstone? God, no. She had the faults to match her virtues. Like every doctor I've ever met, she was convinced she knew better than God. She was stubborn, arrogant and sometimes flippant about things that are never funny. And when she got a bee in her bonnet about something, she wouldn't leave it alone until everybody had agreed to go along with her ideas.'

'Did you see much of her socially?'

'A bit. We'd end up at the same parties, barbecues, benefits, you know the sort of thing.'

Only by reputation, thank God. 'Was she involved with anyone when she died?' I asked. If Maggie was going to block me, this was where it would start.

'I don't think so,' Maggie said. She appeared to be sincere. 'The last relationship she was in ended round about the end of last summer. The woman she was seeing, Diana, moved to Exeter to start a new job, and there wasn't enough between them for the relationship to survive. They'd been knocking around together for the best part of a year, but not in a committed kind of way. There was always something a bit aloof about Sarah, as if she didn't want to let anyone too close.'

'Did that include Helen Maitland?'

Maggie's eyebrows shot up. 'That's been over for years. How did you hear about Helen and Sarah?'

'Sarah used Helen's name as an alias. I wasn't sure whether the connection between them went deeper than colleagues.' All perfectly truthful, as far as it went. There really wasn't any need to tell Maggie that my suspicions had been confirmed by the Land Registry. Before Helen Maitland's house had been registered in her sole name, it had been jointly owned by Dr Maitland and Dr Sarah Blackstone. I don't know many people who buy houses with anyone other than their lover.

Maggie's mouth twisted into a rueful grimace. 'And I just told you it did, didn't I?'

'Well, I had my suspicions,' I said. 'What was the score there?'

'Oh well, in for a penny . . . Let me see now . . . It must be six or seven years ago that they first got together. Helen was already in Leeds when Sarah arrived, and it was one of those thunderbolt things. I remember the night they met – it was at a Lesbian Line benefit. Somebody introduced them and they looked at each other like they both had concussion. They moved in together within a couple of weeks, and eventually bought a house together. Then it all fell apart.'

'Why?'

Maggie squeezed the bridge of her nose between her thumb and forefinger, like a woman who's suddenly discovered she's got a sinus headache. 'I had a lot on my mind,' she said quietly. 'It was around three years ago. Not a good time for me.'

I stayed silent, remembering. It had been hard enough for me to accept Moira's death. For Maggie, it must have been a waking nightmare. I waited without impatience for her to fast forward from the worst days of her life. Some things even I'm sensitive to. After a few moments, she stopped massaging her forehead and tuned back in to the here and now. 'I don't know if I ever knew the exact details, but I certainly don't remember them now. I've got a feeling it had something to do with Helen wanting kids and Sarah not. Whatever it was, it was serious. As far as I know, they never spoke again after the bust-up except through their lawyers. A mate of mine acted for Sarah and she said she'd never seen anything like it. It was as if they went from total love to total hatred overnight.'

'That's interesting,' I said, my brain working overtime. My first thought was that she'd got the bit about the kids the wrong way round. Then I thought about what it would mean if she hadn't.

Before I could pursue that line, Maggie shook her head wonderingly and said, 'Oh, so that's what this is about, is it? Looking for a suitable dyke to replace your client on the suspect list?'

'You know I don't work like that. If I did, I'd have told the police about a certain incident three years ago . . .'

Her embarrassment was obvious even if it didn't stretch to an apology. 'Yeah, well,' she said. 'Helen's not the type. Believe me, I know her. She went out with my best mate for about a year not long after she came to Leeds. Anyway, Helen's had stuff to deal with in the last year that must have seemed a hell of a lot more significant to her than whatever Sarah Blackstone was up to.'

'Like what?'

'Like cervical cancer. She had to have a complete hysterectomy. She's only been back at work for about three months.'

I felt like a fruit machine with two lemons up and a fistful of nudges. 'And has she been involved with anyone since Sarah?' I thought I knew the answer, but it's always worth checking.

'Oh yes,' Maggie said. 'She's got a girlfriend in York. Flora. A librarian at the university. Masses of black hair, like one of those Victorian maidens in distress.'

'I think I've met her. Looks like she'd break if you spoke too loud?'

'You'd think so to see her doing that vulnerable innocent routine. But when you watch her in action, you soon see she's tough as old boots. If St George had rescued her from a dragon, he'd not have had her home long before he realized he'd spared the wrong one. And when it comes to Helen Maitland, that Flora's besotted. You could see from early on. Flora had Helen in her sights, and she was going to have her. A ruthless charm offensive, that's what it was. You never get the chance to get Helen on her own these days. Flora's never more than a heartbeat away.'

'How long have they been together?'

Maggie frowned, trying to recall. 'It's been a while now. Since before Helen was diagnosed. Mind I get the impression that if it hadn't been for the cancer and the fact that she needed the emotional support, Helen would have dumped Flora a long time ago. You often see it in relationships – you get the one who worships and the one who's not much more than fond. Well, Helen's not the worshipper here. But she definitely wasn't hankering after Sarah, if that's what you're thinking. That relationship was dead and buried well before Sarah died,' she added definitely.

Before I could say more, the front door opened and a tall woman in her twenties wearing an ambulance paramedic's uniform walked in. 'Hi, hon,' she said to Maggie, moving into the room and kissing the top of her head. She grinned at me. 'Hi. We've not met.'

'This is Amanda. She's the one who burns your Christmas cards,' Maggie said drily.

The tall woman's face darkened in a scowl. 'You're Kate Brannigan?' she demanded.

'That's me.'

'My God,' she said. 'You've got a nerve. How dare you come round here hassling us! Haven't you done enough?' She took an involuntary step towards me.

I got to my feet. 'It's probably time I was going,' I said.

'You're not wrong,' the paramedic snapped.

'It's all right, Mand,' Maggie said, reaching out and touching her partner lightly on the hip. 'I'll walk you to your car, Kate.'

Amanda stood on the step watching us down the path. 'She thinks you're the one who broke my heart,' Maggie said as we walked up the hill towards my car. 'I thought so too for a while. It took me about a year to realize I'd been idealizing

Moira. She was a wonderful woman, but she wasn't really the fabulous creature I had constructed in my mind. If I'm brutally honest, I have to admit we'd never have gone the distance. There were too many things that separated us. But Amanda . . . With her, I do feel like I've got a future. So on the rare occasions when I remember you're on the planet, I don't think of you with anger. I think of you as the person who probably kept me out of prison so that I was free to meet Amanda.'

We had reached my car. I held out a hand and we shook. 'Thanks,' I said.

'That's us quits now.'

I watched her walk back down the pavement. She took the steps to her front door at a run and fell into the kind of hug that would have got her arrested twenty years before. I hoped I'd still be off her hate list by the end of this case.

I walked up the wide path and stopped by the Egyptian temple, sitting down on a stone plinth between the paws of a sphinx. Over to one side, I could just see the columns of a Graeco-Roman temple, complete with enough angels for a barbershop quartet, if not a full heavenly choir. I leaned back and contemplated a Gothic spire like a scaled down version of Edinburgh's Scott Monument. The watery spring sunshine greened the grass up in sharp contrast to the granite and millstone grit. There's nothing quite like a Victorian cemetery for contemplation.

I didn't have to be back in Manchester until eight, and I needed a bit of space to think about the fragmented pieces of information I'd picked up about Sarah Blackstone's life and death. I'd persuaded myself without too much difficulty that I didn't really have enough time to nip over to Leeds and start interrogating the IVF-unit staff. Instead, Undercliffe Cemetery, out on the Otley Road, seemed the perfect answer, with its views across Bradford and its reminders of mortality. Surrounded by obelisks, crosses, giant urns, elaborately carved headstones and mock temples, thinking about death seemed the most natural thing in the world.

According to Alexis, the burglar who had allegedly been

disturbed by Sarah Blackstone hadn't actually stolen anything. The only thing missing from the scene was the murder weapon, believed to be a kitchen knife. I found it hard to get my head around that. Even if he'd only just broken in when she walked in on him, there should have been some sign that a theft was in progress, even if it was only a gathering together of small, portable valuables. The other thing was the knife. If the murder weapon came from the kitchen, the reasonable burglar's response would be to drop it or even to leave it in the wound. That's because a burglar would be gloved up. A proper burglar wouldn't need to take the knife with him in case he'd left any forensic traces. Even the drug-crazed junkie burglar would have the sense to realize that taking the knife was a hell of a risk. It's harder to lose good-quality knives than most people think. They've got a way of getting themselves found sooner or later.

So if it wasn't a bona fide burglar, who was it? I shivered as a cold blast of moorland wind caught the back of my neck. I turned my collar up and hunched into the lee of the sphinx. Sarah Blackstone posed a risk to the future of her colleagues, there was no denying that. But the more I thought about it, the less likely it seemed that she'd been killed for that. Even if her secret had been discovered, presumably no one else was directly implicated. In spite of the truism that mud sticks, in my experience it dries pretty quickly and once it's been whitewashed over, nobody remembers it was ever there in the first place. So I could probably strike the angry/frightened colleagues.

There was no doubt in my mind that some of the babies Sarah Blackstone had made owed more to the doctor than the exercise of her skills. Her eggs had gone into the mix, and I had the evidence of my own eyes that she had cruelly duped some of her patients. Even though I'm a woman who'd rather breed ferrets than babies, I can imagine how devastating it would be to discover that a child you thought came equipped with half your genes was in fact the offspring of an egomaniac. I could imagine how Alexis would react if the child Chris was carrying was the result of so wicked a deception. It would be as well for Sarah Blackstone that she was already dead. So there was a group of women out there who, if they'd managed to put two and two together and unravel Sarah Blackstone's real identity, had an excellent motive for murder.

And then there was Helen Maitland.

21

The hardest part had been getting Tony Tambo to play. Briefing me was as far as he had wanted to go. Tony and his friends didn't mind pitting me against DI Lovell and his thugs, but they drew the line at taking too many risks themselves. I knew there was no point in simply phoning him and asking him to cooperate in a sting. What I needed was a pressure point. That's why I'd taken a trip to a certain Italian espresso bar before I'd gone to Bradford.

Every morning between eleven and twelve, Collar di Salvo sits in a booth at the rear of Carpaccio, just round the corner from the Crown Court building. Collar likes to think of himself as the Godfather of Manchester. In reality, the old man's probably got closer links to the media than the Mafia. Even though he was born in the old Tripe Colony in Miles Platting, Collar affects an Italian accent. He has legitimate businesses, but his real income comes from the wrong side of the law. Nothing heavy duty for Collar; a bit of what Manchester calls taxing and other, less subtle, cities call protection rackets; counterfeit leisurewear, mock auctions and ringing stolen cars are what keeps Mrs di Salvo in genuine Cartier jewellery and Marina Rinaldi clothes. And definitely no drugs.

The story goes that Collar got his nickname from his method of persuading rival taxation teams to find another way of earning a living. He'd put a dog collar round their neck, attach a leash to it and loop the leash over an overhead beam in his warehouse. Then a couple of his strong-arm boys would take the dog for a walk . . . History tells us that the competition took up alternative occupations in droves.

In recent years, with the rise of the drug lords, Collar's style of management and range of crimes has started to look like pretty small potatoes. But his is still a name that provokes second thoughts for anybody on the fringes of legality in Manchester. Given that young Joey, the heir apparent, was supposedly involved in the flyposting business, Collar seemed the obvious person to talk to. We'd never met and we owed each other no favours; but equally, I couldn't think of any reason why Collar wouldn't listen.

I walked confidently down the coffee bar and stopped opposite the old man's booth. 'I'd like to buy you a coffee, Mr di Salvo,' I said. He likes everyone around him to act like they're in a movie. It made me feel like an idiot, but that's not an unusual sensation in this job.

His large head was like the ruin of one of those Roman busts you see in museums, right down to the broken nose. Dark, liquid eyes like a spaniel with conjunctivitis looked me up and down. 'Is-a my pleasure, Signorina Brannigan,' he said with a stately nod. That he knew who I was simply confirmed everything I'd ever heard about him. The thug sitting opposite him slid out of the booth and moved to a table a few feet away.

I sat down. 'Life treating you well?'

He shrugged like he was auditioning for Scorsese. 'Apart from the tax man and the VAT man, I have no complaints.'

'The family well?'

'Cosi, cosa.'

Two double espressos arrived on the table, one in front of each of us. Never mind that I'd really wanted a cappuccino and a chunk of panettone. Fuelled by this much caffeine, I'd be flying to Bradford. 'The matter I wanted to discuss with you concerns Joey,' I said, reaching for the sugar bowl to compound the felony.

His head tilted to one side, revealing a fold of wrinkled chicken skin between his silk cravat and his shirt collar. 'Go on,' he said softly.

Joey was Collar's grandson and the apple of his beady eye. His father Marco had died in a high-speed car chase a dozen years ago. Now Joey was twenty, trying and failing to live up to the old man's expectations. The trouble with Joey was that temperamentally he took after his mother, a gentle Irish woman who had never quite recovered from the shock of discovering that the man she had agreed to marry was a gangster rather than a respectable second-hand car salesman. Joey had none of the di Salvo ruthlessness and all the Costello kindness. He was never going to make it as a villain, but his grandfather would have to be six feet under before Joey got the chance to find out what his real métier was. Until then, Collar was going to be faced with people like me bringing him the bad news.

'His flyposting business is suffering. I won't insult your intelligence by outlining the problem. I'm sure you know all about Detective Inspector Lovell. I'm sure you also know that conventional means of dealing with the problem are proving ineffective because of Lovell's access to law enforcement. Joey's difficulty happens to coincide with that of my client, and I'm offering to provide a solution that will make this whole thing go away.' I stopped talking and took a sip of the lethal brew in my cup. My mouth felt sulphurous and dark, like the pits of hell.

'Very commendable,' he said, one liver-spotted hand reaching inside his jacket and emerging with a cigar that could have done service as a pit prop, always supposing there were any pits left.

'I need your help to make it work,' I continued as he chopped the end off his cigar and sucked indecently on it. 'I need Tony Tambo's cooperation, and I don't have sufficient powers of persuasion to secure it.'

'And you hope' – puff – 'that in exchange' – puff – 'for you getting Joey off the hook' – puff – 'I will persuade Tony to help?'

'That's exactly right, Mr di Salvo.'

'Why you want Tambo?'

'DI Lovell has been keeping a low profile. Not a lot of people know he's behind these attempts to take over the turf. But Tony's already had a face-to-face with him, so the man's got nothing to lose by coming in to a meeting. All Tony has to do is set it up. I'll do the rest. It's my head on the block, nobody else's.'

Collar nodded. He closed his eyes momentarily. That didn't stop him abusing my air space with his cigar. His eyes opened and he stared into mine. Any more ham and he could have opened a deli counter. 'You got it,' he said. 'Unless you hear otherwise, the meet will be at Tambo's club, half past eight, tonight. OK?'

'OK.' I didn't want to ask how he was going to get it sorted that fast. To be honest, I didn't want to know. I stood up and was about to thank him when he said menacingly, 'You don't like your coffee?'

I'd had enough of playing games. 'It looks like sump oil and tastes worse,' I said.

I thought he was going to bite the end off his cigar. Then he smiled, like a python who finds a dancing mouse too entertaining to eat. I paid for both coffees on the way out, though. I'm not that daft.

Eight o'clock and Della Prentice had her hand down the front of my most audacious underwired bra. We were in an interview room at Bootle Street nick, and Della was making sure the radio mike was firmly anchored to the infrastructure of my cleavage. If Lovell paid the kind of attention to breasts that most Vice cops are prone to, I didn't want anything showing that shouldn't be. Nipples were one thing, radio mikes another altogether.

'Right,' said Della. 'He's not going to spot that unless things get rather more out of hand than we're anticipating.' She stepped back and gave me the once-over. I'd gone for a shiny gun-metal lycra leotard over black leggings and the black hockey boots I normally reserved for a bit of cat burglary. Draped over the leotard was an old denim jacket with slashed sleeves that revealed the temporary tattoos I'd got stencilled on both biceps. The make-up aimed for the recovering-junkie look; the hair was gelled into a glossy helmet. 'Very tasteful,' she commented.

'You can talk,' I muttered. Della wore a white shirt with the collar turned up and the buttons undone almost as far as her navel. The shirt tucked into a black lycra skirt a little wider than the average weightlifter's belt. Her legs were bare, her feet sensibly shod in flat-soled pumps. From her vantage point washing glasses behind the bar, no one would see more than the tarty top half and immediately dismiss her. With her hair loose and enough make-up to change the shape of eyes and mouth, Lovell was never going to recognize a woman DCI who might have been pointed out to him a couple of times across a crowded canteen. 'Did you manage to pick up anything on the grapevine about Lovell?' I asked.

She pulled a face. 'Not a lot. I didn't want word getting back to him that I was interested. I heard his wife divorced him because he was too handy with his fists, but that's hardly exceptional in the Job. What I did find out, though, was that he claims to have a couple of weeks' time-share in a villa in Lanzarote. Very tasteful property up in the hills, swimming pool, terraced garden, half a dozen *en suite* bedrooms. A little bit of poking around and the calling in of a couple of favours reveals that the holding company that owns the villa is in turn wholly owned by Peter Lovell. Since the property's worth the thick end of quarter of a million, it does raise one or two questions about DI Lovell's finances.'

'Nice one, Della,' I said.

'That's not quite the end of it,' she said as we walked up to the waiting car. 'An old school friend of mine is married to a chap who manages one of the vineyards there, so I gave her a call. Her husband knows Lovell. Clothes by Versace, car by Ferrari, part owner of a restaurant, a bar and two discos in Puerto del Carmen,' she said, her voice tight with anger.

'Obviously not the kind of life style one could sustain on a police pension.'

'Quite. And about bloody time his gravy train hit the buffers. Let's go and make it happen.'

The plan was simple enough. Della would be inside the club watching what was going down. Three of her most trusted lieutenants would be hidden within yards of the main bar where the meeting was scheduled for – two in the ladies' loo, one behind the DJ's setup. Another four hand-picked officers would be stationed outside the club, listening to the transmission from my radio mike. When they had enough on tape to hang Lovell out to dry, they would move in and relieve him of his liberty. A classic sting.

Considering Tony had only had eight hours to sort everything out, he'd come up with a credible cover story for me. I was the keyboard player in a new all-female band. We'd allegedly got together in Germany and we'd been touring in Europe, so successfully that we already had a recording contract with a small indie label in Hamburg. But we wanted more, so we'd come back to Britain to make a full-frontal assault on the music scene in a bid to get a major label contract. Because we were already fairly established, we didn't want to piss around. We wanted promotion, we wanted exposure. We wanted it fast and we wanted it top quality. And we'd told Tony Tambo we wanted to talk to the top man because we weren't going to waste time or money. Now I just had to pray that Lovell would give us enough to pull him on, or I was going to owe so many favours the only solution would be to leave town.

Thinking of favours reminded me of my grave robbers. 'Did you turn over Sell Phones?' I asked.

Della nodded. 'We sent a team in this morning. The shop was clean, but one of my bright boys noticed there was a trap door for a cellar. And lo and behold, there was a phone room down below.'

'A phone room?'

Della raised her eyebrows. 'You mean I've finally found a scam you haven't heard about?'

'Try me.'

'OK. There's a little electronic box you can buy that allows you to eavesdrop on mobile phone calls. What it also tells you is the phone number of the mobile phone that's being used, and its electronic code number. With that information, you can reprogram the silicon chip in a stolen phone and turn it into a clone of a legitimate phone. You can then use that phone to call all over the world until the cellphone company cottons on and cuts you off. Normally, you can get a few hours' worth of calls, but if you're making international calls, sometimes they cut you off within the hour. So if you're cloning phones, you set aside a room with a dozen or so cloned phones in it, and hire the room out for, say, £20 per person per hour, and as soon as one phone gets cut off, the hirer just moves on to the next phone on the table. The hirer gets their calls dirt cheap and untraceable. And the crook's got virtually no outlay once they've got the original scanner and stolen phones.'

'And you found one of these at Sell Phones?'

'We did.'

'So I'm flavour of the month?'

'Let's see how tonight goes down.'

At ten past eight, Della and I descended into the club via the fire escape, as I'd prearranged with Tony. He was waiting for us, nervously toking on his Camel. 'Your friends got here,' he said, his unease and resentment obvious.

'Where are we going to do this?' I asked.

Tony pointed to a small circular table in the far corner, surrounded on three sides by a banquette. 'That's my table, everybody knows that. Anywhere else and he's going to be even more suspicious than he is already.'

I followed him across the room while Della made for the bar and the dirty glasses stacked ready for her. The lights were up, stripping Manassas bare of any pretensions to glamour or cool. In the harsh light, the carpet looked stained and tacky, the furnishings cheap and chipped, the colours garish and grotesque. It was like seeing a torch singer in the harsh dressing-room lights before she's applied her stage make-up. The air smelled of stale sweat, smoke and spilled drink overlaid with a chemically floral fragrance that caught the throat like the rasp of cheap spirit.

Tony gestured for me to precede him into the booth. I shook my head. There was no way I was going to be sandwiched between him and Lovell. It wasn't beyond the bounds of possibility that I was about to become the victim of a classic double-cross, and if Tony Tambo had decided to hitch his wagon to the rising star rather than the comet starting to dip below the horizon, I wasn't about to make it any easier for him. 'You go in first,' I told him.

He scowled and muttered under his breath, but he did what he was told, slipping over upholstery cloth made smooth by

202

hundreds of sliding buttocks. I perched right on the end of the seat, so Lovell wasn't going to be able to corner me without making a big issue of it. Tony pulled the heavy glass ashtray towards him. 'I hope you know what you're doing,' he said.

'So do I. Or we're all up shit creek.'

'I fuckin' hate you women with the smart mouths, acting like you've got balls when all you've got is bullshit,' he said bitterly, crushing out the remains of the cigarette with the sort of venom most people reserve for ex-lovers.

'You think I like hanging out with gangstas? Get real, Tony. It'll all be over soon, anyway.'

He snorted. 'So you say. Me, I think this'll be rumbling round for a long while yet.' He leaned forward and shouted in Della's direction. 'Hey, you!' Della looked up from the glass she was polishing. 'Do something useful and bring me a fuckin' big Southern Comfort and lemonade.'

Della's look would have shrivelled Priapus, but Tony was too tense to care. 'You want the usual, Kate?' she asked me. I nodded.

The door at the far end of the club crashed open with the force that only a boot can produce. All three of us swung round, startled. In the doorway stood a tall, thin man dressed in the kind of warm-up suit top tennis players wear when arriving at Wimbledon. He was flanked by two men who could have played line backer in an American football team without bothering with the body padding. Their shoulders were so wide they'd have had to enter my house sideways. They looked like they were built, not born, complete with suits cut so boxy they could have been constructed out of Lego.

The trio moved across the room at a measured pace and I had the chance to take a proper look at Peter Lovell. He had a narrow head with the regular features of a fifties matinée idol, an image nurtured by a head of thick brown hair swept straight back like Peter Firth's. It was an impression that crumbled at closer range, when skin wrecked by teenage acne became impossible to disguise or to deflect attention from. He stopped a few feet away from me, his minders closing ranks behind him. His eyes were like two granite pebbles, cold and grey as the North Sea in January. 'Segue,' he said contemptuously, his voice like hard soles on gravel. 'What kind of a name is that?'

'It's Italian,' I said. 'It means "it follows". Which means my band is the next big thing, yeah?'

'That depends. And you're Cory?'

'That's right. Tony says you're the business when it comes to getting a band on the map.'

Lovell slipped into the seat opposite me. 'A brandy, Tony,' he said. 'Best you've got, there's a good lad.'

'A large Hennessy over here, girl,' Tony shouted. 'What's keeping you?'

I didn't even glance at Della. 'So what can you do for us, Mr . . . ?'

'My company's called Big Promo. You can call me Mr Big or Mr Promo, depending how friendly you want to be,' he said without a hint of irony.

I acted like I was deeply unimpressed. 'The question stands,' I said. 'We're really cooking in Europe, but this is where the serious deals get made. We want to be noticed, and we don't want to hang around. We don't want to be pissed about by somebody who doesn't really know what they're doing, who isn't up to playing with the big boys.'

Something approaching a smile cracked his face. 'Attitude, eh? Well, Cory, attitude is no bad thing in its place.' Then he leaned forward and the smile died faster than a fly hitting a windscreen at ninety. 'This is not the place. I'm not in the habit of dealing directly with people. It wastes time I could be using to make money. So the least, the very least, I demand from you is respect.'

'Fine by me,' I said. 'So can we stop wasting your time? What can you do for us that makes you the one we should do business with?'

'Why don't you have a manager?' he demanded.

'We never found anybody we trusted enough. Believe it or not, I'm a qualified accountant. I can tell a good deal from a bad one.'

'Then we're not going to have any problems. I'm offering

the only good deal in town. This is my city. In exchange for forty per cent of your earnings, including any record deals you sign, I can place you in the key venues. I can make sure your tickets get sold, I can get you media coverage and I can paper the whole city with your tits.' Lovell leaned back as Della approached with our drinks on a tray. Sensibly, she served Lovell first, then me, then Tony. As she walked away, Lovell said, 'Since when did you start employing pensioners?'

'All she does is sort the glasses and stock the bar. She's out of here before the punters start coming in. The girlfriend's auntie,' Tony said dismissively.

'I hear on the grapevine that there's been a bit of bother lately. Posters getting covered up, bands having their gigs wrecked, that kind of shit. What's to stop that happening to us?' I asked.

Lovell drummed his fingers on his brandy bowl. 'Signing with us, that's what. You stupid cow, who do you think has been handing out the aggravation? I told you, this is my city. Anybody who thinks different has to take what's coming to them. You stick with me and nothing bad will happen to you. Ask Tony. He pays his taxes like a good 'un. You never have any bother, do you, Tone?'

'No,' Tony said tonelessly, reaching for his cigarettes and lighting up. 'No bother.'

'Let me get this straight, then. You're saying if we pay you forty per cent of everything we make, you'll sort it for us. But if we choose somebody whose prices are more in line with the rest of the planet, we'll live to regret it? Is that what you're saying?'

Lovell picked up his glass and wasted the brandy in one swallow. 'Sixty per cent of something's a lot better than a hundred per cent of fuck all. There's a lot of things can go wrong for a band trying to make a break in this town. Posters that never make it onto walls. Tickets that mysteriously don't sell. Riots at the few crappy gigs they manage to pick up. Vans full of gear burning up for no obvious reason.'

'You saying that could happen to us if we don't sign up with you?'

He replaced the glass on the table with infinite care. 'Not

could. Will. It was you asked for this meeting,' he reminded me, stabbing his finger towards the centre of my chest. 'You need what I can do for you. Otherwise you might as well fuck off back to Germany.'

I jerked back from his finger. I could relax now. Lovell had just nailed himself to the wall. 'OK, OK,' I said. 'No reason why we can't do business. I was just checking.'

Lovell got to his feet. 'Well, you've done your checking and now you know what the score is. You don't ever get smart with me, bitch, you hear? I tell your poxy band where they play and when; you do no deals without consulting me first.' He put a hand in his pocket and tossed a small mobile phone on the table. 'Keep it on you. My number's programmed in at number one. That's the only number you call, you hear? I get any bills that say otherwise and you pay a service charge I guarantee you won't like. You can buy a charger unit anywhere that sells phones. I'll let you know when your first gig is.'

Whatever he was going to say next was lost. The door to the club crashed open again and two men piled in, shouting, 'Police. Don't move.' The door to the ladies' toilet opened and the other two rushed into the room, heading for the minders. A fifth cop jumped over the DJ's turntables as Della ran out from behind the bar towards Lovell. Everybody was screaming, 'Police. Don't move.' The acoustics of the club had a strange effect on their voices, almost swallowing them in the vastness of the space.

Lovell's face went deep red from the neck up, like a glass filling with coloured liquid. 'Fucking bitch,' he yelled. 'Let's get the fuck out of here.'

But before he could go anywhere Della's sergeant, a rugby prop forward from Yorkshire, misjudged his run from the DJ's platform and cannoned into him. Seeing their boss floored and themselves outnumbered, the muscle decided that the game that had been keeping them in made-to-measure suits was over. Lovell was dead in the water. But that didn't mean Tweedledum and Tweedledee had to sink with him. In perfect sync, two right hands disappeared inside their jackets and emerged holding a matching pair of semiautomatic pistols.

Suddenly, everything went quiet.

22

It's not just the immediate prospect of being hanged that concentrates the mind wonderfully. Staring down the barrel of a gun does the trick just as well. For a long minute, nobody moved or said a word. Then Tweedledum gestured with his pistol towards Della. 'You, bitch. Over here.'

At first she didn't move. I knew what she was thinking. The more spread out we were, the harder it would be to keep us all covered. 'I said, over here,' the gunman screamed, dropping the nose of his pistol and firing. A chunk of wood from the dance floor leapt into the air inches from Della's feet and frisbeed away across the room. 'Fucking do it,' he shrieked. I've never understood why it is that the guys with the guns always sound more scared than those of us without them.

Slowly, cautiously, Della moved towards him. As soon as she came within reach, he pulled her to him by the hair, back against his chest, gun muzzle jammed into her neck. I knew then that these guys were the real thing. The neck is the professional's option. Much more sensible than holding it to the temple. The muzzle buries itself in the flesh of the neck rather than sliding on bone covered by sweating skin. Guns to temples are amateur city, a mark of someone who's watched more movies than they've committed crimes.

The man holding Della turned so that he and his companion were almost back to back. 'Nobody fucking move,' the other one screamed.

'Get this fucker off me,' Lovell yelled.

'I said *nobody* fucking move, and that means you.'

'You fucking *work* for me, shithead,' Lovell screeched, his face purpling now with sheer rage.

'We just handed in our notice, OK?' the gunman shouted, his gun pointing at Lovell and the cop still sprawled on top of him. 'OK, Let's go.' He took a step backwards as his buddy moved forwards. Awkwardly they made their way over to the fire exit. Given that only two cops had burst in the main door, I guessed that the remaining two men were outside the fire door. I sincerely hoped neither of them was the heroic type.

The gunmen had nearly made it to the fire door when Tony Tambo suddenly erupted into action. I don't know if he was playing at knights in shining armour or if it was just sheer rage at seeing his club abused like this, but he jumped up on the seat, ran straight across the table, leapt to the floor and went for the heavies. The one facing us didn't even pause for breath. He just let off two shots. The first caught Tony in the thigh, his leg bursting into shattered fragments of flesh and bone in a spray of blood. The second caught him in the abdomen as he fell, the exit wound bursting out of his back like someone had used a morphing program on his suit. His scream was like every nightmare you hope you'll never have. The groans that followed it weren't a whole lot better.

'I fucking warned you,' the gunman shrieked, sounding like he was about to burst into tears. 'Let's get the fuck out,' he added.

His companion kicked the bar on the fire exit, which sprang open. I could just see the corner of the basement stairs that led up to the street. Then he shouted, 'Get the fuck down here now, or the bitch gets it, you hear?' He stepped back, yanking Della with him. Nothing happened, so he sidestepped her, still holding her hair, leaned into the doorway and fired. I heard the singing whine of a ricochet against the stone walls of the stairway. Then he hauled Della in close again. 'Get them down here,' he snarled.

'Come down quietly,' Della shouted. 'That's an order.'

By now, Tony had stopped groaning, so I was able to hear the sound of heavy feet on the steps. Two men edged through the door into the club. They followed the gestures of the man with Della and the gun and moved round the walls until they were almost parallel to Lovell and Della's sergeant. 'OK. Nobody follow, you hear? Or the bitch dies,' he screamed, rushing the door, followed by his companion.

As they disappeared, Lovell made a superhuman effort that caught the sergeant unawares. Suddenly he was wriggling free. I jumped onto the table and launched myself in a flying kick that would have got me suspended for life in any legitimate Thai boxing club. I hit Lovell in the side, and as we crashed to the ground together, I heard the satisfying crunch of snapping ribs and his simultaneous squeal of pain before the wind was completely knocked out of him. I rolled free and left him to Della's sergeant. I ran for the fire exit, along with one of the cops. The others were already out of the main door and heading for the street in a desperate bid to cut off the gunmen.

We reached the door at about the same moment the gunmen, slowed by an uncooperative Della, reached the street. With a roar that King Kong wouldn't have been ashamed of, the one trying to control her picked her up bodily and threw her down the flight of narrow stairs.

No amount of training in how to fall drills you for that sort of experience. Della tumbled down the steps in a loose ball, head defended by her forearms, bouncing off the walls. The cop and I stepped forward to break her fall. It was probably the worst thing we could have done. As she hit us, her leg shot out and snagged the wall. I heard the crack as bone snapped. Then we were a tumble of limbs. We settled with her face a couple of inches from mine. 'What a fuck-up,' she breathed. Then she fainted. I managed to free one arm from under her in spite of the excruciating pain that ran like a flame up to my shoulder. When I saw the tattered sleeve of my jacket drenched in blood I fainted too.

It had been a quiet night in Casualty until we hit the infirmary. Tony Tambo was on the critical list, having blood pumped into him and hanging onto life by sheer willpower, according to the nurse strapping up the wrist I'd merely sprained in the crush at the foot of the fire stairs. The blood had been Tony's.

I'd landed in it when I'd rolled free of Lovell. Mr Big Promo was under arrest with four broken ribs and a collapsed lung, and I was half expecting one of Della's zealots to charge me with assault. Della herself had been sent down to the plaster room to have her ankle set and immobilized. The cop whom we'd both landed on was being kept in for observation with a double concussion, two unlovely black eyes and a missing front tooth. You couldn't get near the coffee machine in Reception for uniformed cops.

When the nurse had finished with the bandages, I walked down to the plaster room, taking it slowly to avoid jolting any part of my protesting body. I'd only just pushed the swing doors open when I heard a familiar Scouse accent. Alexis's cheerful raucousness was to my headache what Agent Orange is to house plants. Della's head swung round with all the belligerence of a punch-drunk boxer who's gone one round too many and we chorused, 'Go *away*.'

'Well, that's a charming way to greet your friends. Soon as the newsdesk hears there's a bit of a fracas involving DCI Prentice and a private eye called Brannigan, I say to them, "I'll take care of this, the girls need to see a friendly face,"' Alexis said self-righteously.

'If you're here as a journalist, go away, Alexis,' I said wearily. 'If I said this has not been a good night, it would be the understatement of my life. Things have gone so wrong in the last hour that I'm desperate to hit somebody. Now, we might be in the right place for the aftermath of that sort of thing, but I really don't want it to happen to you.'

'Me, I'd just settle for somebody to arrest,' Della said, her voice sounding as emotionally exhausted as she had every right to feel. 'So, as Kate said, Alexis the journalist can take a hike. Alexis the friend, however, is welcome to stay provided she has a set of wheels that can take us all home after this little fiasco has run its course.'

'I'm sorry,' I said.

Della shook her head. 'It really wasn't your fault. I should have had the sense to realize he'd be walking around with armed minders. We should have let them all walk out of there then picked Lovell up in the middle of the night when he was on his own. I misjudged it.'

That should have made me feel better. Instead, I felt infinitely worse. Della was on the point of being promoted to superintendent and an operation like this that could be painted as a screw-up wasn't going to help. Add to that the pariah status automatically granted to any police officer who puts other cops away, and it looked like my bright idea might have put Della's next promotion into cold storage. 'You'd better come back and stay with me,' I offered as the first stage in what was going to be a long apology. 'You won't be able to manage the stairs at your place for a few days.'

She nodded. 'You're probably right. Won't Richard mind?'

'Only if you try to arrest him for possession.'

Della managed a tired smile. 'I think I can manage to restrain myself.'

'So what actually happened?' Alexis chipped in, unable to restrain herself indefinitely.

'Gun battle in Manchester's clubland,' I said. 'Police officer held hostage. Man helping police with inquiries, two gunmen sought. Club owner seriously injured, two police officers with minor injuries. One private investigator who wasn't there.'

Alexis grinned. 'I hate it when you come home with half a tale.'

Later, a lot later, when Della was asleep in my bed and Richard in his, I sat in the dark in the conservatory with a strong mixture of Smirnoff Black Label and freshly squeezed grapefruit juice and contemplated the capital D of the moon. Tony Tambo hadn't made it; one of Della's colleagues had rung to tell her not ten minutes after we got home. I sipped my drink and thought about how far reality had diverged from the simple little sting I'd envisaged. I'd gone in all gung ho and full of myself, and now a man was dead. He'd had a girlfriend and an ex-wife and a little daughter who was the apple of his eye, according to Richard. He wasn't supposed to behave like a hero, but then, I hadn't imagined there was going to be any need for heroics.

If my life was like the movies, my character would be planning vengeance, putting the word out in the underworld that she wanted those guys so bad she could taste it. And they would be delivered to her in such a way that she could decide their fate. But my life isn't like the movies. I knew I'd be doing nothing to discover the identities of the gunmen, where they hung out or who they ran with. That was the police's job, and I couldn't do it without placing more lives in danger. After what had happened to Tony Tambo, I was through with setting myself up against the major players.

I took a long cool swallow and tried not to think about Tony's daughter. Tried not to despise myself too much. Tried desperately to remember why I'd been working so hard to find a way to stay in this destructive game.

I woke around half past seven, just as the sun climbed over my back fence and hit the end of the wicker settee where I'd finally lost consciousness. I was still wearing the T-shirt and jogging pants I'd put on after the shower I'd needed to get the last of Tony Tambo's blood off me. If there's a female equivalent of unshaven, I felt it. I rubbed the grit out of my eyes, wincing at the arrow of pain in my left wrist, and stumbled through to the kitchen. I was just filling the coffee maker with water when I heard Della call me. 'Be right there,' I said, finishing the job.

Della was propped up on my pillows looking ten years older than she had done the day before. According to my wardrobe mirror, that still gave her a few on me. 'How are you feeling?' I asked.

'You see it all.'

'That bad? Shit, I'd better take your shoelaces and belt then.'

Della reached out and limply patted my hand. 'Do I smell coffee?'

'You do. Life-support systems will be available shortly.'

Ten minutes later, we were sharing the first pot of coffee of the day. I even relaxed the house rules enough to let her smoke in my bed. 'What have you got on today?' she asked.

I shrugged. 'I thought I might go down to the university and see if I can sign up to finish my law degree this autumn.'

212

Della was suddenly alert. 'Part time?' she said suspiciously. 'Full time.'

'Tony Tambo's death was not your fault,' she said firmly.

'I know that. I just don't know if I want to do this job any more. I didn't think it was going to be like this. Come to that, it didn't use to be like this. I don't know if it's the world that's turning nastier or if it's just that I've had a run of cheesy luck, but some days I feel like there should be a task force of counsellors, undertakers and paramedics in the car behind me.'

Della shook her head, exasperated. 'My God, you are feeling sorry for yourself this morning, aren't you? Listen, I'm the one who screwed up royally last night. A man died, and other people could have. The only way I could feel worse than I do now is if it had been you lying there on the mortuary slab. I've also probably kissed goodbye to my next promotion. But I'm not about to hand in my resignation. Even though I make mistakes, the police service needs people like me more than I need to gratify my guilt. I don't have to tell you about the dozens of sleazy, creepy exploitative PIs there are out there. Your business needs you, just like the police needs me. What about all the times when you've changed people's lives for the better? You got Richard out of jail, didn't you?'

'Yeah, but if it hadn't been for me, he wouldn't have been there in the first place,' I reminded her.

'You've saved businesses from going down the tube because you've identified the people who were stealing their money and their ideas. You've done work that has helped to clear up major drug syndicates.'

'Oh yeah? And that's really made a difference to the amount of drugs rattling around the streets of Manchester.'

'What about that case you were working when I first met you? The land fraud? If it hadn't been for your work, Alexis and Chris would have been comprehensively ripped off and they wouldn't be living in their dream home now. You've made a real difference in their lives,' Della insisted.

Her mention of Alexis and Chris reminded me forcibly of one job I still had to finish. Even if I was going to throw the towel in and sell my share of the business along with Bill, I couldn't walk away from Sarah Blackstone's murder.

When I failed to respond to Della, she gave my arm a gentle punch. 'You see? It breaks my little police heart to say it, but this city needs people who don't carry a warrant card.'

I swallowed my coffee. 'You sound like Commissioner Gordon,' I said acidly. 'Della, I'm not Batman and this isn't Gotham City. Maybe I could make just as much difference as a lawyer. Maybe Ruth would take me on.'

Della snorted. 'Listen to yourself. You want to go from cutting the feet from under the villains to defending them? You couldn't be a criminal lawyer. It's not possible only to defend the innocent, and you know it.'

'I sure as hell couldn't be a Crown Prosecutor either,' I growled.

'I know you couldn't. It's just as impossible only to prosecute the guilty. The trouble with you, Kate, is you understand the moral ambiguity of real life. And you're lucky, because the job you do lets you exercise that. You decide who your clients will be. You decide to defend the innocent and nail the guilty. You're too moral to be a lawyer. You're a natural maverick. Exploit it, don't ignore it.'

I sighed. Now I knew why Philip Marlowe didn't bother with buddies.

23

I'd got as far as Leeds before my determination ran out. It wasn't entirely my fault. Sherpa Tensing would have a job unravelling the roads in the centre of Leeds fast enough to take the right turning for the police admin building where I'd find the press officer I needed. Since I found myself inevitably heading for Skipton, I pulled off at Hyde Park Corner and killed some time with a decadent fruit shake in the radical chic Hepzi-bahz café while I reviewed where I was up to on the case that stood between me and a new life.

The more I looked at Sarah Blackstone, the more I grew convinced that this murder was about the personal, not the accidental or even the professional. Sure, one of her patients might have her suspicions about the biological coparent of her daughter, but to confirm even that much wouldn't be easy for a lay person. And even if it were confirmed, it was still a long way from there to murder, given that her patients didn't even know her real name. Logically, if a patient had killed her, the body should have been in the Manchester clinic, not the Leeds house.

That thrust Helen Maitland into the position of front runner. I knew now that she had wanted a child but that Sarah Blackstone had refused her. God only knew why, given what she'd been doing for two of the three years since they split up. But since that separation, Helen had lost the capability to have children. If I'd learned one thing from Chris's relentless drive towards pregnancy, it was the overwhelming, obsessive power of a childless woman's desire for motherhood. Chris once described the feeling as possession. 'It's there as soon as you wake up, and it's there until you go back to sleep,' she'd explained. 'Some nights, it even invades your dreams. Nothing matters except being pregnant. And it stops as soon as your body realizes it's pregnant. Like a weight lifting from your brain. Liberation.'

If Helen Maitland had been feeling like that before her cancer was diagnosed, the arrival of a card from Jan Parrish with a photograph of a baby girl and a lock of silky hair must have seemed a grotesque gift, cruel and gratuitous and, at first glance, bewildering. But when she'd examined it more closely, she couldn't have failed to see the child's undoubted resemblance to Sarah Blackstone. Helen was nobody's fool. She must have known Sarah's work was at the leading edge of human fertility treatment. Seeing a photograph of a baby who looked so like Sarah must have set her wondering what her lover had done now, especially coming so soon after the final dashing of her own hopes.

For a doctor involved in research, tenacity is as necessary a virtue as it is in my job. Faced with a puzzle, Helen would not simply have shelved it any more than I would. Given her specialism in the area of cystic fibrosis, she would have routine access to DNA testing and to researchers working in the field. I knew it wasn't standard practice to obtain DNA from hair shafts – it's difficult, technically demanding and often a waste of time because the DNA it yields is too poor in quality to be meaningful. But I knew that it was possible. It was the sort of thing some eager-beaver researcher would doubtless be happy to do as a favour for a consultant. Having met Helen Maitland, I didn't doubt she could be both charming and terrifying enough to get it done.

Getting a comparison sample of Sarah's DNA wouldn't have been so difficult either – a couple of hairs from the collar of her lab coat would be enough, and probably easier than cut hair, since they would have the roots still attached. Checking the two DNA profiles against each other would tell Helen a truth that for her in particular was a stab to the heart.

Given her probably fragile state, who knew how she might react? She could easily have stormed round to Sarah's, determined to have it out with her ex-lover. It didn't take much to imagine a scenario ending in Sarah's heart pumping her blood out on to the kitchen floor instead of round her arterial system. Now I had two problems. The first was proving it.

The second was what I did with that proof.

When the Yorkshire TV crowd started to pile in for lunch, the women in striped men's shirts and tailored jackets, the men in unstructured linen and silk, I decided it was time to go. I still had no idea how to deal with the second question, but it was academic if I couldn't answer the first.

This time, I decided to abandon the car in the Holiday Inn car park and make for the police station on foot. I hoped I wasn't going to be there long enough to be clamped. Just in case, I stuck my head into the restaurant, spotted a table where the half-dozen business lunchers included a couple of women. Then if I came back and the car was clamped, I could pitch the hotel into setting me free on the basis that I'd just had lunch, that table over there, no I didn't have the receipt because one of the others had paid for me. Usually works.

After I'd left Hepzi-bahz, I'd called ahead to warn the press officer I wanted to see not to go to lunch until I got there. At the front desk, I presented my official press card to the officer on duty, who gave it a cursory glance. It was, of course, a complete fake, based on a colour photocopy of Alexis's card plus a passport photograph of me, all shoved through the office laminating machine. Must have taken me all of ten minutes to cobble it together, and it would take close comparison with the real thing to tell the difference. I'd never try to get away with it in a police station in Manchester, where my face is too familiar to too many coppers, but over the Pennines it seemed a chance worth taking.

Ten minutes later, Jimmy Collier and I were nursing glasses in a busy pub which was a rarity in northern city centres in that it preferred customers to hear the sound of their voices rather than loud music. Jimmy was a dapper little man who could have been any age between thirty and fifty and dressed like he thought men's magazines had to have dirty pictures in them. He looked a bit like a penguin and walked like a duck, but there was nothing birdlike about the appetite with which he was attacking a cheese and onion barm that was approximately the size of a traditional Yorkshire flat cap. Along with his lunch, I fed him a story he swallowed as easily as the sandwich.

I told him I was working for one of the women's weekly magazines on a feature about burglary and home invasions. 'What we want to do is give them a "what you should do" guide, using real-life cases as an indicator of what you should and shouldn't do.' I smiled brightly. 'I thought the Sarah Blackstone murder was a perfect example of what you don't want the outcome to be,' I added, letting the smile drop.

Collier nodded and mumbled something indecipherable. He swallowed, washed his mouthful down with a draught of Tetley, then said, 'You're not kidding.' It hardly seemed worth the wait.

'So . . . what can you tell me about this case?' I asked.

He wiped his mouth on the back of his hand. 'Sarah Blackstone had been working late in the IVF laboratory at St Hilda's Infirmary. As far as we can ascertain, she left the hospital at around half past nine. At 10.27, we got a treble niner from a call box on the corner of her street. A woman who didn't give her name said she'd just been nearly knocked down by a black youth with what looked like a knife in his hand. He'd come running out of a house, leaving the door wide open. We took it seriously, because let's face it, between you and me, you don't get a lot of blacks living in a street like Pargeter Grove. We got there at 10.40, four minutes after the ambulance. Dr Blackstone was already dead. The knife had gone straight under her ribs and into her heart.'

I took notes as he spoke. 'And you reckon she disturbed a burglar?' I asked.

'That's right. A pane of glass in the back door was smashed. The key was in the lock. That's something to remind your readers about. Unbelievably stupid, but you'd be surprised how many people do that.'

'I read that nothing appeared to have been stolen,' I said.

'That's right. We reckon he'd just walked in the back door when she walked in the front. She were still wearing her mac. He didn't have time to do anything except strike out at her. I doubt he even had time to think about what he were doing, he just lunged at her. She was really unlucky. Not many stab wounds kill you as fast as that. When he saw what he'd done, he legged it empty-handed.'

'Wasn't the house alarmed?'

'No, it was just a bit nervous!' He guffawed. I'd heard the riposte too many times to find it funny any more, but I smiled nevertheless. 'She did have an alarm fitted,' he continued. 'But like a lot of people, I suppose she just left it switched off. People never think it's going to happen to them. You should stress that to your readers. If you've got an alarm fitted, never leave the house without setting it.'

'Good point,' I said appreciatively. He wasn't to know, after all, that Sarah Blackstone was so security conscious it bordered on the paranoid, and with good reason. Another argument against the random burglar. There was no way Sarah Blackstone would leave the alarm switched off. 'This woman that phoned in – wasn't it a bit funny that she didn't give her name?' I asked.

He shook his head. 'More often than not, they don't, around there,' I deciphered through a mouthful of barm cake. 'They don't want to get involved. Even when they're the only proper witness we've got. They don't want to have to miss work to come to court to give evidence, they're frightened that if they stick their necks out, it'll be their house the bad boys come to next. Far as they're concerned, their civic duty stops with the 999 call.'

'That's your middle classes for you,' I said.

'You're not wrong. Especially after the riots down Hyde Park. They're terrified of repercussions. We tell them they're safe to give evidence, but they don't believe us.'

Neither did I. I'd heard too much about West Yorkshire Police. I know a woman whose house was being broken into by three teenagers with a sledgehammer in broad daylight. The next-door neighbour dialled 999 and the police arrived a full half-hour later, protesting that there wasn't a lot they could do since the burglars had already gone. I flicked back through my notes. 'Fascinating case, this one. No forensic, I take it?'

'There are some indicators that the forensic team are

working with,' he said guardedly. 'But they won't even tell me what they've got. All I know is that it's a bit of a struggle to make it look like one of the usual suspects.' He winked.

'She took her time coming home from St Hilda's,' I commented. 'Can't be more than fifteen minutes' drive at that time of night.'

'She'll have stopped off on her way home for a drink or fish and chips,' he said confidently.

'Or popped round to see somebody who turned out not to be in,' I suggested. 'So you've no other eye witnesses except for the mystery caller?'

'That's right. It was chucking it down, so the usual dog walkers and drunks would have been head down and hurrying, that time of night. We were a bit surprised that no one saw him going over the back wall on his way in, since it's overlooked by the student residences, but we've not had a lot of luck all round with this one. Something else to tell your readers – set up a Neighbourhood Watch scheme if you want to cut down the risk of violent burglary in your street. It really works, according to our Community Security team.'

'Community Security?'

He had the grace to look embarrassed. 'What used to be called Crime Prevention,' he admitted sheepishly.

Only it didn't. So in the same way that 'closing hospital beds' became 'care in the community', a quick name change had been necessary. I asked a few anodyne questions, bought Collier a second pint, then made my excuses and left before I had to watch him demolish a slice of Black Forest gateau about the same size as its namesake.

I sat on the top floor of the city art gallery under the huge Frank Brangwen panels representing the horny-handed sons of toil of the industrial revolution, their bodies suspiciously like those of the desk-bound Stallone wannabes you see down every designer gym in the country. Today, though, I wasn't thinking about social change. I was staring at *The Rolling Mill* without seeing it. All I could see was the picture in my mind's eye of Helen Maitland's face, ugly with anger and pain as she

220

lashed out at the woman she had once loved and who had deprived her of her dream of motherhood.

I had a pretty clear idea now what had happened. The results of DNA testing would have confirmed Helen's guess at what Sarah had been doing. This wasn't an experiment that had come out of nowhere; I could imagine the conversations as the lovers had snuggled together under the duvet, Sarah fantasizing about the day the technology would be there to make babies from two women, Helen dreaming of what it would mean to them, to her. But Sarah had refused, for whatever reason. And the refusal had driven a wedge so deeply between them that it was impossible to continue their relationship.

The scenario was as vivid as film to me. When she realized the truth, Helen must have gone round to confront Sarah. But Sarah hadn't been home. She'd been working late. I could picture Helen sitting in her car, impotent rage building like a bonfire. When Sarah had eventually arrived, Helen had probably been beyond rational conversation. She had insisted on being admitted and the two women had gone through to the kitchen. There, the argument had raged before Helen had snapped, seized a knife and thrust it deep into Sarah's body.

The act of murder must have sobered her. She'd had the sense to go to the back door and make it look like someone had broken in. If they'd had drinks, she had cleared glasses or cups. Then, making sure she was hidden by darkness, she'd slipped out of the house, back to her car, and driven to the phone box where she'd made the spurious 999 call.

It accounted for the awkward facts that spoke against it being a burglar. It covered the time gap between Sarah leaving the hospital and being found dead. It explained why the killer had taken the knife; she wouldn't have been wearing gloves and for her there was less risk in taking it home, sterilizing it and dumping it in her own cutlery drawer. She'd probably been bloodstained, but it had been raining that night and she'd likely been wearing a mac or raincoat that she could simply take off and dispose of later.

Helen Maitland had done a good job of covering her tracks. Lucky for her that West Yorkshire Police are crap. But if the police did start to take a serious interest in her rather than doggedly chasing their mystery burglar, there would be proof for the taking. A voice print of the 999 tape would match hers. A new mac would be another circumstantial nail in her coffin. And, of course, she'd have no alibi. They might be short on motive, but if they started to push Helen Maitland, the truth might pour out. If that happened, it was only a matter of time before they started knocking on Alexis and Chris's door. And that was what I'd been hired to prevent.

I sighed. It must have been louder than I thought, because the middle-aged attendant strolled casually into my line of vision, concern producing a pair of tram tracks between her eyebrows. 'You all right, lovey?' she asked.

I nodded. 'I'm fine. Just something I'm trying to work out.'

She inclined her head. Now she understood. 'We get a lot of that,' she said. 'Especially since Alan Bennett did that TV programme about the gallery.'

Like a character in one of Bennett's screenplays, she walked on, nodding to herself, her shampoo-and-set hair as rigid as one of the Epstein busts next door. I roused myself and looked at my watch. Just gone four. Time to head for another confrontation. At least this time I could be fairly sure that I wouldn't end up staring down the barrel of a gun.

I parked about fifty metres down the street from Helen Maitland's house and settled back to wait. By six o'clock, I knew the news headlines better than the newsreaders. Seven o'clock and I was expecting Godot along any minute. As the numbers on the clock headed towards 20:00 I decided I'd had enough. I needed to eat, and Bryan's was frying a haddock with my name on it not five minutes' drive away.

When I returned nearly an hour later, there were lights showing in Helen Maitland's house. When she opened the door to see me on her doorstep, she looked momentarily annoyed, then resigned. 'The return of Sherlock Holmes,' she said wryly.

'I have things to say you should listen to,' I said.

Her eyebrows quirked. 'And they say etiquette's dead. You'd better come in. Ms Branagh, wasn't it?'

222

'Brannigan,' I corrected her as I followed her indoors. 'Branagh's the actor. I do it for real.' Sometimes I hear myself and think if I was a punter I'd laugh at me.

'Sorry, Ms *Brannigan*,' Helen Maitland said. 'Have a seat,' she added as we arrived in the kitchen. I ignored her. She leaned against the worktop, facing me, one hand absently stroking a tortoiseshell cat sprawled on the draining board. 'Well, you have my undivided attention. I presume this is to do with Sarah?'

'I know you were lovers,' I said bluntly. 'I know you wanted children and she refused to go along with you. But after you split up, the technology was perfected that allowed Sarah to build babies from the eggs of two women rather than using sperm. But the immortality of being the first to do it wasn't enough for Sarah. She wanted her genes to carry on too. So she started mixing her own harvested eggs in with the patients'. And one of those patients was so grateful that she broke the injunction of secrecy and sent a photograph with a lock of hair to the doctor who'd helped her make her dream come true. To nice Dr Helen Maitland. How am I doing so far?'

Her face had remained impassive, but the hand stroking the cat had stopped, fur clenched between her fingers. She tried a smile that came out more like a snarl. 'Badly. I don't have the faintest idea what you're talking about.'

'Somewhere there will be a record of the DNA tests you ran on that lock of hair and on Sarah's DNA. You can't lose something like that. The police would have no trouble finding it. A lot of legwork, perhaps, but they'll get there in the end.'

Her eyes were cautious now, watching me like a hawk's, hardly blinking. 'I'm sorry, I must have missed a turning somewhere. How did we get to the police?'

'Don't, Dr Maitland. Neither of us is stupid, so stop acting like we both are. I can imagine how distressed you were when you discovered what Sarah was doing, especially after she had denied you the chance to be the first to try the treatment. Even more so since your own operation. You went round to see her, to confront her with the outrage she'd perpetrated against you. And she dismissed you, didn't she? She didn't take your emotions seriously, just like before when she'd dismissed your desires for motherhood.'

Helen Maitland shook her head slowly from side to side. 'I thought you said you were for real, Ms Brannigan. Sounds to me like you need treatment.'

'I don't think so. I think you're the one with the problem, Dr Maitland. You might give the impression of being cool, smart and in control, and God knows, you're good at it. But then you'd have to be, to kill your ex-lover and get away with it.'

She pushed off from the worktop and stood bristling at me, like one of her cats finding a strange tom on the front step. 'You've gone too far. It's time you were leaving,' she said, her voice low and thick with anger.

'I knew there was a temper lurking in there. It's the same temper that flared when you confronted Sarah and she dismissed your pain. It's the same temper that made you grab the nearest knife and thrust it under Sarah's ribs right into her heart.'

'Get out,' she said, anger and incredulity fighting in her. 'I don't have to take this from you.' She took a step towards me.

'You can't get away with it, Helen,' I said, my hands coming up automatically, palms facing her. 'Once the police start looking at you, they'll find the evidence. It's all there, once you accept that Sarah wasn't killed by a burglar. As soon as they match your voice against that 999 call, you're right there in the frame.'

'That's not going to happen.' The voice wasn't Helen Maitland's. It came from behind my right shoulder. I whirled round, straight into fighting stance, poised on the balls of my feet.

It was Flora. And in her hand was a shiny long-barrelled revolver.

24

Her small pale hands looked too fragile to wield a big cannon like that, but the barrel wasn't trembling. Whatever was driving Flora, it was powerful stuff. 'Flora,' Helen said calmly.

'It's all right, Helen,' Flora said, not taking her eyes off me.

Not with me it wasn't. I'd had enough of people waving guns at me. And frankly, I didn't think Flora was in the same league as Peter Lovell's gunmen. I glanced over at Helen Maitland and let my jaw go slack.

'My God!' I exclaimed.

Out of the corner of my eye, I saw Flora's hand jerk as her eyes swivelled towards Helen. On the instant, I launched myself, right leg jabbing up and out at shoulder height, my own voice roaring in my ears like Bruce Willis on heat. Everything suddenly seemed to be in slo-mo: my foot connecting with her shoulder, Flora toppling towards the floor, her gun arm flying out to one side, her finger tightening on the trigger as I landed on top of her, my body tensing against the expected blast of the gunshot.

A tongue of flame spurted from the gun barrel, then died as Flora released her pressure on the trigger.

I'd been scared shitless by a cigarette lighter.

I'd been scared, no two ways about it. But now I was really, really cross. When I'd walked through the door, I'd been feeling sympathetic. My instincts had all been to find a way out of this situation that didn't mean Helen Maitland spending the rest of her useful life behind bars. Now I wasn't so sure that was what I wanted.

'That was really silly, Flo,' Helen remarked in an offhand tone I'd never have been able to manage in the circumstances.

I disentangled myself from Flora's hair and limbs and pushed myself back to my feet. 'It was a lot more than silly,' I said. 'For fuck's sake, I could have really hurt you, you pillock.'

Flora threw the gun across the room. It clattered into the kitchen unit next to Helen. Then she curled up into a ball and burst into tears.

Helen picked up the lighter and laid it on the kitchen table, then moved to Flora's side. She crouched down and put her arms around her. It felt like Flora wept for a very long time, but it was less than five minutes by the kitchen clock. I didn't mind. It gave my heart time to return to its normal speed and rhythm.

Eventually Helen steered Flora into a kitchen chair and sat down beside her. 'Even a real gun wouldn't stop the police running those voice comparisons,' I said. 'I'm not daft enough to embark on a confrontation like this without leaving a bit of insurance behind in case some idiot pulls some brainless stunt where I actually do get hurt.'

'Then it's all over,' Flora said dully.

'How can you say that?' Helen demanded, pulling away. 'How can you think that I . . . That's crazy.'

'It's not crazy, actually.' Flora's voice was shaky. 'You see, if the police did start to run comparisons on that 999 tape, they would find a match.'

'Look, Flora, I don't know where you've got this idea from. I didn't kill Sarah,' Helen protested. 'I'm appalled you could think so.'

'I *don't* think so. No one knows the truth better than me.'

There was a silence as Helen and I digested the implications of Flora's words. Then the enormity of my second screw-up in two days hit me. I'd been right about the obsessive power of love being responsible for Sarah Blackstone's death. But I'd picked the wrong candidate for the killer. I'd been so convinced that Helen was the killer I hadn't even paid attention to Flora.

'Are you saying what I think you're saying?' Helen asked. There was an edge of horror in her voice.

'It was you, wasn't it?' I asked. Flora said nothing. She

226

didn't have to. We both knew the truth now. 'So tell me. Was I close? The scenario I painted? Was I on the right lines?'

Flora pushed her hair back with her free hand. 'Why are you so keen to know the details? So you can run to the nearest police station and turn me in?'

I sighed. 'The reason I became a private investigator was because I like to know the reasons why things happen. I understand the difference between the law and justice. I know that handing people over to the police isn't always the best way of ending things. If you want to prevent me going to the police, you've got more chance talking to me than you have trying to terrorize me. I have a client who has an interest in Sarah Blackstone's death. She has her own, very pressing, reasons for wanting to know the truth here.'

While I had been speaking, Helen Maitland had been rummaging through a drawer in the kitchen table. As I got to the end of a speech that owed more to the British commanding officer in *The Great Escape* than any innate nobility of spirit, she pulled out a bashed packet of Silk Cut. 'I knew there was a packet in here somewhere.' She ripped the cellophane off, flipped the top up, tore out the silver paper, shoved a cigarette up with her thumb and drew it out with her lips. She picked up the gun and lit the cigarette. Pure bathos.

'I think we're in deep shit here, Flora,' she said through a sigh of smoke, 'but from what I've seen of Ms Brannigan, it seems to me she's the person who can best deal with that. I think you should tell us what happened.'

Flora started crying again. I still wasn't impressed. 'I didn't *mean* to kill her,' she said through a veil of hair and tears.

'I know that,' Helen soothed in her practical, no-nonsense way. There was going to be a reckoning between these two, I could see that in her eyes. But Helen Maitland had the sense to realize this wasn't the time or the place. 'It's not your style, Flo.'

Flora did a bit more weeping, and Helen just sat there smoking, her eyes never leaving her lover. It was impossible even to guess at what was going on behind that blank stare. Finally Flora sat back, pushed her hair away from her face and scrubbed her eyes with her small hands, like a child who's been crying from tiredness. She took a deep breath, gave Helen a pleading look, then turned to face me. 'I really didn't mean to kill her,' she said. 'I didn't go there with that intention.'

'Tell me about it,' I said. Helen only crushed out one cigarette and lit a second.

Flora breathed out heavily through her nose. 'This isn't easy,' she complained.

'Easier than killing someone,' I remarked.

'Not really,' Flora said tremulously. 'That happened in the heat of the moment. Before I even knew I had the knife in my hand, she was dead. Telling you is a lot harder, you have to believe that, Helen.'

Helen nodded curtly. 'So what happened, Flora? I want to know just as badly as Ms Brannigan does.'

Flora pushed her hair back from her face and adopted a beseeching expression. I couldn't get a handle on this woman at all. The image she projected was of a fairly timid, vulnerable innocent. Then I'd get a flash from those dark eyes and I'd feel like an entire brigade of dark, supernatural nasties were dancing on my grave. I realized exactly what Maggie had meant about the dragon and the maiden. I could see that it might be a powerful erotic mixture, but it left me feeling pathetically grateful that the gun hadn't been for real. Flora was a woman who could easily have pulled the trigger then pulled the same 'I didn't mean it' routine over me that she was giving us now over Sarah Blackstone.

'Can't it wait till we're alone?' Flora pleaded.

'Ms Brannigan already knows too much for us to throw her out now,' Helen said. Somehow her words didn't scare me like Flora did. 'I suspect that telling her the whole story is the best chance we've got of salvaging something from this mess.' I couldn't have put it better myself.

Flora looked as if she was about to protest, then she registered the determination in her lover's face. 'It all started when Helen was diagnosed with cervical cancer,' she said.

'I know about that,' I interrupted her, not wanting to let her get into a flow of pathos too early in her narrative. 'It resulted in a complete hysterectomy. What had that to do with the murder of Sarah Blackstone?'

Flora darted me a look of pure malice. It wasn't lost on Helen Maitland. This time, when she spoke, her voice was more brisk. 'Helen was desperate to have a child, and as soon as she was diagnosed, she got a gynaecologist friend of hers, not Sarah, to harvest her eggs for the next three months.'

'Why?' I asked.

Helen stared at the table and spoke rapidly. 'Part of me hoped that a full hysterectomy wouldn't be necessary, that even if I couldn't produce fertile eggs any more, I might just be able to have a child by artificial insemination, or even surrogacy. You know, get someone else to carry my child. So we took what eggs we could harvest before my surgery and froze them. It's dodgy, freezing eggs; nobody really knows yet how successful it is. But I had this crazy idea that even if I couldn't have a child myself, at least my genes might continue. And if all else had failed, at least I could have made an egg donation to someone who needed it.'

Not for the first time in the past few days, the desperate nature of the need to reproduce hit me between the eyes. I said a small prayer to the goddess of infertility that it would continue to avoid taking up residence in my soul. 'Right,' I said, determined to move this along and keep the emotional level as low key as possible. 'So Helen had her eggs frozen. How does that get us to murder?'

'One morning a couple of months ago, Helen had a really strange letter in the post. It was from Manchester –'

'I know about that too,' I interrupted, partly to maintain control over events, partly to impress both of them with how much I'd already found out. 'It contained a baby's photograph and a lock of hair and a message of thanks.'

Helen's composure showed a crack for the first time. 'The baby was the spitting image of Sarah at the same age. I couldn't believe the similarity. I'd heard Sarah talking about the technical possibility of making babies from two women's eggs, and I realized that's what she was probably doing. I work with cystics, so I have access to DNA-testing facilities.'

'They were able to get DNA from the cut hairs?' I asked.

'There are always researchers who love a challenge and one of the women at St Hilda's relished the chance to extract viable DNA from the hair shafts. I bribed one of my students to get a blood sample from Sarah. He told her it was for random testing in some experiment he was doing into some obscure aspect of blood chemistry, and she let him take it. The DNA test was very clear. Sarah was one of the parents of the child.' She was smoking now like she'd made it her life-long ambition to be a forty-a-day woman.

This time, it was Flora who reached out, gripping Helen's free hand tightly. Helen continued, almost talking to herself. 'It was all the more bitter because that was the issue that split us up. I wanted a child desperately, but Sarah didn't. I knew subfertility treatment was close to the stage where it would be possible to make a child from two women. And she refused point-blank to do it with us. She said she wasn't prepared to experiment with my body. That if the experiment produced a monster, or even a handicapped child, she wouldn't be able to live with herself. Me, I thought it probably had more to do with the fact that she absolutely didn't want to share her life with a child. I eventually came to the conclusion I'd rather have the possibility of a child than the certainty of life with her. You can imagine the kind of rows . . .' Her voice tailed off into a quiet exhalation of smoke.

'You must have been devastated to discover she was experimenting with other women,' I said in the crass mode of television news reports.

Helen pulled a face. 'I think if she had been in front of me when I got the DNA results through from the lab, I might have killed her. But the more I thought about it, the more I realized that I was actually glad that I hadn't had her child. That I didn't want a daughter of mine to consist of half Sarah's genes. Distance doesn't lend enchantment, you know. It allows you to put things in perspective. I hadn't stopped wanting a child, but I'd stopped caring about Sarah. I didn't even hate her any more. Despised her, yes, because there wasn't anything in her life she wouldn't betray. So I didn't actually want to kill her for very long.'

'Long enough to tell Flora?' I asked softly.

Flora turned on me then, eyes wide and angry. 'Don't try and blame Helen. She said nothing of the sort to me. It was my idea to go and see Sarah. Helen didn't even know I was going.'

'So why did you go, if it wasn't to confront Sarah with her double-cross?'

'Yes,' Helen said. 'Why did you go to see her?'

Flora gave a weary smile. 'I went to try to persuade her to do for us what she'd done for those other women. My eggs and yours. So we could share a child.'

There was a long silence. Helen's eyes raking Flora's face as if she was trying to scour any falsehood from her words by reading her features. Then her head dropped into her hands. She didn't cry. After a few moments, she looked up, dry-eyed, and said, 'That is an extraordinary thing to say.'

'It's the truth,' Flora said. 'Why else would I have gone to see her?'

'I had no idea you felt like that.'

'What? That I loved you that much, or that I wanted a child that much?' Flora challenged, chin up.

'Either or both,' Helen said, her voice tired. 'What did Sarah say?'

Flora looked away, her face clouding over. I was starting to feel seriously redundant here. 'She laughed in my face. She said she wasn't going to give a baby to a brainless bimbo and a compulsive obsessive. So I told her that if she wouldn't cooperate, I'd go to the authorities and tell them exactly what she was doing.'

'Not a clever move,' Helen said, reaching for another cigarette. 'Sarah and threats were never a comfortable mix.' Her cool irony was starting to get to me. Sooner or later, an explosion was going to come. The longer she kept the lid on, the worse it was going to be. I hoped I'd be well out of the fallout zone when it did.

'How did she react to your threat?' I asked.

'She grabbed me by the lapels and shoved me up against the kitchen counter,' Flora said, still incredulous that someone in her world would do such a thing. 'She kept banging me against the counter, telling me I was a dirty blackmailing bitch and that she knew a lot of women who'd happily kill to keep the children she'd given them. I was terrified. She kept twisting her hand in my coat, it was so tight it was strangling me. I was desperate. I groped about on the worktop behind me and my hand touched a knife. I just grabbed it and thrust it up into her. I wasn't thinking, I just did it. And she sort of fell back onto the floor. I was standing there, holding the knife, watching her die. And I couldn't do a thing about it.'

'You could have called an ambulance,' Helen said, her voice cold.

'I did. I went straight to the phone box down the street and called an ambulance.'

'Not then, you didn't,' I said. 'You did one or two other things first. You cleared up any signs of a struggle. You unlocked the back door, leaving the key in the lock, went outside and smashed a pane of glass to make it look like a burglary. You took off your bloodstained mac and checked nobody was about, then you walked calmly out of the front door and up to the phone box on the corner. And then you phoned 999 and told the operator you'd just seen a black man running out of an open door on that street with a bloodstained knife. By which time Sarah Blackstone was dead.'

'It wouldn't have made any difference if I'd phoned straightaway,' Flora said desperately. 'She died so quickly. Honestly, Helen, she was dead in seconds.'

'Not that quickly,' I said coldly. 'She can't have been dead for long otherwise the ambulance crew would have told the police there was a discrepancy between the time of death and the time of the call-out.'

The way Flora looked at me, I was glad there wasn't a knife handy. 'Let's face it, Flora, you couldn't really allow her to live, could you?' Helen said bleakly. 'Not after what you'd done. No wonder you said to me the next day that you'd give me an alibi if the police came asking. You wanted to make sure you had one, didn't you? Just don't you dare ever say you did it for me.'

Flora said nothing. Helen faced me. 'I suspect there's a tape recorder whirring away in your handbag.'

My jacket pocket, actually, but I wasn't about to tell them

that in case either of them got any clever ideas. 'Technology's got a bit smarter than that these days. I wouldn't still be alive if I didn't believe in insurance,' I said.

'So now you go to the police, is that it?'

'Helen!' Flora wailed. 'I can't go to jail!'

'I don't think that's necessary,' I said. 'The way Flora tells it, it sounds pretty much like self-defence that got out of hand. I don't think she's a risk to anyone else. I don't see a need for this to come out into the open.'

A cynical smile curled Flora's lip. 'You mean you don't want the world to know what that bitch Sarah was doing. I bet your client's one of those women she gave a baby to. She won't want that can of worms opened, will she?'

'Don't push your luck, Flora,' Helen said. 'Ms Brannigan holds your freedom in her hand. Or wherever she has her tape recorder stashed.'

I nodded. 'There are conditions to my silence,' I said. 'If anyone else is charged with Sarah's murder, I can't stand idly by. And if Sarah's secret work becomes public knowledge and I think it's anything to do with you, the tape goes to the police. Is that a deal?'

EPILOGUE

The cops picked up Peter Lovell's thugs a couple of weeks later in a routine raid on an after-hours shebeen in Bradford. They charged them with Tony's murder. The Crown Prosecution Service, who love bent coppers about as much as the police do, also added murder to Lovell's list of charges under the 'joint enterprise' principle. According to Della, who was on the point of giving up the elbow crutches and moving back into her house, it looks like they're all going to go down for a very long time. Oh, and Dan Druff and the Scabby Heided Bairns signed a deal with an indie record company on the strength of their first Nazi-free gig. They've promised me the first pressing of the first single to roll off the production line. I can hardly wait. It'll look great framed on my office wall. Not.

The law on fraud being what it is, Alan Williams and Sarah Constable probably thought they were unlucky to do any time at all. But the police did a good job, tying them into ripping off the bereaved in Birmingham, Durham and Plymouth. They each got eighteen months, which they'll do easy time in an open prison. It probably won't stop them dreaming up another nasty little scam when they come out, but at least it's got them off the streets for a few months. Their boss at Sell Phones did a bit better; all they could get him on was obtaining phone calls by deception, on account of the laws in this country affecting telecommunications are so archaic it's hard to nail anybody on anything to do with cellular phones. And since nobody much likes phone companies, he only got a suspended sentence. He lost the business, though, which is a kind of rough justice.

I also got round to talking to Josh. He gave me a load of toffee about how he wanted to devote some of his capital to working with small businesses, and I told him to cut the crap and get to the horses. The deal we worked out meant he bought Bill's share of the business, but in recognition of my sole contribution to the profits, my stake in the partnership was upgraded to fifty-five per cent. So I got an extra twenty per cent for nothing except running the agency and doing all the hard graft ... Josh also promised me that when I can afford it, I can buy him out for what he'd paid plus the rate of inflation. I know a good deal when I see it. I nearly bit his hand off. The best part about it was that overnight I stopped wanting to rip Bill's arm off and hit him with the wet end. That Sheila's a really good laugh when you get to know her.

Alexis was happy with the way I sorted things out with Helen and Flora. With the single-mindedness of all parents-to-be, she didn't much mind who'd killed Sarah as long as it wasn't going to bounce back and wreck her happy little idyll. I never did tell her about Sarah Blackstone's nasty little trick of dropping her own eggs into the mix. I couldn't bring myself to say anything that would poison Alexis's happiness.

It's just as well I didn't. When Chris gave birth six months later, there was no mistaking the genetic source of Jay Appleton Lee's shock of jet black spikes. I swear the child cries with a Scouse accent.

I wish I could close the account there. Everything in credit, almost a happy ending. It's never been that neat in my experience. About two months after the showdown in her kitchen, Helen Maitland turned up at my office one afternoon around close of business. I left Shelley in charge and took her up to the café at the Cornerhouse for a herbal tea and a flapjack. Sometimes it's dead handy having an art cinema so close to the office.

Over a cup of wild strawberry she told me that Flora had just got a job in a university library in Wyoming. 'I didn't know they had universities in Wyoming,' I said. Cheap, I know, but I never claimed to be otherwise.

'Me neither,' Helen said, smiling with the half of her mouth that wasn't clamped around a cigarette.

'You looking for jobs, then?'

'You mean am I going with her?'

I nodded. 'I wondered if this was goodbye, don't worry, we're out of your life.'

'I suppose it is, in a way. Flora won't be back, and the one thing I'd pray for if I had any religion left is to be allowed to forget the whole sorry mess. So you can rest assured you won't be hearing any more of this from me. And Flora . . . well, she has too much to lose. The police never arrested anyone, never even seriously questioned them. The case is going to die now, just like Sarah did.'

'Better that way,' I said.

'Better all round,' she agreed. Her green eyes looked distantly over my shoulder. 'I'm not going to join Flora, though. Ever since she told us what had happened, I've scarcely been able to tolerate being in the same room as her. I may have stopped loving or hating Sarah, but I never wanted her to die, not even in our most terrible fights. And I hate the thought that I was the instrument of her death.'

'Don't be daft,' I protested. 'It was Flora who knifed her, not you. You didn't even know she was going to see her. You certainly didn't suggest it, that much was obvious from your reaction to Flora's confession.'

'Maybe not overtly. But she'd never have dreamed up the idea if my obsession hadn't planted it. If I hadn't told her the meaning of the photograph and the lock of hair, she'd never have gone near Sarah. I may not have held the knife, but I carry the guilt.'

I could tell there was no point in trying to get her to change her mind about that. We finished our drinks, talking about anything except Sarah and Flora. Then she excused herself, saying she had someone to meet. I sat by the first-floor window and watched her stepping out across Oxford Road, dodging cars and buses. I watched her long stride as far as the corner of Princess Street, where she turned left and disappeared.

The story was in the next night's *Chronicle*. DOCTOR DIES IN HOTEL PLUNGE. She'd taken a room on the top floor of the Piccadilly Hotel. She'd even brought a club hammer in her overnight bag in case the window didn't open far enough. At the inquest, they read out a note where she'd quoted that bit from Keats about ceasing on the midnight with no pain.

Some nights, I dream of Helen Maitland falling through the air, morphing into a bird and suddenly soaring just before she hits the ground. I hope someone somewhere is making babies with her eggs.

The Mermaids Singing

Val McDermid

You always remember the first time. Isn't that what they say about sex? How much more true it is of murder...

Up till now, the only serial killers Tony Hill had encountered were safely behind bars. This one's different – this one's on the loose.

In the northern town of Bradfield four men have been found mutilated and tortured. Fear grips the city; no man feels safe. Clinical psychologist Tony Hill is brought in to profile the killer. A man with more than enough sexual problems of his own, Tony himself becomes the unsuspecting target of a battle of wits and wills where he has to use every ounce of his professional skill and personal nerve to survive.

A tense, brilliantly written psychological thriller, *The Mermaids Singing* explores the tormented mind of serial killer unlike any the world of fiction has ever seen.

Winner of the 1995 CWA Award for Best Crime Novel of the Year

'Truly, horribly good'   *Mail on Sunday*

ISBN 0 00 649358 0

Clean Break
Val McDermid

Manchester-based private eye Kate Brannigan is not amused when thieves have the audacity to steal a Monet from a stately home where she'd arranged the security. She's even less thrilled when the hunt for the thieves drags her on a treacherous foray across Europe as she goes head to head with organized crime. And as if this isn't enough, a routine industrial case starts leaving a trail of bodies across the North West, leaving Kate with more problems than she can deal with.

Cleaning up the mess in *Clean Break* forces Kate to confront harsh truths in her own life as she battles with a testing array of villains in a case that stretches love and loyalty to the limits.

'Tough, funny and intensely topical, McDermid stands out as one of the few contemporary writers actually nourished by the here and now'   *Literary Review*

ISBN 0 00 649772 1

Crack Down
Val McDermid

There was only one reason Manchester-based private eye Kate Brannigan was prepared to let her boyfriend help out with an investigation into a car sales fraud – nothing bad could happen. But by now Kate should know that with Richard you have to expect the unexpected.

With the unexpected being Richard behind bars, Kate seems to be the obvious choice to look after his eight-year-old son – who proves even more troublesome than his father. Kate finds herself dragged into a world of drug traffickers, child pornographers, fraudsters and violent gangland enforcers . . . bringing her face to face with death in the tensest, toughest and most terrifying investigation of her career.

'Tough, funny and intensely topical. McDermid stands out as one of the few contemporary writers actually nourished by the here and now'   *Literary Review*

ISBN 0 00 649008 5